CW00862938

T

About Maddie!

Maddie

Best Wishes

Irene Lebeter

Irene Lebeter

Also by Irene Lebeter - 'Vina's Quest'

Vina's Quest is the story of one woman's epic search for her roots, stretching over six decades and two continents. Everybody craves love, family and romance in their lives and Vina is no different from the rest. The reader is taken on a rollercoaster ride of highs and lows, accompanying her on her quest. Seeking closure from the past, her journey includes both pain and happiness as she searches for answers.

Maddie

By **Irene Lebeter**

Published by Author Way Limited through CreateSpace
Copyright 2016 author

This book has been brought to you by -

Discover other Author Way Limited titles at -
http://www.authorway.net
Or to contact the author mailto:info@authorway.net

ISBN-10   1539132269
ISBN-13:   978-1539132264

For my grandsons

Daryl, Mark and Joshua

with thanks for adopting me

Acknowledgements

With thanks to

Author Way, Publishers.
Pat Feehan, for his time spent in proofreading the story.
Fiona McLellan, John McLellan and Marjory Holmes, for information about life on a dairy farm in the 1950s/60s.
Mark Garrity, owner of German Shepherd, Zeus.
Nicky Neill, owner of German Shepherd, Star.
Fiona McLellan, owner of Daisy the cat.
Patricia Harper, for allowing me to use her name for one of the characters.
Zen Boyd, Librarian, Heritage Centre, Rutherglen for information on Rutherglen in the 1950s.
Alan Fraser, for advice about characters' health issues.
Campbell Thomson, for advice about police issues.
Rachel and Erin McLaren, for inspiring me to have twin girls among my characters.
Jan Ladd, for loaning me her book on trees.
All members of Strathkelvin Writers' and Kelvingrove Writers' for their valuable feedback.
Julie Smith, Librarian, Rutherglen and Eryl Morris, Librarian, Bishopbriggs for offering venues for a launch of *Maddie*.

Chapter One

November 1955

It was on the third Sunday of the month that Maddie Granger killed Will Benson. She lifted the heavy brass candlestick off the communion table and struck the back of his head with it, over and over again, satisfaction in every hit. He dropped like a stone at her feet, blood pouring from his wounds, and she inflicted another couple of blows to make sure the job was properly done. She rolled his body over; his eyes were craving the forgiveness she couldn't find.

Maddie was deciding how best to dispose of the corpse when Mr Dunwoodie thumped the pulpit ledge, jolting her back to reality. Seated between her mum and the hateful Will in their family pew at St Luke's, she forced a swift glance at her stepfather's profile. His crooked nose and thin, mean mouth made her shudder.

Long-standing and intense hatred of Benson filled her soul; it rose up and choked her. After all he'd inflicted on her in her younger days, he was now a pillar of the Kirk. What would Mr Dunwoodie and his elders think if they knew the Will Benson she knew?

The sullen clouds clung tenaciously to the windowpanes, allowing no vestige of daylight in to brighten the colourless interior of the sandstone walls and dark wooden pews. Maddie's eyes were drawn to the stained glass window to the right of the pulpit. She loved the bright-blue and purple hues on the glass and its inscription, 'In the beginning was the Word and the Word was with God'.

Having long since lost the thread of the minister's sermon, Maddie picked at her chipped nail polish; the shade was pretty peach. Her stepfather hated painted nails, saying they made her look cheap, but she wasn't interested in his opinion.

She edged away from Benson and closer to her mother, smelling the mothballs from Mum's fur coat. Wisps of hair escaped out of the sides of Mum's blue felt hat, curling up to rest on the fabric. Pulling a handkerchief out of her pocket, her mother began to cough into it, the feathers on her hat waving around with the movement. Maddie glimpsed a flash of blood when her mother took the hankie away from her mouth. The cough was getting worse and Mum had also lost a lot of weight recently, although she pooh-poohed Maddie's concerns. Sensing Maddie's anxious eyes on her now, she smiled reassuringly and squeezed her daughter's hand.

Poor Mum had been easy prey for Will Benson. She must have found it hard to cope after Dad's death at Dunkirk, with little money or help with child-minding. As an engineer, Benson had been in a reserved occupation and his offer of marriage must have seemed heaven sent.

He'd only moved in with them a couple of months when it had started. Even now all these years later Maddie still felt her stomach churn. Her hands were in a tight fist on her lap as she recalled the brushing sound of her bedroom door in Rowan Avenue being pushed open across the thick pile carpet. It had continued into her school years and she'd been terrified to say anything to Mum because of Benson's violent temper and threats of what he'd do to both of them if she did tell. Mum wouldn't have believed her anyway as she could see no wrong in Benson and reporting him to the police would have meant answering too many painful questions.

By now Mr Dunwoodie's words had faded into the distance and Maddie stopped even trying to listen to what he was saying.

She looked up at the bulbs on the light fittings hanging from the ceiling. Cleaning them must be difficult; surely scaffolding would be needed to get up to that height. She counted seventy two bulbs in total; six sets of lights, each with twelve bulbs. Three bulbs had gone out but she guessed they wouldn't be replaced until others joined them; too much effort otherwise.

The sermon over, Mr Dunwoodie said a final prayer and gave out the announcements. While they were singing the last hymn, 'Onward Christian Soldiers', Mum started coughing again and had to dig into her bag for a boiled sweet. She always kept them with her for this purpose. After the Benediction, they moved out of the pew and made their way downstairs where Mr Dunwoodie was waiting at the front door to shake hands with his parishioners.

Maddie linked arms with her mother on the five minute walk to their terraced home in Rowan Avenue. The coughing fit had abated for the moment but she decided to persuade her mother to contact Dr Harvie, their G.P., first thing tomorrow morning.

Chapter Two

March 1956

'Your hands are so cold, Mum,' Maddie smiled through her tears at the skeletal figure lying on the bed, while she rubbed her mother's paper thin hands between her own. When some warmth began to creep back into the frail fingers Maddie placed them underneath the blankets, noticing how the colour of her mother's skin matched the white sheets. Mum was tiny, 5'2" in her stocking soles, but the outline of her body under the covers made her look even smaller. At 5'7" Maddie had taken her height from her dad, the dad that sadly she couldn't remember.

Her mother's blue eyes looked up at her. 'Happy Birthday, Maddie,' she whispered, then began coughing with the effort of speaking. Stretching over for the glass of water sitting on the bedside table, Maddie held it to her mother's pale lips. Her mother sipped it slowly and when the coughing ceased she lay back on the pillow, exhausted.

'Don't worry Mum, you'll be able to help me celebrate my next birthday.' Both knew Maddie was lying; mother and daughter were equally aware that there was little time left for Mum in this life. It was on a cold wintry day, almost three months ago now, that Dr Harvie had diagnosed pulmonary tuberculosis. Even although Maddie had suspected that tuberculosis was the cause of her mother's cough, hearing it put into words still came as a shock. The disease had taken too great a hold for Mum to benefit from treatment in a sanatorium, even if she could have afforded the fare to go to one.

Dr Harvie had visited Rowan Avenue about an hour

ago to give Mum her injection of streptomycin and as he sounded his patient's emaciated body, Maddie could see that he was visibly upset.

The door was pushed open and Will Benson came into the bedroom. His eyebrows arched but Maddie shook her head. Tensing up at the sight of him, she turned away to avoid meeting his eyes. When Mum's diagnosis had been made, Benson's behaviour towards Maddie had changed, due she suspected to his fear that she would speak out once her mother could no longer be hurt by the revelations. But his efforts to redeem himself were wasted as she knew that she could never forgive him for her stolen childhood.

He came closer and made to lay a hand on her shoulder but she quickly moved aside, out of his reach. 'Do you want something to eat, Love,' he whispered, 'you've been up here for hours and you really need a rest. You'll make yourself ill.'

His words grated and, without looking at him, she shook her head. 'No, I'm staying with Mum,' she said abruptly, and turned away, holding her mother's hand under the blankets.

Her shoulders relaxed once the door closed behind him and she stroked her mother's sweaty brow and dark stringy hair, now liberally sprinkled with grey. She glanced at the clock above the door. 'It's time for your cough medicine, Mum,' she murmured, picking up the bottle from the bedside table. She poured some of the foul-smelling treacly solution on to a spoon and raised her mother up into a sitting position. Supporting her mother with one hand, she held the spoon to the pale lips with the other. Her mother made a face but valiantly swallowed the medicine. Maddie wiped a drip of medicine off her mother's pink nightie before capping the bottle and returning it to the table.

When her mother's eyes closed soon afterwards, Maddie patted the white cheek. 'You have a sleep now Mum and I'll be here beside you when you waken up.'

Over the past week, during which her mother's condition steadily worsened, Maddie had had little sleep and even when she went to bed she lay there for hours wide awake. Thankfully her boss at work was understanding and allowed her as much time off as possible to be with her ailing mother. But now, sitting here, with her mother lying peacefully in bed, Maddie soon drifted off, dreaming that Benson was sobbing but she could feel no pity for him.

A strange noise wakened her and when she jerked back to full wakefulness she realised it had come from her mother. Guilt at falling asleep washed over her and she took her mother's puny hand between her own two. Panic arose inside her when she heard a rattling noise coming from her mother's throat. Maddie wiped the sweaty brow again and drew her fingers gently down the waxen cheek. The rattle came again and, as Maddie leaned closer, her mother's eyes flew open.

'No Mum, no,' she whispered. She sobbed quietly as she laid her cheek against her mother's. When she raised her head again, her tears dripped down on to the bedclothes as she gently pushed the eyelids down.

Chapter Three

July 1956

Maddie scuffed her way over the cobblestones, carrying a brown case containing as many of her possessions as would fit into it. The blue sky was at odds with the leaden grey smoke belching out of the chemical factory chimneys. This, mingled with the pungent smell of hops from the local brewery, became almost suffocating.

On her way to the bus stop down on the main road she stopped outside Bonnycross primary school, which she'd attended until the age of twelve. Maddie stared for a few minutes at the sign beside the gate; West Lothian County Council, Bonnycross Primary School. She'd been unhappy there and had difficulty in mixing with other children. Her problems accompanied her to Bonnycross High, where once again she found herself ostracised from her fellow pupils. Although aware that she herself was the problem, it hadn't made her feelings of isolation any easier to bear.

'Good riddance,' she yelled to both the school and the empty street. Maddie was happy to bid farewell to this drab town, where she'd spent the entire eighteen years of her life so far. Bonnycross, she thought as she trudged along. Nothing bonny about it.

Keen as she was to be rid of Bonnycross, the relief of escaping from Will Benson was even greater for Maddie. Her hatred and fear of her stepfather was such that she couldn't bear to be in the same house as him, never mind the same room.

Today she'd taken the chance to put her plan into action while he was sleeping following a nightshift. She crept

9

out of the house, her case packed and hidden for the past few days until the time was right. In the case she had pictures of her real dad wearing his Army uniform. She wondered what had happened to his war medals, trophies that Mum had proudly kept in the bureau. No doubt Benson sold them, she thought bitterly.

After Mum's death, she'd discovered that her mother and Will Benson weren't in fact married at all but living together in a common-law arrangement. Looking back, Maddie recalled as a young girl wondering why her surname was Granger and not Benson but she'd been too scared to ask any questions.

Maddie draped the strap of her leather bag over her shoulder. She'd bought it with the money Mum gave her for her eighteenth birthday, the very day Mum had died. Tears welled up at the memory. She wiped them away, leaving her clean handkerchief covered in black smudges of mascara.

The smell of soot wafted over to her from the factory chimneys. No wonder people here have lung problems, she thought, in no doubt that the environment had contributed to Mum's early death. She drew a hand across her forehead, feeling a headache coming on, only partly due to the smoke. She hoped the headache wouldn't develop into a full-blown migraine, something she was subject to.

'Mind where ye're going,' an irate passer-by growled, as she almost collided with him. Recognising him as Jimmy Frame from the next street and a bad-tempered old so and so to boot, Maddie's only response was to make a face. She knew that no-one in Bonnycross would mourn her going and she certainly wouldn't miss the town or its residents.

She couldn't wait to start a new life in a different part of the country, free of Benson. She'd left no note and as she was over sixteen the police would not investigate her whereabouts should he report her missing.

Putting her case down on the ground beside the bus stop, she sat on it to wait for the Glasgow bus. She pulled her hair away from her face, hair that had been almost white as a child but had darkened gradually over the years to its present brown shade. Grabbing the hair firmly with one hand, she tightened the blue elastic band holding it into a ponytail.

She took a sheet of paper out of her bag, on which she'd written down the name and address of a hostel in Glasgow she'd seen advertised in the local paper. When the Glasgow bus drew up a few minutes later, Maddie boarded it without giving even a backward glance at the town that had been her home for eighteen years.

Chapter Four

When she got off the bus in Glasgow, the enormity of what she was doing hit Maddie. Outside the bus station in Waterloo Street she turned right and wandered around, unsure of her bearings. She walked in a haphazard way, weaving in and out of people crowding the pavements. Most of them seemed to be in a hurry. Glasgow was such a huge place that she'd need to get used to the streets teeming with people. Mum had come from Glasgow before she met Dad and she'd always told Maddie what a friendly city it was. That thought heartened her slightly and she turned to a grey-haired woman with a round, cheery face, who was walking along the pavement towards her.

'Excuse me, can you tell me how to get to Clyde Street from here?'

The woman stopped and beamed at Maddie, showing the gaps in her blackened front teeth. 'Aye hen, it's no far. This is Waterloo Street and along there is Hope Street and if ye turn right and walk doon the hill,' the woman moved her shopping bags to her left hand and pointed with her right, 'that'll bring ye tae the Clydeside. I'm walkin' that way masel, so I'll see ye get there.'

Maddie fell into step with her and the woman kept up a constant stream of chatter as they walked. 'Ah' got some great bargains in Livingston's in Sauchiehall Street,' she said, holding out the large bags with the name of the store on them. 'If ye plan to stay in Glasgow for a bit, ye should go there.' Without waiting for a reply, she went on. 'Their school claes are a' reduced an' ah' got a couple o' skirts for ma granddaughter an' socks for 'er wee brother. Ma daughter'll be fair pleased wi' them, it costs her a fortune tae buy their uniforms.'

Maddie was relieved when they parted company at Clyde Street and, thanking the woman for her help, she hurried along to the Scottish Girls' Friendly Association Hostel, glad of her own company again. The foyer was dark and dingy, with the wallpaper hanging off in places and the carpet threadbare in parts. The place looked as if it needed a total redecoration.

'Hello, I'm Madeleine Granger and I'd like to book a room for a week,' she said to the woman at the desk. She'd decided to stay for a week and then re-assess her situation at the end of it. She was hoping to get a job quickly as her meagre savings in the Trustee Savings Bank wouldn't last long.

'If you could sign our register, Miss Granger?' The prim, middle-aged receptionist, dressed in a smart navy suit, seemed to scowl at Maddie as she pushed the book towards her. Ignoring the woman's attitude, Maddie signed, putting a dash in the column marked address.

The woman took a key from the board behind her and laid it down on the counter beside Maddie. 'Your room key, Number 23, on the first floor at the end of the corridor. Breakfast is from 7-8.30 a.m. and dinner between 6-8 p.m., both are self-service. And we have strict rules about no animals and no men and the front door is locked at 11 p.m.'

'Is there a lift?'

'It's broken,' Miss Frosty Face told her and returned to something she was writing.

Maddie picked up the key and headed towards the stairs. So much for the friendly city, she thought. Upstairs, she popped into the communal toilet and bathroom halfway along the corridor where, on entering, she was hit by a strong smell of disinfectant. The walls were painted bright yellow and on the floor in front of the bath was a scrubbed wooden board, presumably for residents to stand on when they stepped out of the bath.

When she emerged from the bathroom, a dark-haired

girl a couple of inches taller than herself came along from the opposite direction. The girl smiled and disappeared into a bedroom.

Maddie's room was small and narrow. From its single window she had a view over the River Clyde, to what looked like warehouses on the opposite bank. Some small boats bobbed around on the water. A bigger craft, its name unclear from this distance although the first letter looked like a 'C', was moored close to a nearby bridge that spanned the river. She watched a red double decker bus drive over the bridge and when she turned her head to the right she could see more bridges further along the river.

The room felt stuffy and she tried to open the window but no matter how hard she yanked, it seemed to be stuck fast. She wasn't game to report it to Miss Frosty Face so decided to ask a member of staff to open it for her later.

Although the room was spartan, the wallpaper had some pretty pink flowers on it. The single divan bed was covered with a pink candlewick bedspread and the curtains were of a similar shade. A few cigarette burns decorated the eiderdown, the bedside lamp had no bulb and one of the drawers was missing a handle. The whole room wore a look of having seen better days. At least the carpet was clean and the furniture had been dusted. She folded back the bedclothes to reveal freshly laundered white sheets. Mum had always said the first thing you did in a hotel was to check the bed. Thinking of her mum brought on tears.

She laid her dad's old case on top of the eiderdown. When she lifted the case lid, the musty smell coming out of it confirmed its age. She'd brought the case down from the loft in Rowan Avenue a few nights ago when Benson was on a nightshift. A quick blow of the dust off the top and she'd hidden it under her bed until it was required.

Inside the case, she'd found a photograph. It seemed to have been taken at the local Bonnycross tennis courts and there were four men in the picture, all wearing white flannels and Fair-isle pullovers and holding tennis rackets. One of the men she recognised as her dad from his Army pictures but the other three were strangers to her. In clear writing, which she assumed was Dad's, it said 'The Wee Crowd, 1934'.

Maddie hung her few items of clothing in the wardrobe and folded her underwear into the drawers. On the table at the side of her bed she stood her dad's framed Army picture along with the little alarm clock she'd received as a leaving gift from her workmates in the insurance office in Falkirk. Benson had been unaware that she'd resigned from her job; she'd only left a couple of days before she came to Glasgow. She took a book of poetry out of the case. It was a school prize for Dad. She rubbed her hand across the front page where his name, *Robert Granger*, was printed in a fine copperplate handwriting, before laying it down beside the clock.

At the bottom of the case was Mum's dusky pink flannelette nightdress, still bearing the stain from the spilled medicine shortly before her death. Maddie had rescued the soiled garment from a pile of clothes after her mother's death, before Benson disposed of everything. She'd kept it hidden and had packed it unwashed. It was much too small for Maddie but she needed to have something of her mother's to keep. Tears glinted as she buried her face into the folds of the material and breathed in deeply the slight scent of Mum, before carefully placing the garment in the bottom drawer of the bedside cabinet.

Maddie went outdoors again to have a walk around the area before dinner. A brisk wind had whipped up by now and an empty paper bag whooshed past her legs, no doubt from the nearby litter bin overflowing with papers and other rubbish.

A few doors along from the hostel a queue had formed inside a fish and chip shop. The smell coming through the open doorway reminded Maddie that she'd last eaten at breakfast time in Bonnycross. Hunger gnawed at her and she decided to search out a place to eat.

She turned right, which led up to a large square. St Enoch Railway Station was on the right and to her left she spotted 'Luigi's Café'. There was a tinkling sound as she pushed open the door and went inside. She chose a window table with bench seating. The table was covered in a blue and white gingham cloth and a vase of artificial flowers sat in the middle of the table. They might have passed for real blooms except for their bright blue colour.

The waitress, wearing a frilly apron and white lace cap, approached the table and smiled at Maddie. 'What can I get you?'

'A fruit scone with butter and jam and a cup of tea please.'

Pulling up the pad that hung on a string from her waistband, the waitress licked the tip of the pencil and jotted down Maddie's order. In no time at all she returned and laid the scone and the tea in its pyrex cup and saucer in front of Maddie. 'Sugar and milk are on the table,' she said, before turning away to serve a new customer who was seated nearby.

In the hostel that evening Maddie went down to dinner during the last half hour they were serving in the hope that she'd be left in peace and wouldn't have to enter into conversation with strangers. Her plan worked and she had the dining room almost to herself. While she was eating, the hostel staff clattered around in the kitchen clearing up. No doubt all rushing home to their families, she thought bitterly.

Her meal over, she got up from the table. The evening sun hadn't yet fully set and from the dining room window she noticed the pretty reflections on the river as it did so.

Despite Maddie's earlier depression, she felt her mood lifting a fraction, and she pumped herself up to face any challenges tomorrow may bring.

Chapter Five

The following morning when Maddie walked into the Ministry of Labour office in Waterloo Street, or the Buroo as most folk called it, a Commissionaire directed her to the correct department. Staff members were seated in a row like bank tellers behind a dark wooden counter. The partitions between each staff member offered some privacy to the people seeking work.

Although it was only a few minutes after nine o'clock, a large crowd had already gathered in the reception area. Preparing herself for a lengthy wait, Maddie took her seat at the back of the queue beside a large plant, its leaves yellowed and curled up. The hot sun streaming in through the windows behind Maddie roasted her and any air generated by the fans positioned around the room was totally ineffectual.

To help pass the time, Maddie observed the people round about her. She was entertained by two claimants having a punch up while another man was escorted out of the building by the Commissionaire for swearing at a female staff member. Eventually Maddie's turn came and she was called over to one of the booths.

'I arrived in Glasgow yesterday and need to find work,' she told the middle-aged woman behind the counter, when asked to state the reason for her attendance.

The woman, whose hair was pushed back into a French roll, peered at Maddie from behind the largest pair of specs she'd ever seen. 'Have you been in employment previously?' she asked in a pleasant enough voice.

'Yes, I left my job last week.'

'What kind of experience do you have?'

'Office work. I was with an insurance company in

Falkirk. Here's my P45.' Maddie slid the certificate across the desk.

The woman wrote Maddie's name from the P45 on to a card. 'And can you confirm your date of birth, Miss Granger?'

'27th March, 1938.' Some hair had come loose from her pony tail and Maddie flicked it away from her face, winding the longest strands behind her ears.

'And what's your address in Glasgow, Miss Granger?'

'I'm staying in the Scottish Girls' Friendly Association Hostel in Clyde Street. Until I can get a job and a place of my own.'

'Do you have any qualifications?'

Maddie opened a brown envelope and removed two certificates which she pushed towards the woman. 'I've got a Pitman's shorthand certificate for 100 wpm and an RSA typing certificate for 40 wpm.'

The woman checked the certificates and added the details on to the card. 'Is it office work you're seeking? Or would you consider another type of employment?'

'I'm willing to take anything I can get but I'd prefer office work.'

'As you have experience that shouldn't be a problem.'

'I'd like to find a job quickly as I don't have much in the way of savings.'

'Maybe you'll get a position quickly and won't need to go on to benefits,' the woman continued, her tone sympathetic. 'We'll send you word of openings as they come up, Miss Granger. It's important you attend for interviews as non-attendance can affect you receiving benefits at a later stage.'

Maddie thanked her and got to her feet while the woman filed her card into a box before calling out 'next please'. And so it goes, Maddie thought as she left the building, we're all just numbers to them.

Not wanting to spend the rest of the day in her room at the hostel, she wandered along Argyle Street, one of the main shopping streets in the city, looking in the shop windows she passed. She reached the entrance to the Argyle Arcade; a plaque on the wall told her that it had been built in 1827 and was Scotland's first ever indoor shopping mall.

She strolled through the Arcade which seemed to contain mainly jewellers' shops, apart from a baby shop, a shop selling ladies' fashions and the Clyde Model Dockyard. There was a rather posh-looking restaurant, Sloane's, situated near the entrance, with a board outside advertising the dishes on the menu. Maddie looked longingly in the windows of the jewellers' shops. Fabulous rings and pendants sparkled up at her from their velvet trays on the other side of the glass. 'Maybe one day I'll own jewellery like this,' she said under her breath.

The Arcade was L-shaped; she entered from Argyle Street and emerged at the other end of the 'L' on to Buchanan Street, which was crowded with shoppers.

Crossing the street, she entered Henderson's department store. It was like an Alladin's cave. She wandered round all five floors, gazing at the racks of clothes from London fashion houses, dreaming of being wealthy enough to purchase something.

She felt herself drawn towards the perfume counters near the store entrance, where she tried out the various scents. The very air in this part of the store seemed to be perfumed. Under the scrutiny of a watchful assistant, looking shapely in a tailored wool dress, Maddie dabbed scent on to her wrists and her neck. Finally the assistant, her sleek black hair cut into a neat bob, headed over to Maddie. 'Can I help you Madam?' With her supercilious tone, the last word came out like Modom.

Realising how long she'd been standing at the counter, Maddie shook her head and scurried away towards the rear of the store. When she stumbled across a counter displaying a rack with sale goods on it, she noticed the blouses hanging there had been marked down by 50%. Even at that, they were still way beyond her means.

A pink and white candy striped shirt blouse caught her eye and when she checked the label, it was her size. The blouse would be ideal to wear to an interview if she was lucky enough to get one. The assistant working on the counter had just sold a cashmere cardigan for a vast sum of money to a well-dressed customer.

The assistant's attention was taken up with placing the money into a cylinder which would go up to the Counting House on the top floor by conveyor belt. When the customer turned her face away for a few moments Maddie, on impulse, grabbed the striped blouse and stuffed it into her roomy shoulder bag.

She dashed past the perfume counters once more and breathed a sigh of relief as she emerged out on to Buchanan Street unhindered after her first foray into shoplifting. Checking that no staff member was following her, she vanished into the crowd of shoppers and made her way down to St Enoch Square.

Guilt washed over her, aware that Mum would have disapproved of such behaviour but she consoled herself that she was on her own now and had to live by any means she could.

The station clock was at half past one and hunger enticed her into Luigi's café once more. She needed to watch she didn't overspend but she'd never last out without food until dinner. She sat at the same table as yesterday. The waitress came over straight away, giving her a smile of recognition. 'Hello again, what can I get you today?'

'I'll have a ham sandwich and a cup of tea.'

Maddie was halfway through her sandwich when a girl about her own age came into the café. She vaguely recalled having seen the girl in the corridor of the hostel yesterday.

The newcomer slipped her floral headscarf off her shiny black hair and began to move towards Maddie's table. Maddie looked away immediately and the girl hesitated, then walked over to a table on the other side of the café.

Maddie relaxed again, happy to keep to herself right now.

Chapter Six

August 1956

Maddie stood in front of the mirror trying to pull the uneven strands of hair into her pony tail. But it was a thankless task; no sooner had she wound the elastic band tightly round them, when the shorter strands had once again come loose to hang untidily at the sides of her face.

She looked at her dull, lifeless hair and sighed. She, who'd always taken a pride in having shiny, healthy hair, was well aware of how badly it needed a trim. But her meagre savings had depleted to an alarming degree and she couldn't justify the cost. She had to accept that right now eating was more important than her appearance, no matter how she hated it.

Two weeks had elapsed since her visit to the Ministry of Labour and, although they'd sent her for two interviews, the first as a cleaner in the Post Office and the second as an assistant in a children's nursery, she hadn't been successful on either occasion. They weren't the kind of jobs she wanted and, in hindsight, she was sure that had probably been apparent to the interviewers. But as her savings were beginning to dwindle to almost nothing, she decided she couldn't any longer be so choosy but would need to take on any work that came her way. Hopefully soon she'd get word of more job vacancies.

Maddie had been brought up to believe it was right and proper to work for her living and not expect handouts, but she had to adapt her thinking to fit her circumstances.

Today, after wandering around the town centre for a few hours, she'd come into Henderson's to use their ladies' room. As she returned her comb to her handbag, she felt a

21

twinge of guilt about the blouse she'd stolen the last time she was in this store. She certainly wasn't game to steal anything more and hoped to find a job soon before she got herself a criminal record.

The plan had been to call in at Luigi's on her way back to the hostel, however, she came across another café, The Pantry, before she got there. She ordered tea and a plain cookie and butter, the cheapest item on the menu. She could have eaten lunch back at the hostel but it wouldn't have worked out any less expensive and the food would have been very similar to this evening's menu.

On her arrival back at the hostel, Maddie collected her room key from the torn-faced receptionist at the front desk. As well as the key, the woman took an envelope out of one the pigeonholes and laid them both on the counter. 'Mail for you,' she said to Maddie in her expressionless voice.

'Thank you,' Maddie replied and walked towards the stairway.

Closing the door behind her, Maddie opened the envelope and whooped with joy when she read the letter from the Ministry of Labour requesting that she attend for a job interview the following day. The job was as an assistant in a tobacconist's shop, not really what she wanted to work at but she'd make that less obvious at this interview. She gave a wry smile, recalling one of her mother's favourite sayings, beggars can't be choosers.

Chapter Seven

September 1956

'Goodnight ladies, see you tomorrow.' Mr Jackson, who'd owned the tobacconist's shop in St Enoch Square for almost twenty years, drew the shutter down over the shop door and padlocked it, before heading over to his car parked nearby.

'Goodnight, Mr Jackson,' his two assistants returned the greeting. They giggled as they watched him stride it out, his rigid gait resembling that of a tin soldier. Both were certain that his magnificent head of hair was a wig. Yet they were both fond of him as he was a true gentleman and treated them very courteously.

The two women said their farewells and headed off in different directions, Cathy to catch the Baillieston bus in Argyle Street and Maddie to the hostel. She walked through the square, admiring the trees around her, all clothed in their autumn colours. Autumn had always been her favourite season of the year. The shop opened until seven o'clock on Thursdays and she had to get down to the dining room quickly before they stopped serving at eight o'clock.

Tying her blue headscarf tighter under her chin, Maddie lowered her head against the stiff wind blowing through the square. The narrow part leading to the river was like a tunnel and you were treated to the full blast. As she walked, Maddie counted back the weeks and realised that she'd been working for over a month now in Mr Jackson's shop.

Even though it wasn't the job she wanted, it had been a stop-gap to give her money until she found something better paid. Mr Jackson treated her well and Cathy was pleasant enough too. She didn't know Cathy's exact age but guessed she was around the middle forties. Because she got on so well with them, she hadn't made much effort to find something else although she still wanted a better job. Her plans of moving into her own place were thwarted because rents in Glasgow were so high, especially near the city centre.

Back at the hostel, she hurried upstairs to her room and hung her coat in the wardrobe. The blouse she'd stolen from Henderson's, or 'liberated' as she preferred to think of it, was also hanging in there, a bit crushed looking. She'd washed the blouse a couple of days ago and reckoned if the garment hung in the wardrobe for a few days the creases would disappear and the heat of her body would also help to smooth out the material. There were ironing facilities in the hostel but that would cost money she didn't have.

After giving her face and hands a quick wash, she smoothed down her pleated skirt, a blue and black checked one she'd sewn in the dressmaking class during her last year at secondary school. The material had lasted well and she should get a lot of wear out of it yet. Then she tightened the blue elastic band around her pony tail and made her way downstairs for her meal. The dining room was almost empty and there was little left on the hot plates. Plumping for macaroni and chips, she played with it and left almost half. She chose a portion of trifle as a dessert and finished up with a cup of tea. Only a couple of kitchen staff remained by the time she left the dining room.

Cathie had lent her Alistair MacLean's novel 'The Guns of Navarone' but, after an abortive attempt at reading the first chapter, Maddie decided to go out for a walk to clear her head before bed.

The nights were drawing in and the streetlights were on when she got down to the front door of the hostel. She crossed the road and walked along at the side of the river. She turned left on to the suspension bridge and made her way to the middle.

From her position on the bridge, she could see the

Carrick rocking gently on the water. It was the boat she'd noticed on her first night in the hostel. Mr Jackson had told her that it was owned by the Navy and when she was passing one day she'd stopped to read the sign on it, which said Royal Naval Volunteer Reserve Club. Right now light showed from inside the vessel and voices and laughter drifted over to her through the quiet night.

She watched the reflections of the streetlights dancing on the inky black water below her. The river was flowing quite fast and she thought she saw a silver flash skimming over the surface. Perhaps it's a fish, she thought, but remembered the polluted river in daylight and was sure no fish could survive in it. Cathy had told her that the source of the Clyde was a trickle of water in the Leadhills in Lanarkshire.

As she stood there, a tidal wave of sadness engulfed her and she saw her mother's face smiling up at her from the murky depths. Missing her mum's voice and gentle smile, Maddie's defences broke and tears flooded down her face. Her bitter sobs were carried away by a sudden strong gust of wind. Dark thoughts had been churning around her mind during the past few days when she was unable to see any future ahead. Her days were routine, work, eat and sleep, one boring day following another, with nothing special to look forward to at weekends.

A wall of loneliness hit her, a feeling she hadn't admitted to herself previously. That's it, she thought, I'm lonely and unloved. Her breath caught as the wind increased, moving the water below.

She looked down at the swirls and felt herself being drawn into the river. 'Come,' she heard her mother's voice whisper. 'Escape from your unhappiness and be with me.'

The urge to jump was strong. She clutched the top of the rail and pulled herself up to her full height. Leaning her hands heavily on the rail, she started to swing her right leg up when something nuzzled her other leg. She came down off the rail and looked into the soft brown depths of the Golden Retriever's eyes. The dog rubbed its wet nose against her hand and, with its tongue hanging out, wagged its tail to say hello.

'Golda, come back Golda.' Next minute the dog's owner appeared at Maddie's side. The woman, who looked in her sixties, was out of puff and breathing heavily, and a gust of wind caught at her white rain mac, ballooning it out until she resembled a Michelin man. 'I hope Golda hasn't been bothering you,' she said once she'd caught her breath again. Unaware that Golda had just saved Maddie's life, the woman went on, 'she's very friendly and thinks everyone likes dogs.'

'It's alright, I do like dogs.' Maddie smiled at the woman. She knelt down and patted Golda's thick coat and played with her long ears, receiving some more licks in response.

They chatted for a few more minutes before Golda and her owner made their way over to the other side of the bridge. Maddie, now recovered from her previous feelings, walked back towards the street and safety.

Chapter Eight

November 1956

Although not yet half past four, the street lamps were already on, bubbles of rain clinging to their glass orbs. The sky had steadily darkened in the ten minutes Viv Kingston had been standing in the hostel doorway, sheltering from the sudden heavy shower. The tip of her cigarette glowed like a beacon in the November gloom. She edged further under the hostel canopy, keen to avoid going into the cinema in wet clothes. Taking another draw, she inhaled deeply and released the smoke down her nostrils, a trick she had copied from her dad.

She'd heard good reports of 'To Catch a Thief' and with two of her favourites starring in it, she was sure the film would come up to her expectations. The Hitchcock thriller starred Cary Grant as a retired cat burglar, preying on wealthy tourists visiting the French Riviera. With Grace Kelly as his co-star it was certain to be a winner. As Tuesday was their half day at work, she and her workmate Lily had decided to go to the five o'clock showing at Green's Playhouse in Renfield Street.

She inhaled again, studying the girl on the opposite side of the road. Viv had seen her quite often in the hostel and she seemed a real loner. The girl had come out of the hostel about five minutes ago and crossed the road without even glancing at Viv standing at the entrance. Since then she'd been standing like a statue in the pouring rain, staring at the river. Viv held her breath for a moment when it looked like the girl might be about to jump into the water but then she turned round and headed back to the hostel once more.

Drawing her feet wearily over the cobblestones, which

shone brightly in the drizzle, the girl seemed oblivious to her dripping wet coat and hair. When she got closer Viv saw that long strands of hair had come loose from her pony tail. They were plastered against the sides of her face, a face that wore the same strained look that Viv had noticed in the past.

Thinking back, Viv recalled seeing this girl in the corridor the day she'd arrived at the hostel sometime during the summer. Over the months that had elapsed since then, Viv had often smiled at her but had never received any response.

Approaching the doorway now, the girl slouched past and into the hostel, making Viv feel invisible. Her downcast expression and empty eyes saddened Viv. Maybe what was troubling her would have been helped by sharing it with someone.

Viv stubbed out her cigarette when she saw Lily approaching. Lily's head and shoulders were hunched under a large blue and white golf umbrella. 'Sorry,' she apologised, 'the bus was late. Thank God I'm going to get away from this foul weather soon.'

Viv hated when Lily spoke about her impending departure with her family to start a new life in Australia. It was so far away and Viv was sure she'd never see Lily again. For over a year now the two girls had worked on the haberdashery counter at Marshall's emporium in Argyle Street and during that time they'd become firm friends.

'We've plenty of time. The film doesn't start for another half hour.' Viv linked arms with Lily and they squeezed together under the brolly.

'Did you notice the girl who went past me into the hostel just as you arrived?' Viv asked while they were waiting in the queue for tickets.

'I caught a glimpse of her disappearing inside. Who is she?'

'I don't know. She's a strange girl, keeps herself to herself. I've tried a couple of times to start up a conversation but she doesn't seem interested.'

'Her loss. Think what excitement she's missing not knowing you.'

Viv gave her a friendly prod in the ribs. 'Seriously though, she looks really sad and downcast. There's a desperate look on her face. I'd like to help her if I could. I saw her in Luigi's café one day but she didn't look like she'd welcome company so I didn't speak to her.'

'That's you all over Viv. Always looking for a lame duck to care for.'

They reached the cinema cash desk and Lily pushed two shillings and sixpence, better known as a half crown, through to the cashier seated behind the glass. 'Two for the stalls, please,' she said. The balcony seats cost one shilling and sixpence so the girls contented themselves with the one shilling and threepence seats in the stalls. When they'd moved away from the cash desk, Viv gave Lily the cost of her ticket, counting out a silver shilling coin and a threepenny piece into her friend's hand. The threepenny piece was much larger than the silver sixpence and, because of its bronze colour, was known as a wooden threepenny.

Moving into the darkened cinema, they found seats not too near the screen and, for the moment, Viv forgot about the sad-looking girl in the hostel.

*

An ambulance was driving off, its siren going full blast, when Viv arrived back at the hostel. When she got into the entrance hall Morag, the evening receptionist, was standing with a member of the catering staff.

From what little Viv could make out of their conversation, it was obvious they were discussing the person who'd gone off in the ambulance.

'What's happened?' she asked. 'I saw the ambulance.'

'It's one of the residents,' Morag told her.

The other woman took up the story. 'She swallowed some tablets but the ambulance men think she'll recover. They said it was more a cry for help than a definite suicide attempt.'

Morag turned to Viv. 'Jenny here said the resident seemed very down in the mouth at dinner time and suggested that I should check if she was alright. When I knocked her door, I couldn't get a reply and used my pass key to get in. I found her lying on the bed with the tablet bottle at her side.' Morag pressed her hand over her brow and sighed. 'I got such a fright when I saw her.'

'And they weren't her tablets,' Jenny said.

Morag gave her a sharp look and turned back to Viv. 'No they were sleeping pills. The name on the bottle was Janet Benson and the girl's name is Madeleine Granger. Anyway the police and doctors in the Royal Infirmary will sort it out.'

Viv had remained silent, open mouthed, while they were speaking. She couldn't imagine ever wanting to kill herself; surely a person in their right mind wouldn't take such drastic action. 'Is that the girl in Room 23? Wears her hair in a ponytail.'

'Yes, it is. Do you know her?'

'Not to speak to but I've seen her in the corridor. I saw her earlier tonight outside the hostel and she looked awful. I've tried to smile and be friendly but she doesn't seem to want to enter into a conversation.'

Morag nodded. 'I think you're right. Keep her overdose under your hat, will you? The fewer people who know about it, the better. I'll get your key,' she said, moving over to the desk.

'I won't say anything, trust me,' Viv told her, as she took the key. She made her way towards the stairway, avoiding the hole in the carpet where she'd tripped up in the past.

'Maybe you could keep up your efforts with her,' Morag called after her, 'the poor girl seems to be in need of friends.'

'Will do,' Viv threw over her shoulder as she started to climb the stairs.

Chapter Nine

Next morning Viv didn't ask Kate, the daytime receptionist, for news of the girl from Room 23. Kate was different from Morag, who enjoyed a chat. Instead, she'd get a progress report from Morag that evening.

Lily was getting off her bus outside the store when Viv reached the entrance.

'And how's your lame duck today, Viv, did you see her this morning?' Lily asked when they were leaving their coats in the staffroom.

Viv carefully hung her coat on the hook inside her locker. 'She's in hospital. Took an overdose last night. I got back home just as the ambulance drove off.'

Lily re-applied her lipstick and stood back from the mirror to admire her appearance. 'Good God, what leads folk to try and do away with themselves? It's beyond me.'

'That's because you're so confident and happy in your life, Lily. I knew last night there was something wrong with that girl.' Viv's regret at doing nothing was evident in her voice.

'Sorry if I sound heartless, Viv, but it really is her problem. Don't get involved.'

'I know you're right but I can't get her out of my mind. You should have seen her face yesterday, it really haunts me.'

'Well just forget about her, that's my advice. Did you remember we're having a staff meeting at nine o'clock?'

Viv glanced at the clock on the staffroom wall; it was a couple of minutes before nine.

'Yes,' she lied, and put her handbag into her locker before following her friend into their Head of Department's office.

The store was hectic that day with early Christmas shoppers and Viv had no time to ponder any further on the suicidal girl.

Chapter Ten

'I really did mean to kill myself,' John told his fellow group members, two weeks later. 'I could see no other way to escape from my depression and if the rope hadn't snapped then I wouldn't be here speaking to you now.'

'Are you glad that you didn't succeed?' the chap sitting next to Maddie asked.

'I am now, because I'm coming here.' John looked at Brian, the therapist, as he said this.

Maddie was sitting directly opposite John in the circle. She'd listened intently to his story, aware of how desperate she'd felt when she'd turned to the tablet bottle two weeks ago. Having regained consciousness in hospital after the overdose, she'd felt strangely relieved that the pills hadn't killed her, most likely because the bottle had only been a quarter full when her mother died. She'd been given what the staff nurse called gastric lavage on arriving at the A & E department which Maddie understood was to wash the tablets out of her system.

Shortly after her admission, Dr Hepworth from the hospital's psychiatry department visited Maddie in the ward. At well over six feet tall, with a slight stoop and balding, the doctor's eyes behind his dark-rimmed glasses were full of understanding. At that initial meeting Maddie was reluctant to speak to him, embarrassed about her overdose and a bit hostile about accepting help from him. The next day she was interviewed by Dr Hepworth in his office and, with this meeting being in private, she opened up about her problems. Maddie found him easy to talk to and he arranged for her to attend this psychotherapy group on an out-patient basis.

Brian hadn't interrupted John while he was speaking

and it was only after he'd fallen silent, that the therapist asked if any group members wanted to comment on John's story.

Maddie shifted in her seat, wanting to express her admiration for the candid way John spoke about his suicide attempt. But her courage failed her and she remained silent, looking down at her feet. She looked up when she heard someone sobbing. It was Helen, sitting two along from John. Maddie only knew her as Helen; no surnames were known within the group. Through her sobs, Helen began to tell the group members that her mother had lung problems and severe rheumatoid arthritis, resulting in very poor mobility. Helen and her mum lived together and her mother's health problems often necessitated Helen taking time off work. Because of this she was sacked from her job and wasn't working at the moment. Helen loved her mother but everything had got on top of her and she had cut her wrists.

She stopped speaking for a moment and swallowed deeply. 'Mum found me on the bathroom floor,' she went on, 'and dialled 999. It's thanks to my mum that I'm still here,' she finished, her sobbing abated somewhat now she'd spoken about her problems.

'And how do you feel now, Helen?' Brian interjected.

'I feel very weak and disgusted by my action. I know I was being selfish and I've promised my mum that I won't ever try it again but I don't know if she totally trusts me to be left on my own for long. I really need to find another job to help with household bills.'

Seeing the distress on Helen's face, and knowing how close she'd been to killing herself with an overdose, Maddie felt great empathy with her. When she felt the tears welling up in her own eyes, she took out her handkerchief and blew her nose fiercely.

*

When she came out of the counselling session, Maddie stood outside the hospital gates, smoking a cigarette and trying to gather her thoughts. Because the counselling group was on a Tuesday afternoon and the shop closed at lunch time, it meant she didn't need to take time off work in order to attend. She decided to go to Luigi's, now her local watering hole. Although she knew she shouldn't be spending money until she'd found better paid work, Maddie couldn't face sitting in her bare room for the rest of the afternoon.

She walked down Castle Street until she got to the Tolbooth at Glasgow Cross. Cathy had told her this was where in days gone by they used to hang murderers. At the Tolbooth, she turned right into Trongate, which further along became Argyle Street. Reaching Buchanan Street, she crossed the road and went into the now familiar St Enoch Square.

A wall of noise hit her as she entered Luigi's, jam packed with people enjoying an afternoon tea or coffee. The café was a popular venue, being so close to Argyle Street. Looking around as she made her way to the only empty table she could see, Maddie recognised some of the folk as regulars.

The usual waitress served her. 'Hello, how are you today?' the woman asked brightly.

'Okay', Maddie replied, aware of her hollow tone but unable to alter it. She just wanted to be left in peace. While she was waiting for her order, it occurred to her that there had been no word from Benson since she left Bonnycross. He obviously hadn't been able to trace her because she wasn't a child and for that Maddie was truly thankful. Even thinking about him gave her the creeps. She'd been served with her bacon roll and tea when a girl came into the café and then, horror of horrors, after looking around the busy café, she headed towards Maddie's table.

'Sorry to disturb,' the newcomer apologised, 'but do you mind if I join you?'

Maddie's only response was to draw her crockery closer, leaving more room on the table.

As she slid into the bench seat facing Maddie, the girl pulled off her grey serge jacket and lay it down on the seat beside her. The waitress, who seemed to know the girl quite well, came over to take her order. Afterwards the girl smiled over at Maddie, her blue eyes crinkling at the sides. 'I've seen you in the hostel. I live there too.'

Maddie murmured 'yes', a smile almost forming on

her face but not quite. She hoped that would end the conversation but her companion had other ideas.

'Are you settling into the hostel?'

Maddie shrugged and gave another slight nod.

'How long have you lived there now?' the girl persisted, pushing her black curly hair away from her face. 'I'm Viv Kingston by the way.' Her hand shot out across the table.

Maddie reluctantly shook hands. 'Maddie Granger.'

'Is that short for Madeleine?' When Maddie nodded, the girl went on. 'My name's shortened too, it's really Vivienne. I hate it but when my mother was expecting me she read about the American film star, Vivienne Leigh, in a magazine and decided to call me after her.'

'Wasn't she the star of 'Gone With the Wind?'

'That's right. I was about two when the film came out. When I was ten, Mum took me to see it in a cinema in Kilmarnock. She was sure I would be bored but instead I loved the story and didn't move a muscle during the film. So how long have you been at the hostel?' Viv asked once again.

'I arrived in July.'

'I've been there for a year. My family live on a farm in Ayrshire but there was no employment for me that far out in the country so I moved to Glasgow.'

'Do you come into this café often?'

'Yep.' Viv nodded and her earrings, which reminded Maddie of curtain rings, shook when she did so. 'I found it when I first moved to Glasgow. It's handy for the hostel and cleaner than some of the other places around here. I sometimes come in at lunch time, it's a change from our staff canteen.'

Maddie felt her mood lifting a bit and, despite her desire for her own company, found herself warming to this girl. 'Where do you work?'

'In Marshall's Emporium on Argyle Street, I'm in the haberdashery department. The store's been really busy in the past few weeks with Christmas just round the corner.'

'How long have you worked there?'

'About a year now. I got the job a week after coming

to Glasgow. Because it's cheap and quite clean, I've lived at the hostel since I got here. My parents think it's safer for me to be there than living in a dingy tenement flat on my own. How were your folks about you moving to the big city?'

'My parents are dead. My dad died when I was little and Mum passed away a couple of months ago. I miss her.' Maddie's voice dropped and she looked down at the table cover. Saying nothing about Benson, she changed the subject. 'My room at the hostel is fine at the moment until I get a better paid job.'

'What kind of work do you do?'

'I'm working in a tobacconist shop near here.'

Viv decided not to mention the overdose, feeling it would be too intrusive. The way she saw it, Maddie would tell her about that if she wanted her to know.

'And how do you like it there? In the tobacconist's I mean.'

'It's ok. It's the first time I've worked in a shop.'

The waitress appeared with Viv's toast and tea. 'Anything else?' she asked Maddie, picking up her used crockery.

'I'll have another cup of tea, please.' Maddie was surprised to find how much she was enjoying Viv Kingston's company

'What did you work at before?' Viv asked, when the waitress had moved away.

'I've been in an insurance office in Falkirk since I left school but I gave up that job in July to come here to work.' She couldn't believe she'd told so much of her life to this stranger. And yet, the girl didn't seem like a stranger. It was almost as though Maddie had known her previously. She watched Viv buttering her toast, amazed at the length of her fingernails, well-cut and covered in red polish. It's well seen she works in a shop, Maddie thought, having lost count of the number of broken fingernails she'd suffered at the hands of her typewriter in the insurance company.

'Hello, a penny for them.'

'Sorry, I was miles away,' she apologised.

Viv laughed. 'I could see that. I was asking if you come from Falkirk.'

'No, from Bonnycross, in West Lothian. I travelled by bus to my work in Falkirk. I've lived in Bonnycross all my life and was glad to get away to make a new life for myself here.' She stopped speaking when the waitress arrived with her second cup of tea.

'Is Bonnycross as pretty a place as its name suggests?'

Maddie shook her head vigorously. 'No, it's very drab and dirty because of all the smoke from the factory chimneys. And there's always a stink from the brewery.'

Viv popped the last piece of toast into her mouth and washed it down with the remainder of her tea. 'If you're keen to find another job, I could check in Marshall's if there are any staff openings in the store. If you didn't want to work as a sales assistant, we have a large office on the top floor of the building.'

'Thanks a lot.' Maddie smiled, spooning more sugar into her tea.

Once they'd paid their bill, they got to their feet and headed back to the hostel. 'Will I see you downstairs tonight in the dining room?' Viv suggested. 'I usually go down sharp as later on some of the dishes run out and you don't get so much choice.'

'OK, I'll come down early and see you there.'

By the time Maddie reached her room, she was feeling happier than she'd done in a long time.

˙ Chapter Eleven

'There's a job going for a shorthand typist in our counting house, Maddie,' Viv told her the following week when they were having dinner together in the hostel, a habit they'd slipped into quite naturally. 'I enquired about it and if you're interested Miss Edwards, the Manageress, will give you an interview. I explained that you were working at the moment so she would be willing to see you during your lunch hour.'

'Thanks, Viv, you're a true friend. What's Miss Edwards like?'

Viv shrugged. 'I've only spoken to her a couple of times as I was interviewed for my job by Mr Chalmers, the store manager. She comes across as a bit of a tartar but I've heard her bark's worse than her bite.' She pulled a face and pushed the rather sad looking green beans to the side of her plate. 'The food in here's getting worse.'

Maddie also put her cutlery down, having eaten enough of her spaghetti dish. 'I don't know how you've managed to stay here for so long. I can't wait to get a place of my own.'

'It's money that's been the problem Maddie. You'll be surprised at how expensive rents are in a big city like Glasgow, especially if you want to stay quite close to the city centre.'

'I wondered if you and I could share a place to half the rent,' Maddie suggested when they'd collected their coffee and returned to the table. 'Or will Lily want to share with you.'

'Didn't I tell you that Lily and her family are moving to Australia in January? I'm pleased for Lily but I'm going to miss her a lot.'

Viv lit a cigarette and laid her lighter on the table while she took a draw. Then she sat back and blew rings of smoke up towards the ceiling. 'Your suggestion sounds good.'

Maddie pushed the ashtray towards Viv, secretly pleased to hear of Lily's imminent departure for Australia. Viv had introduced them one evening when Lily came to the hostel and Maddie had instantly felt a hostility from Lily. She certainly wouldn't have wanted her as a friend but didn't want to offend Viv by voicing that opinion.

'Maybe we could consider getting a place of our own in the New Year,' Viv said, 'especially if you get the job in our counting house and earn more money.'

*

When Maddie walked through the double doors of Marshall's Emporium on Wednesday around noon, she was hit by a wall of noise. The counters positioned around the entrance were bathed in bright light and the din from the shoppers crowding the place was deafening to the newcomer. A well-dressed lady was choosing perfumes at one counter, several women at the nearby jewellery counter were standing in front of mirrors trying on necklaces and earrings while other customers were looking through the goods hanging up at stands beside the counters.

Maddie stood still for a moment, listening to about a dozen conversations going on at once, catching a word here and there. Viv had wished her luck at the hostel last night and now, as Maddie passed the haberdashery counter, she noticed that Viv was serving a customer. Maddie didn't try to catch her friend's eye but made her way to the lift. The doors closed against the noise and she enjoyed the silence during her ascent to the counting house on the fifth floor.

When the doors opened, she walked along the corridor to the reception desk, her two-inch heels sinking into the deep pile of the rust coloured carpet.

The receptionist, an attractive, well-proportioned blonde of medium height, took Maddie's name and ticked it off in the diary. She had well-manicured and painted nails and a little name badge on her jacket lapel informed Maddie that her name was Patricia Harper. 'If you'd like to take a seat, Miss Edwards shouldn't be long.' She gave Maddie a cheery smile as she pointed to some chairs sitting in a row further along the corridor.

Maddie returned the smile, more a nervous grimace really, and took a seat as requested. Facing her was a door with the name Miss Doris Edwards, Counting House Manager, on it. The nameplate was gleaming and she wondered if the cleaner polished it every day. The whole establishment reeked of richness; admittedly the wood panelled walls and sturdy brown doors were a bit drab but she felt sure they were of first class quality.

Fingers clenched tightly, Maddie stared into space, trying to calm her nerves. She knew how important it was to get a better paid job to allow her to move out of the hostel and into a flat of her own or to share with Viv. Glancing at her watch, she hoped that she would get back to the shop on time to let Cathy go for her lunch break. She hadn't had time to eat before coming here but felt too sick for food anyway.

Her thoughts were interrupted when a girl, dressed in a dusky pink suit, emerged from the Manager's office, closing the door quietly behind her. The girl smiled at Maddie as she passed by and said thank you to Patricia Harper as she left. If this job interview is to be decided on how well dressed the applicants are then there is no competition, Maddie thought, straightening the collar of her blouse and pushing the loose strands of hair away from her face.

A few moments later, the phone on the reception desk rang.

'Yes, I will do,' Maddie heard Patricia Harper say when she answered the call. She replaced the receiver and came over to where Maddie was sitting. 'Miss Edwards will see you now. Good luck,' she said, as Maddie got to her feet.

The Manager's office was smaller than Maddie had expected but afforded a wonderful view down to the street below. Miss Edwards shook Maddie's hand and directed her to an upright chair on one side of the desk.

While Miss Edwards moved round the desk to take

her own seat, Maddie had a quick glance around. The pale green walls were bare apart from one picture which looked like Marshalls' Emporium in earlier times, perhaps even in the last century. The curtains were deep green velvet and there was a plant with red flowers sitting in a tub on the desk. Maddie recognised it as a geranium from the ones her mother used to have in the house. She swallowed deeply to quell the rush of sadness that the thought had brought on.

'So Miss … Granger, I see you are already in employment. Why do you want to move?'

Maddie kept her reply brief. 'I enjoy my job in the tobacconist shop but I would like to earn a better salary.'

'I see. And you're currently living in the Scottish Girls' Friendly Association Hostel?'

'Yes, I moved to Glasgow from Bonnycross, in West Lothian, for a wider choice of employment.' Although not the real reason for her move, Maddie felt she'd given sufficient information to this would-be employer.

Miss Edwards seemed satisfied with that. 'And I see from your application form that you have office experience?'

'Yes, I worked in an insurance office in Falkirk when I first left school and would like to get back into office work. My job in the tobacconist's was just to get me started on my arrival in Glasgow.'

'Are you happy if I contact the insurance company to seek a reference?'

'Yes, I'm fine with that.'

'The vacancy you have applied for is as a shorthand typist in the counting house. There are sixteen girls in all in the typing pool and you would be expected to take dictation from some of our Section Heads. You'd be typing mainly correspondence and invoices. Have you brought your Certificates with you?'

'Yes,' Maddie said and handed over the shorthand and typing certificates she'd already shown to the woman in the Ministry of Labour.

Miss Edwards glanced at them and nodded. 'Good,' she smiled and slid them back across the highly-polished desk to Maddie. 'The hours are 9 am to 5.30 pm Monday to Saturday and the store closes half day on a Tuesday, when you'd stop at 1 pm. You would start on the first rung of our salary scale at three pounds, fifteen shillings a week before income tax. Your pay would rise in yearly increments, payable on the date you start with the Company. There are quite a few rungs in our salary ladder, with the top one for Head of Section.'

She looked at Maddie over the top of her spectacles. 'How does that compare to your present salary, Miss Granger?'

'It's more than I'm getting in the tobacconist's,' Maddie told her.

Miss Edwards nodded and stroked her chin with her hand.

'Holidays are two weeks a year, fully paid, and of course you would get all the major public holidays as long as the store is closed. With regard to the public holidays, when the store remains open, we work them alternately; if you are off the one time, you work the next. We run the store with a skeleton staff on any public holidays we are open.' She checked to see that Maddie understood then wrote something on the paper lying on top of her blotter. 'Are there any questions you'd like to ask me?' When Maddie shook her head, she said, 'I'd like you to type a short letter and an invoice for me. If you follow me through to the main office, you can use one of the spare typewriters.'

None of the girls in the pool looked round when they entered the room. Miss Edwards directed Maddie to a desk at the back of the room, with an ancient Remington machine on it, older looking than the Royal typewriter she'd used in the insurance company. Miss Edwards handed Maddie a shorthand pad and a pencil, then dictated a letter to her. 'Can you please type that letter and then copy the invoice in the basket. I need two carbon copies of the invoice but only one of the letter. Bring them to my office when you are finished.'

Once Miss Edwards had left the room, a couple of the typists turned round and smiled at Maddie but said nothing to distract her. Maddie took her finished work to Miss Edwards, who glanced over it. 'Thank you. When our interviews are over, and we get a reference from your previous employer, you will be informed by letter as to whether or not you've been successful. Will you be able to find your way out?'

'Yes, thanks,' Maddie replied. She smiled goodbye to Patricia Harper on her way back to the lift.

*

'How did you get on with Miss Edwards?' Viv asked when they were having dinner at the hostel later that evening.

'Hard to say. Her expression didn't give much away but I think my typing was alright and she didn't dictate too quickly thank goodness. The receptionist was very pleasant.'

'Oh yes, that's Patricia Harper. She's Miss Edwards' personal secretary. She's very young for the post but rumour has it that Patricia got the job because of her affair with Mr Chalmers, the Store Manager. He has quite an eye for the ladies although his romance with Patricia has been going on for almost a year.'

'Wonder what Miss Edwards feels about the situation. Doesn't seem the type to condone illicit affairs.'

'Can't imagine she was too keen on the idea at first but she and Patricia seem to get on well now. Patricia's a good worker and has a great sense of humour. I think she's very popular with the girls in the typing pool.'

'There were a few girls in the typing pool when I went in there to do my typing test. They didn't say anything although a couple of them smiled at me.'

'I'm sure you've done alright. Did Miss Edwards say when you'd hear?'

'She had some other people to interview and of course she needs to get a reference for me from my previous employer in Falkirk but I'll hear by letter once they make a decision.'

'Fingers crossed then,' Viv smiled at her friend. 'Think I'll try some of that trifle,' she added, her chair legs scraping across the wooden floor as she got up from the table.

Chapter Twelve

December 1956

Maddie was delighted when Viv invited her to spend Christmas with the Kingston family at their farm, Fairfields, in Ayrshire. It was the first time that anyone had asked her to stay with them. And Viv was the first real friend she'd had. It was also the first time in her life that she'd been left alone to fend for herself. So many 'firsts' since leaving Bonnycross six months ago.

Her friendship with Viv had become even closer since Maddie had been accepted for the post in Marshall's counting house. Lily had left the firm a week ago and was due to sail with her family to Australia the first week in January. With Lily off the scene now, Maddie felt that she and Viv were a twosome. It's us against the world, she thought, and smiled at the idea.

Along with the rest of the Counting House staff, Maddie stopped work at lunchtime on 24th December, to return the day after Boxing Day. Viv had cajoled her department head into giving her a half day on Christmas Eve too so that the girls could travel to Ayrshire that day. They caught the two o'clock bus from Waterloo Street Bus Station and got off near Annbank, with a good twenty minute walk ahead. Maddie was glad that Viv had warned her to wear her stout lacing shoes; her lighter ones would have been ruined on these country tracks.

The snow that was forecast for Christmas hadn't arrived yet and with the strong winter sun beating down on them the girls soon had to remove their woolly hats and mitts.

Fairfields was a much larger property than Maddie had expected, even though Viv had said it was about 150 acres. The farms around Bonnycross had all seemed much smaller to Maddie. Viv led the way across numerous fields, all with sturdy wooden gates to unlock and lock again behind them. When they entered the farmyard via the back gate, they were immediately hit by a strong smell of manure from the fields to their right and Maddie just missed putting her foot into a cow pat.

'Oops, that was a near one,' Viv said, laughing as she took her friend's arm. 'Don't worry, we'll fix you up with a pair of wellies while you're here.'

'How many cows does your dad have?'

'Forty five last time I was home. They're mostly Ayrshires but we have some Belted Galloways too.'

A few minutes later Viv pushed open the back door of the white-washed farmhouse. Maddie stood outside looking at it for a few minutes. The farmhouse resembled the scenes she'd often seen on chocolate boxes and on the many jigsaws her mother used to do.

Sheena Kingston was cleaning the oven when they walked in. The smell of manure outside was replaced by the far more pleasant one of home baking. Maddie almost drooled at the sight of the fruit bread, jam tarts and scones cooling on wire trays on the scrubbed kitchen table.

Sheena stripped off her rubber gloves, the mixed smells of flour and scouring powder wafting up as she did so. She pushed a lock of hair off her sweaty forehead and held out her hand, smiling at Maddie. 'Hello, Maddie, Viv has spoken about you a lot and I feel like I know you already. So glad you can spend Christmas with us.'

'Nice to meet you too, Mrs Kingston.'

'Oh just call me Sheena. We don't stand on ceremony here.'

Maddie found this a unique experience as she'd never before known an older person allowing you to use their Christian name. She liked the idea though and sensed that Sheena Kingston was someone she could trust.

Sheena turned and pulled Viv into a tight hug.

'Hi Mum.' Viv laughed and released herself from her mother's strangle-hold embrace. 'Smells yummy,' she said, nodding towards the baking, 'Maddie and I are famished.'

'Right, get your coats off and I'll organise some tea.'

The farmhouse kitchen led off the living room, where Viv's twin sisters were listening to a children's programme on the radio. One twin was stretched out on the settee, her brown hair pleated and tied with red ribbons. The sun coming in through the window glinted off the lenses of her glasses, making her screw up her eyes. A cat lay across her lap, purring loudly, while she absentmindedly stroked its white fur. The cat's body and legs were white, with black and brown stripes running from the top of its head down to just above its eyes and the same stripes appeared on the tip of its tail. When the girl became aware of Viv and Maddie standing behind her, she gave a whoop of delight and jumped up off the sofa, leaving the cat to leap down on to the floor, squealing its protest.

The second twin looked up from where she lay on a rug in front of a blazing fire, a cushion propping up her head. The twins weren't identical; the second girl had short, curly hair and no specs. She resembled Viv more than her twin.

The second girl now rushed over to hug Viv and Maddie noticed that she was an inch or so shorter than her twin sister.

'This is Maddie,' Viv freed herself from their hugs to introduce her friend, 'and these holy terrors, as you will have guessed, are my twin sisters. Aileen,' she said, inclining her head to the taller girl, 'and Elizabeth,' she went on, throwing her arm round the second girl standing at her side.

Maddie smiled at the girls. 'Hello, Viv has told me all about you both.' From the way Viv had described the work they did around the farm, Maddie had expected they'd be older.

'We're ten,' Elizabeth told Maddie, as though she'd read her thoughts.

'We'll be eleven on 14th April,' Aileen said.

Elizabeth smiled at Maddie. 'In August we'll be

starting at big school.'

'That's great. Which one of you is the older?'

'Me.' Aileen shot a smug glance at her twin.

Elizabeth pulled a face. 'Just by thirteen minutes.'

'But I'm still older,' Aileen repeated as the cat padded over and sidled up to Maddie, rubbing itself against her leg. When she bent to stroke its fur, the cat purred happily.

'Daisy likes you, Maddie,' Elizabeth said.

'She's gorgeous, such unusual colouring. And I love her bright green eyes.'

Aileen picked Daisy up and cuddled into her. 'She's a house cat and doesn't mix with all the other cats running about outside. Don't you not?' she crooned, kissing the cat's head.

'Turn off the radio, please.' Sheena came in and sat a tray down on the coffee table.

Aileen made a face but did as she was asked. 'Goody, you've made my favourite jam tarts, Mum.' She lifted one off the plate and plonked herself down on the sofa again, leaving room for Maddie to sit beside her.

Sheena poured out the tea and Viv handed round the cups. 'Help yourself to milk and sugar, Maddie,' she said, laying the jug and bowl on the coffee table.

'The milk's from our own cows,' Aileen told Maddie, when she passed the jug to her. 'Dad's milking at the moment.'

'And do you and Elizabeth help him sometimes?'

'Yes, we sometimes help with the tea-time milking but not usually in the morning. Milking is about six o'clock in the morning and we'd be late for school if we helped him.'

'You have to get the cattle out of the field and across the road to the milking sheds,' Elizabeth explained to their guest. 'Sometimes the traffic's held up for ages.'

'We also help collect the eggs, then wash and store them in the milk house,' Aileen said.

'So you have chickens too?'

'Oh yes, most farmers have chickens. People come from all over the area to buy our eggs.'

They were still drinking their tea and getting better

acquainted when they felt a blast of cold air as the back door opened.

'That you, Charlie?' Sheena called out.

'Aye,' a tall man said as he came into the living room, two dogs at his heels.

'This is Maddie, Dad,' Elizabeth introduced him. 'Viv's friend.'

'Hello, Maddie. Good to have you with us, lass,' he said, smiling at Maddie.

Charlie was well over 6' tall, his dark hair spiked with grey. The hair around his collar had grown long enough to curl up at the ends. Maddie wasn't sure if the dark shadow around his chin meant he was growing a beard or had just not taken time to shave that morning. He had the kindest face Maddie had ever seen and she warmed to him immediately.

The black and white collie lay down in the corner, eyeing Maddie suspiciously through half closed eyes, while the taller dog, a magnificent black and brown German Shepherd, ran over to the settee.

'This is Zeus,' Aileen said, playing with the dog's ears. 'He was a year old yesterday.'

Zeus sat down in front of Maddie and put his giant paw up on her lap. 'Hello Zeus, aren't you gorgeous?' she said, stroking him. The dog's brown velvety eyes stared into hers and he panted, his tongue hanging out, showing his strong teeth.

'You've got a friend there.' Charlie's blue eyes sparkled, leaving Maddie in no doubt where Viv had got her eye colour. He sat on a chair near the kitchen door and pulled off his wellington boots. 'Holly's different, she takes time to get used to folk.' He got up and carried his wellies into the kitchen.

'Do you want a cuppa, Charlie?' Sheena called after him, the teapot in her hand.

'Pour me one while I wash my hands.'

'So will the cows be inside now they've been milked?' Maddie asked.

'Yep, they're in the byre for the night. Cows don't

like outside on cold days,' Viv told her. 'The new milking machine Dad's installed has helped him a lot. It took much longer when the cows had to be milked by hand. I'll show you around tomorrow,' she promised.

'Have you had enough to eat, Maddie?' Sheena asked.

'Yes thanks, I really enjoyed your baking.'

'I'll take you to your room now,' Viv said, picking up her own case and Maddie's. They moved through to the bedrooms at the back of the cottage, followed by the twins and the two dogs.

'Get off.' Viv shooed Zeus away as he jumped up on the bed in the spare room. 'Keep your bedroom door closed,' she advised Maddie, 'otherwise you'll have him for company during the night.'

'He nearly pushes you out of the bed if he gets in beside you,' Elizabeth giggled.

'Even though you've got your own comfy bed in the kitchen.' Aileen wagged her finger in front of the dog's face but he ignored her and chased Holly out into the hall again.

Maddie looked around. 'What a lovely room,' she said to her friend, already feeling at home in this happy family atmosphere. 'And lilac's my favourite colour.' The lilac and white checked curtains toned in with the colourful patchwork quilt.

The cream coloured linoleum was partly covered by a lilac rug for added warmth, a shard of lowering sunlight casting a design on the rug. The bedside lamp had a white frilly shade.

'Mum made the quilt, the curtains and the lampshade,' Viv told her.

'She's made quilts and curtains for all the bedrooms,' Elizabeth said, 'our room is in pink, Mum and Dad's room is peach and Viv chose lemon for hers. I'll show you the other bedrooms later,' she offered.

Maddie sat down on the wooden rocking chair beside the window, its upholstery also in the same lilac colour as the curtains, its framework painted purple.

'Mum painted the chair too,' Aileen told her. 'And

she also made the rug.'

Maddie got up again and stared out at the fields beyond. She knew her own mother's poor health had kept her from doing so many things she'd have enjoyed. But she pushed any sad thoughts from her mind, determined to enjoy Christmas in the warmth of this wonderful family.

'Your mum's a very talented lady, between baking and sewing.'

Viv shrugged. 'When you live this far out in the country and there are no shops nearby you have to be self-sufficient. You'll see we have linoleum floors throughout the house because carpets are a nightmare to keep clean with the dog and cat hair that gets on to them. Mum finds it much easier to brush the floors and she takes the rugs out to the washing line and uses the carpet beater on them.'

When Zeus and Holly ran back into the room, she shooed them out again. 'We'll leave you to unpack Maddie.' She pointed to a small ornate fireplace, with lilac flowered tiles down both sides and on the hearth. The fire nest had some coals on it, with a fireguard placed in front.

'If you feel it cold in here tonight just let Dad know and he'll light the fire for you. Come on you two, let's give Maddie some peace,' she said and ushered the twins out of the room.

Chapter Thirteen

'Christmas Eve and what have I got to look forward to?' Steve Dixon's reflection stared back at him as he looked into the full length mirror in his mother's bedroom, the birthmark at the side of his eye looking red and angry. He took a puff of his fag, then laid it down on the ashtray sitting on the dressing table, while he slicked back his inky black hair with Brylcreem. He loosened his tie a little and sighed; even its pictures of bikini-clad females wearing a Santa hat failed to lift his mood. This time he took a longer draw at his cigarette.

He stared into the mirror, pleased with his new blue suit. He'd liked the colour the minute he unpacked the suits. One of the perks of working in the warehouse was that he could get his pick of what came in at a discount. He pulled at the shoulder pads on his jacket to make him seem even broader and he looked approvingly at the fit of his drainpipe trousers. The black winklepickers finished off his outfit.

Why am I bothering? She won't be there. He'd been smitten the first time he saw her just over a week ago and now no other girl could match up. He'd caught sight of her going into the lift this morning and was frustrated for ages afterwards. He desperately wanted a date with her. He'd noticed her talking to Viv, the girl in haberdashery. Viv was very chatty so next time he saw her he'd ask what the new girl's name was. She might even put a good word in for him.

He heard the key turning in the front door and by the time he got downstairs Ma was hanging her coat and hat on the stand in the hallway.

'You look smart, Son,' she said when she saw him. 'Going somewhere nice?'

'I'm meeting a couple of lads from work and we're

going to St Andrew's Halls. How was the film?'

'The short film was pretty boring but the main feature was terrific. A real weepy. Agnes and I cried our eyes out.'

'What a pair you and Agnes are,' he said, grinning as he spoke. 'Paying good money to sit and greet.'

She laughed and made a face at him. 'Right, you have a nice time, Son, and don't forget your key. And don't make a noise when you come back and waken me up,' she called as the door closed behind him.

*

Will Benson drew on his heavy trench coat. He'd bought it before the war and it was still as good as new. With the sharp drop in temperature over the last couple of hours, he'd be glad of it. He buttoned his coat and threaded the belt through its metal buckle. Then he pulled on his tweed cap and wrapped his thick football supporter's scarf round his neck. Hearts of Midlothian, the team he'd supported since he was a schoolboy. Once outside, he shivered, sure that the snow that had been forecast wasn't far away.

Benson's local pub, The Drop Inn, was decorated for Christmas with a tree, dressed in coloured baubles, sitting at one end of the bar. He'd forgotten how busy it would be on Christmas Eve and had to push through a wall of noise to find a quieter place at the far end of the bar near to the pub's side door.

He sat on a high stool and ordered a pint of heavy and a half. Lost in his thoughts, he paid no heed to the conversations going on around him. Six months on he was still sore at the way Maddie had left, without even leaving a note. It wasn't as if he was unkind to her and he'd never kept her short of money. Any earlier behaviour of his was so long ago that she should surely have forgotten about it by now.

His thoughts were disturbed by a stoutly-built man wearing a Salvation Army uniform who rattled a collecting tin in front of him. 'Happy Christmas, Sir,' the man said, his face beaming with joy, 'can you spare something for people in need this Christmas?'

Without replying, Benson dug into his coat pocket and

dropped some loose change into the box the man held out to him.

'God bless you, Sir.' The man laid a copy of the 'War Cry' on the counter in front of Benson, avoiding the sticky puddle of liquid on the wooden top.

The noise around Benson grew louder and he downed his whisky in one go. Then he moved away from the bar and the partygoers and slipped out of the side door, leaving his beer glass, still half full, sitting on the counter beside the magazine.

He arrived home as the first flakes of snow were beginning to fall.

Chapter Fourteen

Maddie wakened about seven o'clock on Christmas morning to a winter wonderland. Jumping out of bed, she stared at the virgin snow piled up over the fields, some clinging softly to the branches of the trees. The snow on the tree nearest to her window had formed the perfect outline of a sheep, with holes in the snow that looked like eyes and a nose. Even the pile further back on the branch had fallen in such a way as to resemble a stubby tail.

'Maddie, are you awake?' Viv called to her from the hallway.

Maddie opened the door and smiled at her friend. 'Morning, Viv. I see we've got the White Christmas we were expecting. Are the twins up yet?'

'They sure are. They heard Dad going out to do the morning milking about five o'clock and it's taken Mum and me all our time to keep them from running out into the snow in their pyjamas. If you can just pull on your dressing gown and come through as you are, they're desperate to begin opening their gifts.'

'The twins know that Santa is a myth,' Viv whispered to Maddie, when they all trooped into the living room to investigate the piles of gifts lying around the Christmas tree. 'But they're wise enough to say nothing in case they don't get any gifts.'

The next half hour was full of oohs and aahs as wrapping paper was ripped off and the gifts revealed. The twins had some toys and a new cardigan each and Maddie was thrilled with the presents the Kingstons had bought for her.

She had a box of chocolates for Charlie and Sheena, a

necklace and matching earrings for Viv and a book for each of the twins.

The excitement over, they sat down at the kitchen table to enjoy the fresh eggs Charlie had collected from the henhouse this morning, with some of Sheena's home-made bread. 'Did you make this too?' Maddie asked, sticking her knife into the soft, freshly-churned butter.

'Yes, I always use the cream off the top of the milk. I skim it off before we pour the milk into the cans for collection by the milk lorry.'

'It's delicious,' Maddie said, the memory of food rationing fading fast as she sank her teeth into the thickly buttered bread and relished every mouthful.

'When are you going to collect Grandad?' Viv asked her father as they were clearing away the dishes from the table.

'I've arranged to pick him up about twelve o'clock. He always enjoys the Christmas carol service at the church before he comes here.'

'I'll show you around the farm once we're washed and dressed,' Viv said, when they were washing up the breakfast dishes.

'Here, wear my wellies,' Sheena said to Maddie when they were ready to go outside, handing over a pair of green boots. 'There should be a pair of socks inside.' Maddie was glad of the thick hand-knitted socks that were stuffed inside them as the boots were just a fraction too big for her. With the socks inside they were alright and much better than ruining her shoes.

'Watch out for cow pats under the snow,' Viv warned her friend as they crossed the field in a zigzag fashion to avoid the spots where the cows had relieved themselves.

Maddie could see some sheep grazing on fields up the hill behind the farm. 'Are they your father's sheep?'

'No,' Viv told her. 'Farmers usually either have cattle or sheep. Sheep are much hardier and don't mind being left outside. Cows prefer a warm byre, except perhaps the Highland cows up north.'

'So that land up there belongs to another farmer?'

'That's Middleton farm. It's owned by the McKenzie's. Roddy McKenzie was in my class at school. He didn't follow his dad into farming. The last I heard he'd moved to London.'

The girls were greeted by loud moos when they entered the byre. It was a long, low building with stalls against the walls on both sides. Each cow had an individual stall, the floor covered in straw.

'The cows are chained up after the tea-time milking, with fresh straw laid down for them to sleep on,' Viv explained to Maddie. 'Dad cleans out the gutter in the morning,' she went on, 'and any manure is used for fertiliser. We feed the cows hay at this time of year when the grass is poor.' She pointed to the hessian bags hanging on the stalls as she was speaking. 'Dad also grows turnips to chop up and feed to the cows.'

'What else do you grow on the farm?'

'Oats and barley. And Dad has drills of potatoes, some of which we sell but we mostly use them ourselves.'

'Does your dad use a horse to plough the ground?' Maddie asked, remembering the pictures she'd seen of Clydesdale horses.

'No, he drives a tractor. Most farmers use modern machinery nowadays.'

Maddie jumped back and screamed as a field mouse ran over her wellies and shot across the straw and out of the barn.

'Your face,' Viv said, laughing when she saw Maddie's fear. 'Sorry, I didn't mean to sound cruel, it's just that the mouse is more afraid of you.'

Maddie shivered visibly. 'I hate mice.'

'Well, you have to get used to them on a farm, Love. That's why there are so many cats roaming around the place. That wee mouse won't have a long life. Come and I'll show you the cold room.' Viv led Maddie through a connecting doorway into a freezing cold room, with stone floors and mesh on the windows. There was a marble counter along one wall, on which sat rows of boxes full of eggs and some metal milk containers stood underneath the counter.

'Gosh, it's cold in here.' Maddie felt the chill through her thick jersey and she rubbed her hands up and down her arms over the woollen material.

'Yes, this is where we store the eggs once they are washed and boxed and Mum also keeps her bread and cakes on the counter. She tends to bake in batches so this is good storage space. The marble counter keeps everything cool.'

'What's that over there?' Maddie pointed to a large machine in the corner.

'That's our cooling machine for the milk. We pour the milk into the middle section and when it's switched on, cold water runs down the outer section to cool the milk before it's put into the cans for loading on the milk lorries.'

'So although the water cools the milk, none of it gets into the milk?'

'Oh no, it's only for cooling it. We have milk inspectors who come round the farms and they check to ensure that the farmer isn't watering down his milk. There are stiff penalties for anyone found doing that.'

By the time they got back to the farmhouse, Maddie felt she couldn't take in any more information.

Sheena was working at the sink and turned round when the girls entered and pulled off their boots. 'Well how did the tour go?' she asked, smiling at Maddie.

'I didn't know how much work went on in a farm,' Maddie replied, taking off the socks and dropping them into the boots.

'Yes, it's a full time job. Charlie and I have both been brought up on farms though so we're used to it. Charlie's father had a dairy herd and my dad was a pig farmer. Come and meet my dad,' she said, leading the way into the living room.

An elderly man, his white hair gleaming with health, got up from the armchair to hug his oldest granddaughter. 'This is my friend, Maddie, Grandad.'

'Welcome Maddie,' he smiled and shook her hand

vigorously. 'The twins have been telling me all about you, think you've made a hit with them.'

What a delightful old man, Maddie thought, seeing instantly Sheena's resemblance to her father. He'd been widowed two years ago and Sheena and Charlie had been keen for him to move into the farmhouse with them but the old man was determined to remain independent. He'd moved into a small flat in Kilmarnock where he was handy for public transport.

'We all love him like mad,' Viv had told her. 'He's my only grandparent left. Dad's parents died fourteen years ago and I barely remember them. The twins didn't know them at all.'

'When's dinner?' Aileen looked up from the corner of the room where she and Elizabeth were sorting out the furniture in their new dolls' house that Charlie had made them for Christmas.

'After we hear the Queen speaking to the nation on the radio,' Sheena told them. 'I'll make some sandwiches to keep us going until then. When you two girls wash your hands, you could butter some bread for me,' she said to Viv and Maddie.

*

After dinner, they all flopped down in the comfortable living room to listen to the Christmas music on the radio, with the clicking of Sheena's knitting needles as she got on with a jersey for Charlie. Viv and Maddie played a game of Snakes 'n Ladders with the twins. Before long the two men were snoring in their armchairs, accompanied by the shrieks of the twins.

Maddie felt so relaxed in this happy home; it was like she'd known the Kingstons all her life instead of meeting them yesterday for the first time.

When she climbed into bed that night, Maddie was happier than she'd been for a very long time and she quickly fell asleep.

Chapter Fifteen

February 1957

'Hello gorgeous.' The young warehouseman grinned widely and winked, as he passed Maddie in the corridor near to Miss Edwards' office. His handsome looks were spoiled by the ugly birthmark at the side of his eye.

Maddie looked over at the door, scared that the boss would catch them in the corridor together. She still had a healthy respect for Miss Edwards and was determined to do nothing that would lead to her dismissal. But he'd spoken quietly and no-one else in the vicinity would have heard his words.

'Don't worry, the old witch knows I'm up here, she summoned me to her audience chamber,' he whispered, tightening the knot in his tie; a bright pink with silver stripes, the very opposite of the dull coloured ties worn by most of the male employees in the store.

This chap had been chatting her up for weeks now but, although secretly flattered by his interest, she hadn't responded to his advances. He seemed harmless enough, she supposed, but he was still a male. And she'd heard that he drank more than was good for him; shades of Benson returned and she shivered. Viv had told her that his name was Steve Dixon but, apart from him working as a warehouseman for the company, Maddie knew no more about him. And she wasn't remotely interested in finding out.

Patricia Harper came out of Miss Edwards' office at that moment, her shorthand pad stuffed under her armpit and a tray of biscuits and used crockery held between her hands.

'I'll get the door for you,' Steve offered, and moved

nearer to save Patricia having to struggle to close it behind her. Patricia's knee length black straight skirt with the kick pleat at the back showed off her legs to advantage.

'What are **you** doing up here?' she asked him, failing to acknowledge his assistance.

He grinned at Patricia. 'Miss Edwards wants to see me.'

'Oh yes, of course she does. I'd forgotten. Just go in, she's expecting you.'

Steve winked again at Maddie, then knocked on Miss Edwards' door, before pushing it open and vanishing inside.

'Are you settling in alright, Maddie?' Patricia asked.

'Yes thanks, I'm really enjoying my work here.'

'That's great.' Patricia smiled, and went off with her tray in the direction of the staff kitchen area.

*

'Steve Dixon was asking me about you this afternoon.' Viv smiled at Maddie as they were walking to the hostel after work that day. 'Wanted to know if you had a boyfriend.'

Maddie's brow puckered. 'What did you tell him?'

'I said I wasn't sure as I didn't know you very well but I don't think he believed me.'

'None of his business anyway. He tried to flirt with me this morning when he was going into Miss Edwards' office for something. I certainly didn't encourage him and I wouldn't be interested in going out with someone who drinks too much.'

'He is quite handsome though, isn't he?' Viv giggled and raised her eyebrows slightly. 'His black wavy hair and those gorgeous green eyes stop you from noticing his birthmark, don't you think?' she prodded her friend gently.

But Maddie was having none of it. 'If you like him so much why don't you go out with him?'

'He isn't my type and besides it's you he's interested in.' Viv had already confessed to having a crush on the red-haired carpet salesman on the fourth floor. 'What will I say to Steve if he asks about you again?'

'Tell him to get lost. I don't want a boyfriend.'

'Ok, I won't give him any information about you,' Viv assured her, deciding not to tease Maddie any more, aware her friend was becoming annoyed. Maddie seemed to have something against the male of the species and Viv was determined to nose out the reason.

I'll work on it, she thought, as they arrived at the front entrance to the hostel.

Chapter Sixteen

April 1957

'Are you sure?' Maddie asked Viv that Friday morning when they were walking from the hostel to work, something they now did every morning. Usually Viv worked later than Maddie at night but occasionally they walked home together too. 'I mean it sounds too good to be true.'

'No, it's ours if we want it,' Viv assured her. She'd waited until they were some distance from the hostel before she'd dropped the bombshell that they'd been offered a two room and kitchen flat to rent in Rutherglen, less than half an hour's tram ride from Glasgow city centre.

'How come? What's the catch?'

'There isn't one.' Viv smiled broadly at her friend and prospective flatmate. 'You've heard me speak about my Aunt Meg? At least she isn't my real aunt but she and Mum have been lifelong friends and we always look on her as an auntie.' When Maddie nodded, Viv continued with her story. 'Aunt Meg has lived all her life in Rutherglen. Her house is in Clincarthill Road, up behind the town centre. Her next door neighbour, Mr Macdonald, is the landlord of this property at 197 Main Street. Aunt Meg told him you and I were looking for a flat to rent and she recommended us as good tenants.'

'She must know him well, I mean apart from being a neighbour, for him to offer us such a good deal.'

'Their two families have been friends for years.'

'It's really kind of your Aunt Meg to speak to him about us, especially when she doesn't know me.'

'She knows any friend of mine will be alright.' Viv

grinned, pretending to polish an imaginary badge on her lapel. 'But seriously Maddie,' she added, as they walked through the revolving door of Marshalls, 'we're really lucky as flats in Rutherglen are hard to come by. Usually you've to be born and bred in the Burgh to have a chance of getting one there.'

Once inside the store, Viv turned right at the entrance towards the staff room where she had a locker for her coat and bag. 'Maybe see you at lunch time,' she said over her shoulder to her friend.

'Not sure what lunch hour I'll be on today, but I'll let you know,' Maddie called after her, before making her own way towards the staff lift where Julie from the typing pool was holding the door open for her.

*

Two days later it was a bright, sunny Sunday afternoon as the bus took Viv and Maddie to Fairfields for the twins' 11th birthday tea. Charlie had promised to run them back to the hostel in the four wheel drive to save them leaving early to catch the last bus back to Glasgow.

'This weather is more like June than April,' Viv said, shielding her eyes from the strong sun as she looked out of the bus window over the patchwork of fields they were passing on their way along the Ayr road.

Maddie made a face. 'Can't see it lasting until the real summer.'

'You never know, we might have a scorcher this year,' Viv suggested, always more optimistic than her friend. She fell silent and continued to gaze out of the window. She wondered again, as she'd done so often before, about Maddie's early life. Maddie had been reluctant to say much about her past and Viv had gained the impression the she had to be careful not to cross too many boundaries where Maddie was concerned.

On this occasion when the bus arrived at Annbank, Charlie was waiting for them with the two dogs in tow. Holly and Zeus barked a welcome to the girls, running around them in circles, tails wagging furiously. Once Charlie had shooed the animals into the back section of the vehicle, the girls got in, Viv in the passenger seat beside her dad while Maddie sat behind Charlie.

The twins rushed out of the back door the minute they heard the chips on the driveway crunching under the Landrover's tyres and they were waiting on the path for Viv and Maddie when the vehicle stopped.

'Happy birthday, kiddos,' Viv greeted her sisters, hugging them both at the same time.

'Happy birthday, Aileen. Happy birthday, Elizabeth,' Maddie said to each of them in turn. 'Have the cows gone to bed?' she asked, seeing the fields behind the farmhouse empty.

'I got them into the byre before I came to Annbank to collect you two girls,' Charlie told her, as he opened the back section and let the dogs out. The animals ran into the field behind the house, with Charlie on their tail, shouting to them not to stray too far from the back door.

'Grandad's here already,' Elizabeth told Viv and Maddie.

'We got our dumps at school on Friday,' Aileen said, as they pushed open the back door. 'Eleven each.'

Maddie smiled at the memory of this custom when she was at school in Bonnycross. You were thumped on the back by your classmates up to the number of times that corresponded to your age. She often escaped this, as she had so few friends at school.

'Come away in,' Sheena smiled, leading the way into the living room with Charlie taking up the rear.

'Hi auld yin,' Charlie greeted his father-in-law and sat down beside him on the settee.

'Less o' the auld,' Grandad complained, grinning back.

'You two girls must be starving after the long journey,' Sheena said, ever mindful of feeding her guests. 'Grandad and the twins have already had some soup so would you like a bowl of it and some home-made crusty bread?'

'Yes please,' Viv and Maddie said in unison and sat down at the kitchen table.

Maddie looked at the birthday cake sitting on the

table, with the words 'Happy Birthday Aileen and Elizabeth' in pink icing on a white background, decorated by pink roses. 'Did you make the roses yourself, Sheena?'

Sheena nodded.

'Are they edible?'

'Yes. Aileen and Elizabeth have already been squabbling about which one of them is to get the pink ribbon from around the cake.'

'It should be me,' Aileen called through from the living room. 'I'm the one who wears my hair in pleats.'

'But I could wear it as an Alice band,' Elizabeth complained.

'For God sake shush, lassies, we're trying to hear the news on the radio.' Charlie sighed and looked round at Grandad, shaking his head. 'Mum can cut the ribbon in half and you can have a bit each.'

Aileen stood at the kitchen door with her hands on her hips. 'Don't be stupid Dad, then it wouldn't be long enough to tie round both my pleats.'

Elizabeth folded her arms, pouting. 'You know we have to share things in this house.'

'Listen you two,' Viv said, peering round the kitchen door, 'Maddie and I would like to have our soup in peace. That is, if you want the gifts we have brought for you,' she cajoled.

'Oh what are they, can we see them before you eat your soup?' Elizabeth asked.

'No you can't,' Viv said firmly.

The mention of their gifts had the two girls jumping up and down in excitement, the ribbon on the cake forgotten for the moment.

'Thanks, Love,' Sheena mouthed to her older daughter.

'Think I'll go and do a wee bit of work on the roof of the milking shed till dinner's ready,' Charlie said, getting to his feet.

'It's hardly worth it,' Sheena told him, 'dinner won't be much longer now.'

'No matter, I'll at least take a look at what's needing done tomorrow. Anything to get away from all these chattering females,' he said, chuckling as he spoke. 'Will I show you what I'm planning to do?' he asked his father-in-law.

Grandad nodded and followed Charlie out of the back door.

When the twins received their gifts from Viv and Maddie, they pulled at the paper excitedly and squealed with delight when they saw what was inside.

Viv had bought them a toy cooker with plastic pots and pans and a pretend sweet shop with tiny jars of sweets and a pair of scales. 'Now remember you share these gifts, okay, no fighting over who gets what,' she warned them when they'd opened her gift.

'OK,' they agreed and started playing straight away.

'Hello Mrs Brown, what would you like today?' Aileen pretended to be the shopkeeper.

'I'll have a quarter of toffees please.'

'Have you got your ration book?'

'Here you are,' Elizabeth said, handing over the pretend book.

Although the twins were born after the war, ration books were still in use until 1954 so they did remember having to use their coupons for buying sweets.

'Peace for a wee while,' Sheena said, smiling at the two older girls.

Then there was more rustling of paper as the twins unwrapped the gifts from Maddie. She'd bought them items for the dolls' house they'd received at Christmas.

'Thank you Maddie.' Elizabeth and Aileen beamed when they saw their gifts. Both girls ran over to give Maddie a kiss of thanks.

'Look Mum,' Aileen said, showing Sheena the wheelbarrow and garden tools and Elizabeth held up the bookcase with a selection of tiny books for it.

Once Charlie and Grandad arrived back from the shed, the family settled down around the kitchen table for a plate of home-made steak pie, potatoes and peas, followed by sherry trifle.

'That was great.' Charlie, his appetite good after working outside all day, pushed his trifle dish away from him. 'Now what's for afters?' he teased his wife.

'Birthday cake,' the twins yelled in unison. Sheena put eleven candles around the edge of the cake. She lit them and they all sang 'Happy Birthday to you' to each of the twins in turn. Aileen was first in view of her thirteen minutes seniority and then it was Elizabeth's turn. The candles were lit twice as they both insisted on having their turn to blow them out.

'Are you pleased about the flat?' Sheena asked Maddie, once they were back in the living room enjoying a piece of birthday cake with their cup of tea.

Maddie swallowed her cake quickly and nodded. 'Yes, it's great. It's really good of Viv's Aunt Meg to arrange it for us.'

'Meg would do anything for anybody and it's a good rent. It would normally be around £22 a month but Mr Macdonald is giving the flat to you girls for £18 a month.'

'It's fine because there are two of us sharing the rent,' Viv joined in the conversation. 'Maddie's wage is £3.15/- a week and, because I'm on to the second point in the wage scale, I get £4.05/-. So between us we have about £30 a month so that would leave us £12 over to cover the cost of food and heating bills.'

'And you need to keep a little back for entertainment,' Sheena reminded them.

'Don't know if we'll be able to afford entertainment,' Maddie told her.

But Sheena shook her head. 'You should try though. When you're working all week, you want to be able to go to the pictures now and again at the weekend. You know what they say about all work and no play.'

'Once you get the keys, I'll come over and decorate the place for you,' Charlie offered. 'Give the walls a wee freshen up.'

'Thanks, Dad.' Viv threw her arms around his shoulders and kissed him on the cheek.

Maddie felt tears stinging her eyelids, watching the genuine warmth and love Viv and her dad shared, and for a second or two a twinge of jealousy surged through her at this show of affection.

It was a very happy evening but all too soon it was time for her and Viv to get back into the four wheel drive for Charlie to take them back to the hostel. Grandad went with them and Charlie dropped him off in Kilmarnock first.

Chapter Seventeen

May 1957

'I like the size of this room,' Maddie said, standing in the front room of the flat they were viewing at 197 Main Street, Rutherglen. 'And I think we'll feel safer on the top storey.'

Viv nodded. 'Yes, and the building looks in good condition. Aunt Meg told Mum that the landlord, Mr Macdonald, attends to any repairs as soon as they're reported to him.'

'Pity it wasn't a tiled close, they look much brighter and cleaner.'

'Or a wally close as they call it in Glasgow,' Viv told her, 'but the walls in this close look freshly painted.'

The flat they were viewing was a two room and kitchen. It had an L-shaped hall, or lobby as it was known. The rooms looked enormous because they had been emptied of furniture. Light bulbs hung from the ceiling minus lampshades and the windows were without either blinds or curtains. The place was empty apart from an old pair of stepladders and a long-handled brush sitting against the wall in the lobby.

Maddie pointed to some large cobwebs that had attached themselves to the flex of the light fitting in the middle of the room and another cobweb hung down from the ceiling above the door. She fetched the stepladder from the lobby and climbed to the top rung, from where she raised the brush handle and used it to swipe away the cobwebs.

She returned the ladders and brush to the lobby. 'What's that?' she asked Viv, looking at the large wooden box pushed against the wall.

'That'll be the coal bunker.' Viv lifted the lid and sure

enough there were some small pieces of coal down at the bottom of the box. She replaced the lid again, jumping back when some coal dust blew up. 'We could drape a fancy table cover over it and put some plants on top to camouflage its real purpose.'

Maddie went back into the front room and stood at the oriel window looking out over Main Street. Directly across the road from the flat was the Grand Central cinema with the Grand Central café next to it. Then came a row of shops; Greene's the chemist, Venditozzi's fish and chip shop, Denton's shoe shop and at the end of the row was Muir's sweet shop. To the left of Muir's, with a lane between the two buildings, was a double fronted shop, McDougall's the gents' outfitters.

She screwed up her nose when she saw a pile of bird poo on the windowsill. Not really surprising with the number of pigeons sitting on the gutters above and on window ledges. Down at pavement level, loads of pigeons were landing on the litter bins positioned along the Main Street, scavenging for titbits. On the pavement outside their building, flower beds were spaced a few yards apart along Main Street, each containing a magnificent show of late spring/early summer blooms. Tall trees were planted in the spaces between the beds. Maddie thought she recognised them as sycamore trees, recalling the shape and colour of the leaves from the nature rambles she'd gone on with her Girl Guide Company in Bonnycross. Close by each tree was a seat for the public to use. Right now a few people were occupying the seats, enjoying the fresh air and buzz of the town.

'What's so interesting down there?' Viv asked, moving over to stand beside Maddie.

'I was wondering if the trees down there were sycamores. The leaves look about right.'

'Or maybe beech? What a view from up here. We'll never be bored with so much to see. And handy for transport to and from work. There's the tram stop immediately outside this building. And the railway station is a couple of streets behind, in Victoria Street.'

'And I can see a bus stop.' Maddie pointed to the left, 'see, where that lady in the green coat is waiting.'

'Mmm,' Viv murmured. 'We need a kettle and some food to keep us going while we're doing up the flat.'

'I think the newsagents' beside the close might sell bread and milk. Even if we don't get it straight from the cow.' Maddie's joke fell on deaf ears as Viv was on to other things.

'Let's have another look at the kitchen and bedroom.' Viv led the way through the lobby into the large, airy kitchen, its window looking over the back courts towards the tenement buildings in King Street. Below the kitchen window was the sink and the gas cooker sat to the left of it. On the right of the sink was a large shelved cupboard, known as a press.

Maddie pointed to the hearth. 'Bet that coal fire will keep the kitchen warm.'

'I love sitting at a coal fire. Aunt Meg will be able to give us the name of the coal merchant she uses. I think I've heard her talk about Devanney the coalmen but we can check that with her later.'

Maddie's eye caught sight of the bed recess at the far end of the kitchen. We could maybe use the recess for a table and chairs. Unless one of us needs to sleep in there.'

Viv shook her head. 'Think there is plenty of room in the bedroom for two single beds. Let's have another look.'

They went into the bedroom, adjacent to the kitchen and nearer to the front door of the flat. The room had a good sized window. Would you be happy for us to share the bedroom?' she asked Maddie.

'Yep, fine by me. There'd still be plenty of space for a wardrobe and chest of drawers.'

'And maybe a wee table in between the beds with a lamp on it,' Viv said, quite excited by now. 'Hope you don't mind not having a bathroom in the flat. There's a communal toilet on the stair landing, which we'd share with the occupants of the two other flats on this floor.'

'That's no problem for me. None of us had inside toilets in Bonnycross; we had to use one outside the back door in the garden area. Not like you, with your posh bathroom in the farmhouse.'

Viv made a face at her. 'I've got used to sharing the bathroom at the hostel by now, so I think I'll survive here. So you're happy for us to take it then?'

'Definitely,' Maddie replied.

*

'Charlie, it looks great,' Maddie said a few days later, looking around the empty room excitedly. 'And you've done it so quickly too.'

Charlie's paste table was in the middle of the room, a remnant of the recently used wallpaper lying across it.

'Thank you so much,' she added, almost ready to kiss him but she drew back at the sight of his dungarees covered in cream and green paint splashes.

'No problem lass,' he beamed, using his sweaty palms to push his hair back from his brow. 'Careful,' he held up his hand as she almost stepped back into the bucket containing the remains of his wallpaper paste.

'Ooh,' she grimaced when she saw the gooey mess at her feet.

Ignoring Charlie's paint splattered overalls, Viv threw her arms around his neck. 'Thanks, Dad, it's gorgeous. I love the design. We chose well, Maddie, didn't we?'

'Sure did. And I love the colour of the ceiling.'

The background of the paper was a cream colour with a brownish sort of squiggle interspersed with green leaves. Charlie had painted the ceiling, cornices, skirting boards, window frames and door in a complimentary shade of pale green.

Viv disappeared for a moment and returned with a roll of wallpaper, a floral design in varying shades of pink. 'We got this for the bedroom, Dad. Do you think it'll look good?'

'It'll be fine and I can do the bedroom paintwork in white. I'll try and get on to that room over the weekend. Your mum and the twins are going to do the milking to let me get on here. Have you got your paper for the kitchen and the lobby?'

Maddie shook her head. 'Not yet but we'll look over the weekend. I'll go and put the kettle on.' Sheena had given them a spare kettle of hers to use during the period of decorating.

'Great.' Charlie grinned. 'I could murder a cup of tea. I've got a mouth as dry as a …'

'We don't want to hear,' Viv silenced him, aware of her dad's fairly frequent rude phrases. But she laughed while she said it, knowing that there wasn't a bad bone in his body.

'What about furniture? And carpets?' Charlie asked when the three of them were sitting on the bare floorboards with their drinks, eating their sandwiches directly from the box Sheena had given Charlie before he left the farm that morning.

'Yes, we'll need to think about that,' Maddie agreed.

'One of the women who works in haberdashery with me has an old table and chairs that she's willing to give us,' Viv told him. 'I offered to pay for it but she says she's ordered a new set and this lot would be going to the tip anyway so she's glad we can take it off her hands.'

'We'll need to collect it though,' Maddie reminded her.

Charlie smiled. 'That won't be a problem. I'll get my plumber mate, John, to come with me and we can get it into his van for you. I'll give him something for his trouble. You two girls take anything that's given to you. Beggars can't be choosers.'

Maddie smiled, remembering how often she'd heard her mother use that proverb.

She marvelled again at how kind Charlie was, a good person through and through. She was sure he'd never done anyone a bad turn in his life. 'But will you and John be able to get the furniture up the three flights of stairs?'

'Yes, no bother,' Charlie assured her. 'The stair treads in these old tenements are wide and there's plenty of space on each landing for us to get round to the next flight.'

'That's great Charlie, you're a star. We thought we'd check out the second hand shops.'

'Good idea, you can pick up a great bargain there. And don't forget, folk advertise second-hand furniture in the papers.'

Viv thumped her dad on the back. 'Great, Dad, you've reminded me of something.'

She disappeared through to the kitchen and returned carrying a newspaper. 'I bought this paper in the newsagents' down at the close when we arrived today.'

'What paper's that?' Charlie asked.

'It's the Rutherglen Reformer, a local paper. It comes out once a week. Now, let's see,' she muttered as she leafed through the pages. Towards the back she stopped, looked up exultantly and began to read. 'Special offers at the Rutherglen Co-op. Three piece suites for £21.0.0d., and fireside chairs from £4.10.0d. On the bottom it says, 'Easy Payments Available'. She turned the page and read out another advert. 'FOR SALE, moquette suite, rust coloured, cost £95.0.0d. when new but selling for £49.0.0d.'

'Read the prices again?' Maddie asked and when Viv did so, she clapped her hands. 'That means the new suite is cheaper than the second-hand one, even though it's half price.'

Viv's eyes widened in surprise. 'So it is, I didn't notice that.'

'The second-hand one is probably a better quality suite but the cheaper Co-op one would do you fine,' Charlie said. 'You'll be able to pay that one up in smaller monthly payments.'

'We could go into the Co-op tomorrow to have a look at the suites,' Maddie suggested.

'Good idea,' Viv said, then gave a squeal of delight as she looked further down the page. 'There are some adverts here for the local cinemas, Maddie. The one across the road, the Grand Central, is showing a Burt Lancaster film, 'The Crimson Pirate' and the second film is 'The Grace Moore Story'.

'Who's in the second film?'

'It's Kathryn Grayson, I like her.'

'Me too.'

'I think you've more on your plate at the moment than the cinema.' Charlie laughed and got to his feet, stepping out of his overalls. 'Well, that's me done for today, lassies.'

Viv got up too and collected the cups. 'Mum said you haven't thrown out the twins' old single beds yet.'

'That's right, they're still in the shed behind the house,' Charlie said, folding his overalls and laying them on the paste table. 'As long as no dampness has got in, we'll be able to bring them here for you two. And we can see if we can pick you up some cheap carpet squares and maybe a strip of carpet to cover the lobby floor.'

'More problems solved.' Viv smiled at them both in turn. 'Right I'll just rinse these cups through before we go,' she said, and headed for the kitchen.

Chapter Eighteen

August 1957

'Are you going down to Glasgow Cross, Maddie?' Helen Ford asked hesitantly as the two girls came out of the counselling group at the infirmary. She and Maddie had exchanged surnames although they were kept confidential within the group.

Maddie nodded and the two girls fell into step, chatting as they walked down High Street, passing the Necropolis on their left hand side.

'Are you going home?' Helen asked.

'I'm going back to work. In Argyle Street.' Maddie had eventually revealed her attendance at the therapy group to Miss Edwards who, despite her formidable reputation, had given Maddie permission to take time off for these appointments.

'And I should hope so too,' Viv had said when Maddie told her. 'After all you're one of her best workers from what I've heard.'

It always amazed Maddie how Viv knew everything that was going on in Marshall's. She was such an extrovert that people readily confided in her. Not for the first time it crossed Maddie's mind how different they were. She recalled the old saying that opposites attract; she smiled, it certainly applied in their case.

'Pardon', Maddie apologised, becoming aware that Helen had spoken again.

'That's okay. I was just saying it was a good session today, wasn't it?'

'Yes, very positive. I like Brian, you feel he really

listens to what you say.'

Helen nodded. 'Where is it you work, Maddie?'

'In Marshall's store in Argyle Street,' she said, as they reached Glasgow Cross and turned right into Trongate. 'I work in the Counting House there. Have you managed to get a job yourself?'

Helen shook her head, sighing. 'Unfortunately nothing so far but I keep applying for anything I think I might be able to do.'

Maddie felt sure that Helen was more capable than she was letting on. 'If it's any help, I could watch out for something in our place and let you know,' she offered, aware of how grateful she'd been to Viv for getting her the interview in Marshall's.

'That's really kind, Maddie, thank you. Will I see you at the next session?' Helen asked as they neared Marshall's.

'Not the next one but the one after. Can I phone you if a job comes up before then?

'We don't have a phone in the house but Mr Neilson our next door neighbour does and I can give you a note of his number.' Taking the pen Maddie held out to her, Helen wrote her neighbour's name and phone number on the back of an old bus ticket.

'That's great Helen.' Maddie put the paper into her bag. 'Look after yourself.'

'You too,' Helen said and walked on towards the bus station.

Chapter Nineteen

October 1957

'Think you've had enough, Will,' Tom, the barman in The Drop Inn said that Saturday afternoon when Benson asked for his fourth whisky. 'Why don't you call it a day? Go home and sleep it off, eh?'

Benson slammed his glass down on the bar counter, by some miracle not smashing it. 'I said another half,' he thundered, his face scarlet from booze and rage.

'Okay, okay, anything you say,' Tom said, his tone placatory, shrugging as he went over to the gantry to pour a refill. He placed the whisky in front of Benson, who chucked the money at him, before storming over to a table in the corner with his drink.

Shaking his head, Tom left Benson's change on the counter. He'd known Will Benson for years. A good engineer and a hard worker, Will used to be a heavy drinker but once he'd become involved in his local church his intake had gone down considerably. Nowadays he tended to keep himself to himself and didn't cause any problems while he was in the pub. Today, however, he was drinking more than his normal and seemed unusually aggressive.

Tom had seen a difference in Benson's consumption after his stepdaughter Maddie disappeared over a year ago and no-one in Bonnycross had heard from her since. She'd left shortly after her mother's funeral but Tom wasn't sure what had happened between her and Will.

Rather than worry about how Maddie was faring, Will seemed more incensed and aggrieved by her going. Of course now that his firm was closing down and he'd been made redundant as of yesterday, Benson's anger had risen further and probably accounted for his behaviour today.

A short time later, a crowd of redundant workers came in to drown their sorrows. Tom was kept busy attending to their orders. He listened to their moans about the suddenness of the company going bust and, because it wasn't mandatory, the firm had laid them off without any severance pay.

It wasn't until most of them had left the bar and taken themselves off to a table that Tom had time to pay attention to the other punters sitting around the pub. That was when he noticed Will Benson had vanished, no doubt to stop off at the town's other pubs on the way home.

Tom shook his head once more, glad that Maddie wasn't there to deal with her drunken stepfather when he finally got home.

*

Instead of taking the bus straight home after work that Saturday afternoon, Steve Dixon got off at the corner of Duke Street and Foundry Row. He walked halfway up the lane to where Pete Douglas, the bookie's runner, conducted his business. One of Steve's fellow storemen had given him a tip that morning, saying that Rocky's Boy was a sure cert for the four o'clock race.

'Hi, Stevie, thought you were giving up gambling.' Pete grinned at him, knowing that Steve was a loser. As ever, Pete had one eye on the punters while keeping a look out for the police who frequently chased him away because of illegal gambling.

'I'm on to a sure thing this time,' Steve told him, pushing back his guilt at having promised his ma he'd stop gambling.

Ma worked hard, with long hours, to make ends meet and he'd promised to stop gambling and give her more of his wages to help with the household bills. He'd vowed time after time not to visit Pete again but, try though he might, he always succumbed and ended up here. This time though, as before, he was certain he'd found a winner.

'I want to place a bet on Rocky's Boy for the four

o'clock,' he told Pete.

'Okay, how much do you want to bet?'

Steve was about to say a pound but then heard himself say, 'I want £5 each way.' His mate had been certain that, going on the nag's previous performance, it would romp home in the lead. And even if it didn't come in first, Steve reasoned, he'd get something for it being placed. He couldn't lose, he convinced himself, and held out a £10 note.

'You sure?' Pete's voice pulled him back into the moment.

'Sure.' He'd tried for months now to get Maddie Granger to go out with him but she'd refused constantly so he might as well spend his money on the horses instead. 'I'll come back later for my winnings.'

Pete shrugged and handed Steve his betting slip. 'Good luck.'

Chapter Twenty

'Dave Tucker has asked me to go to the staff dance with him,' Viv said on Monday evening when she and Maddie were in the flat listening to some popular music on their favourite radio station, Radio Luxembourg.

Maddie lifted the iron from the muslin blouse she was working on and raised her head, her eyebrows arched. 'When did he ask you?'

'He was standing next to be me in the lunch queue today and I knew he was going to ask me something.' Viv and Maddie very rarely had lunch together as they were usually on different lunch hours. 'He spoke in a whisper, I think he was scared anyone heard me saying no.'

'As if you would,' Maddie smiled, remembering how long Viv had had a crush on the carpet salesman. She flattened the sleeve of the blouse down on to the ironing table and laid a damp cloth over it before she pressed it.

'But he didn't know that. I've always been careful not to let him see how much I fancy him.' Viv put the two pieces of lemon meringue pie, leftovers from their visit to the farm the previous day, on to dessert plates. 'Good old Mum with her carry outs. Do you want to stop ironing while you eat this?'

'Leave mine on the table. This is my last blouse so I'll eat my pie when I'm finished it. So when's the dance?'

'Four weeks on Friday. It's to be held in the Plaza Ballroom at Eglinton Toll.'

'I've never been there.'

'Neither have I but I've heard it's a beautiful dance hall.'

'Will you need to get a new dress for the dance?'

'Yes, it's quite a dressed up affair. I think the men wear dinner suits and bow ties. The women need a ball gown. I might ask Mum if she could make me a dress.'

'I'm sure she will. A ball gown would cost a fortune in the shops.'

'You might be needing one yourself.'

Maddie lay the iron on its metal plate to cool down and put the blouse on to its hanger. She looked at her flatmate. 'Why would I need a dress?' she asked, wrinkling her face.

'Because Dave told me that Steve Dixon wants to ask you to the dance.' Viv stopped speaking to push a spoonful of her mum's delicious lemon meringue pie into her mouth. 'Ooh', she mumbled as she swallowed it. Viv was certain that she'd never be as good a baker as her mum.

Maddie brought her back to their previous conversation. 'No way. I hope you told him I wouldn't go.'

'I didn't actually, I suggested Steve ask you?' Praying that she wasn't crossing the line with her friend, she held her hand up, palm facing Maddie. 'Honestly, Maddie, it's time you stopped all this anti-men nonsense. Not all men are monsters you know.'

She realised at once that she'd hit a raw nerve.

'Viv, you've been lucky in your life. I mean your dad and grandad and all the other men in your family are lovely and so kind.'

Viv waited for her to continue but Maddie said no more, instead making a temple of her fingers, something the twins had shown her the previous day. Viv knew Maddie wasn't prepared to explain further. If only she'd open up to me, she thought, I could try and help her with her aversion to men.

Maddie was still attending her counselling group from time to time but she never spoke about the sessions at home afterwards and Viv felt she was prying if she asked anything. She knew Maddie had become friendly with a girl from the group, Helen Ford, who seemed to suffer from depression. Maddie was hoping a job would come up for Helen in

Marshall's.

Maddie appeared to be considering Viv's comments. 'The only way I would go to the dance with him is in a foursome with you and Dave,' she finally said.

'Of course we can go in a foursome.' Viv beamed at her. 'Oh Maddie, I'm so pleased. I'll put a word in Dave's ear. And I'm sure Mum will make a dress for you too. After all, as Mum and Dad always say, you're one of the family now.'

Chapter Twenty-One

November 1957

'Hello, there,' Helen said, as Maddie slid her tray along the metal bars attached to the serving counter in Marshall's canteen. 'What can I get you?'

Maddie quickly scanned the menu written on the board beside the serving hatch. 'Sausage and mash please, Helen.'

After telling Helen about the canteen vacancy she'd seen advertised on the staff notice board, Maddie was delighted to hear that her interview had been successful. Looking at Helen now, so efficient and cheery, it was hard to believe she was the same person. She wondered if Brian, the therapist, had noticed the difference in Helen. Maddie herself was attending the therapy group much more infrequently.

'How are you going?' she asked quietly, while Helen spooned her meal on to the plate.

'Really great.' Helen carried the plate over and placed it on Maddie's tray. 'Thanks to Molly, the manageress, who's been keeping me right in the way things are done. She's such a sweet lady and the staff are very friendly. I'm glad it's a female staff in here as I always get tongue-tied and awkward around men,' she whispered as she leaned forward to place the glass of milk Maddie had ordered on to the tray.

'Snap,' Maddie held out her hand and grasped Helen's, giving her a knowing wink.

'See you later, Helen,' she added, moving on quickly when she saw a couple of girls from the cosmetic counter had begun to form a queue behind her. The last thing she wanted was to get Helen into trouble when she'd only been working in the canteen for a couple of weeks.

*

'Helen served me in the canteen at lunch time,' Maddie announced, when she got home after work that day. As she stopped an hour earlier than Viv on a Friday, Maddie tended to use her extra hour to buy what provisions they needed. By the time she got home with the shopping, Viv was already in and had changed out of her work clothes.

'How's she getting on in the job?' Although Viv had spoken to Helen one day in the canteen, she hadn't yet built up a rapport with the girl. She seemed nice though and Maddie liked her and spoke well of her.

Lifting the heavy bag off the floor where she'd dropped it, Maddie dumped it on to a dining chair. 'Oh, she loves it and says Molly has been helping her a lot.' She started to unpack the groceries and fruit. 'Hannah gave me a few extra apples. And I'm sure she gave me more than a pound of grapes although she just charged for a pound.'

Hannah and her sister Susan, the two unmarried ladies who rented the fruit shop on the opposite side of their close from the newsagent, had both taken a shine to Maddie and constantly gave her extra fruit and vegetables when she went in there.

Viv started to put the fruit into the bowl which sat in the middle of the table. 'Fantastic. You should do all our fruit shopping as they never give me extra. We might as well take the chance of a bargain when we're getting it.'

'They don't look like sisters at all. Hannah is really tall and straight as a ramrod. As well as being small and tubby, Susan's quite a hunchback. I often wonder if the poor woman was born slightly deformed.' Maddie carried the potatoes and cabbage over to the press in the corner and put them into the basket on the bottom shelf until they were needed.

'She might well have been born with a deformity or maybe she simply has bad posture.' Viv laughed. 'Aunt Meg used to make us kids walk around the room with a book on our head to help with posture. Didn't do me much good, mind you, and the book kept slipping off my head. Do Hannah and Susan live together?'

'Yes, Hannah told me they live in what was their family home when their parents were alive. I understand their parents had the shop before them.'

'So a real family concern. Aunt Meg said that there are lots of family owned or rented businesses in Rutherglen. Some of them have been in the same family for generations. Glad we don't need to cook tonight.' Ever since they'd moved into the flat, she and Maddie had made it a rule that they didn't cook on a Friday night. Instead they went to Vendetozzi's for fish suppers.

'Will I go for the fish suppers while you butter our bread and lay the table?'

'Yep, that's fine. Remember and get mine in fish dressing rather than batter. And some pickled onions too.' Maddie filled the kettle and lit the gas ring beneath it, to allow time for it to boil before Viv arrived back with their meal.

Chapter Twenty-Two

I'm glad I told Dad not to meet us,' Viv said, as she and Maddie were walking to Fairfields from the bus stop on Sunday afternoon. 'I need the exercise to make sure my dress fits at the dance on Friday night.'

'Same here.' Maddie puffed slightly as they climbed the hill, her shoulder bag swinging at her side as she walked. 'It's so kind of your mum to make my dress too.'

'Oh, she'll have enjoyed doing it. She looks on you like another daughter, you know.'

Aileen and Elizabeth ran across the field to meet them as they opened the back gate into the farm.

'Your dresses are hanging up in Mum's bedroom,' Aileen told them, as Viv was latching the gate behind them.

Elizabeth jumped up and down in excitement. 'Can we see you wearing them?'

Maddie smiled at her. 'Of course, that's why we're here. Your mum wants a final fitting in case she needs to make any alterations.'

Aileen took Maddie's hand and hurried her towards the farmhouse. 'They're gorgeous dresses, you'll be like fairy princesses.'

Elizabeth followed behind with Viv. 'With your beautiful dresses, will you wear tiaras in your hair?'

Viv threw an arm around her sister's shoulders. 'No silly, it's a staff dance we're going to, not a fancy ball.'

'Aw.' Elizabeth's pretty face crumpled in disappointment.

Sheena was waiting at the open door for them. 'Great to see you both. Do you want a cuppa before you try on the dresses?'

'I'd rather try my dress first,' Viv said. She looked at Maddie who nodded her agreement.

'Good that the dogs are both out in the fields with Charlie,' Sheena said when they got to her bedroom. 'You two stay in the living room until I see how the dresses fit,' she told the twins, who reluctantly did as they were told.

About fifteen minutes later, Sheena called through to the twins. 'Right girls, you can come in now.'

Aileen and Elizabeth raced into the bedroom, almost colliding with one another in the process. Then they held their breath, staring at the vision of loveliness facing them.

Viv and Maddie were both standing on chairs, posing. Viv was exquisite in her royal blue calf-length dress; its taffeta material was covered by matching coloured lace across the shoulders and set off by three-quarter length lace sleeves. She wore a silver Alice band in her thick black, curly hair and silver medium-heeled shoes finished the outfit.

Maddie's tangerine coloured dress was in a satin material; it was a straighter style, sleeveless, and had a bolero. Due to its style, Maddie would have to wear a strapless bra, which she could buy in Marshall's before Friday. Her hair, out of its pony tail, hung loosely around her collar area. She wore a gold coloured artificial rose in her hair and gold high-heeled sandals.

'Oh, you're both so beautiful.' Awestruck, Aileen's voice was reduced to a whisper, while Elizabeth simply stared at them in wonder.

Sheena smiled proudly at the two girls. 'And you'll look even better when you have your hair done on Friday. Now, when you take your dresses off, I've got a box we can pack them in and we'll wrap them in tissue paper. Dad is going to run you home to save you having to take the boxes on the bus.'

Chapter Twenty-Three

The evening of the dance was bitterly cold with a forecast of snow during the night to come. Viv and Maddie were glad that Dave's father had offered to take them to the Plaza in his car and they'd get a taxi home again.

'I hope it doesn't snow until after we get home.' Viv was standing in front of the mirror brushing her hair and playing with her curls to get them to sit the way she wanted.

'Will you stop messing about with your hair, Viv, leave it be, it's perfect.'

Viv smiled at her reflection in the mirror. 'I don't know why I bother going to the hairdresser as I always come home and do it again myself.' She turned to face Maddie. 'Your hair is lovely the way it falls around your neck. You should keep it like that?'

'I can't be bothered with the hassle, I find it easier just to push it back into a pony tail.' Maddie picked up her jacket, a lovely wool one that Sheena had lent her, and pushed her arms into its cosy sleeves. 'I'll get it,' she said, when there was a ring at the doorbell.

'We're ready,' she told Steve, when she opened the door to him. He stood inside the lobby for a moment and, despite the unsightly birthmark, Maddie was surprised by how handsome he looked dressed in a dinner suit.

'Dave and his dad are waiting downstairs in the car.' Steve sounded a bit breathless from bounding up the tenement stairs. 'We want to get there early so that we can find a table close to the dance floor.'

'Right, let's go,' Maddie replied and she followed him out on to the landing, while Viv pulled on the fur jacket she'd borrowed from her mum and turned the key in the lock.

The car was sitting at the kerb outside the close entrance. Dave sat beside his dad in the front while the two girls and Steve squeezed into the back seat. Maddie tensed up slightly when she felt the closeness of Steve's leg against her own but she couldn't do anything about it when they were all crushed up together.

Once inside the Plaza, the girls joined the queue to leave their jackets in the cloakrooms. As they stood there, the band started to play one of Elvis' numbers released earlier that year. The singer made a good job of impersonating The King of Rock nRoll as Elvis was known. The two girls began to keep time to the music, dancing on the spot, and singing aloud as they did so.

> *A well' a bless my soul*
> *What's a wrong with me?*
> *I'm itchin' like a man in a fuzzy tree*
> *My friends say I'm actin' wild as a bug*
> *I'm in love*
> *I'm all shook up*
> *Mm, mm, mm. mm. yay, yay, yay.*

So engrossed were they in the music that they arrived at the cloakroom check-in before they knew it. They were each given a raffle ticket with a number on it that they needed to reclaim their jackets at the end of the evening.

The boys were waiting for them at the edge of the dance floor and they gave wolf whistles when they saw the girls. 'Let's grab that table over there.' Dave indicated towards the only remaining empty table among those at the edge of the dance floor.

They walked along the carpeted area between the tables near the floor and the others on their left against the wall, and settled down at the table Dave had suggested. There were four chairs placed around it, with a small lamp sitting in the centre of the table. Wall lights halfway up the rose pink painted walls added more illumination.

'That's gorgeous,' Maddie said to no-one in particular, pointing to the fountain that stood in the middle of the dance floor. Its base had a pink marble covering and water trickled down from the fountain into the bowl-shaped container on top of the base. Coloured lights had been placed around the outside of the container which gave the effect of the water changing colours.

'What would you girls like to drink?' Dave asked, standing up and taking his wallet out of his pocket.

Maddie was first to answer. 'I'd like to try a Pimms please.'

'O.K.,' Dave nodded. They come in Nos 1, 2, 3 or 4. They all have a different spirit in them, whisky, brandy, vodka or gin. What will it be?'

Maddie didn't want to admit that she'd never tasted spirits before. 'Vodka for me.'

'What about you Viv?'

'I'll have the same as Maddie.'

While Dave and Steve went to the bar on the opposite side of the ballroom, the girls listened to the music of the band, their toes tapping under the table. They watched the dancers already on the floor, interested to see what the other females were wearing.

'There's Patricia Harper,' Maddie said, her voice rising over the music, and she waved to Patricia and her partner waltzing around the fountain.

Maddie had known Patricia wouldn't appear at a staff dance with Eric Chalmers; he'd be with his wife. Patricia, looking glamorous in an emerald green dress with lots of sparkly jewellery, finally caught Maddie's eye on her and waved back.

'She's a real stunner, isn't she?' Viv opened her silver sequined evening purse and took out a mirror and comb to check if her hair was sitting in place. 'Will that be her husband or her boyfriend?'

'I don't know, don't think she's married though.' Maddie glanced round. 'Viv, will you leave your hair alone. It's fine as it is.'

Viv made a face at her and put the items back into the purse.

'Hello girls, are you having fun?' a voice said at

Maddie's side. She and Viv both turned round to see Miss Edwards smiling down at them.

'Yes thanks, Miss Edwards,' Maddie stammered, unable to believe that her boss was actually speaking to them outside of work.

Smiling again, Miss Edwards sat at a table beside the wall, well away from the dance floor. She wore a tailored navy dress, edged with white; her companion was in a dinner suit.

'God, she's human after all,' Viv whispered. 'Wonder if that's her boyfriend?'

Maddie shook her head. 'Julie in the typing pool told me that Miss Edwards always comes to the staff dance with her brother. Neither of them are married and they live together.'

'Who lives together?'

Dave laid the two glasses of Pimms down on the table while Steve followed behind, carrying their pints of beer.

'It's Miss Edwards from the Counting House,' Viv told him quietly. 'She and her brother live together and he's here with her tonight.'

'Oh, is that all, I thought it was scandal. What about a dance?' he asked, holding out his hand to Viv as the band started playing a quickstep.

'Maddie,' Steve said shyly, 'would you like to dance?' His flirty manner was gone now and he looked a bit scared that she would reject his offer.

She'd never danced formally before and was afraid she would make a fool of herself but since she'd come with him she didn't think she could refuse. She held herself rigidly in his arms as they danced and tripped over his feet a couple of times within the first few minutes. 'I'm sorry,' she apologised, 'I don't know the steps.'

'Just relax,' he smiled, 'and let me lead you. I don't know the steps either but we'll soon get the hang of it,' he assured her. Once she did as he suggested, she began to enjoy herself. As he was whirling her round the fountain in the centre of the hall they almost collided with Patricia and her partner.

'Hello Maddie,' Patricia shouted to be heard above the music. 'Frank, Maddie works in the Counting House with me and Steve is in the warehouse,' Patricia said by way of introduction.

'Pleased to meet you.' At well over six feet, Frank towered above all three of them. When other couples began to bump into them, they stopped chatting and danced again.

Maddie found it difficult to keep her strapless bra in place and after any strenuous dance, such as the Gay Gordons, she and Viv had to go to the ladies room, where Viv would unzip her dress so she could pull the bra up into position once more.

On the third occasion this happened, Maddie went into fits of giggles. 'Dave and Steve must be wondering what's wrong with us.'

'Maybe they think we've got upset stomachs,' Viv suggested and they both fell about laughing. It took all their efforts to keep straight faces when they returned to the ballroom.

Midway through the evening the music stopped and they had supper, which was laid out on tables near the bar. This also allowed the band members to have a rest from playing. Towards the end of the dance, Maddie found that she'd enjoyed herself after all and before she knew it the four of them were on their way home in a taxi.

'Could you wait for us please?' Dave asked the taxi driver, who nodded and left the engine running. They saw the two girls into their tenement close and Dave gave Viv a goodnight kiss, which she returned in full measure. When Steve made to kiss Maddie, she turned her face away from him and drew back. She saw the hurt look in his eyes but she couldn't help herself. That was going too far and the mere thought brought on nasty memories.

She mumbled, 'thanks for tonight, Steve, see you on Monday,' and began to climb the stairs to the flat, leaving Viv to say goodnight and hurry after her.

Chapter Twenty-Four

On Monday morning Viv had to go into work early to help
with a consignment of extra Christmas stock that had come in
late Friday afternoon. 'There're piles of boxes lying around so
it'll take us all our time to get everything sorted out before the
first customers come in,' she said to Maddie, wolfing down
her last piece of toast and marmalade. She washed it down
with the remainder of her tea. Then she got up and left her
dishes in the sink, as they did all the washing up at dinner
time. 'It was your Steve and another guy who brought the
boxes to us on Friday.'

'He isn't my Steve,' Maddie said immediately.

'Sorry, I just know how much he fancies you.' Viv
said, as she checked she had everything in her handbag that
she needed. 'I forgot to tell you,' she said, as casually as she
could manage, 'on Friday night Dave said he couldn't see me
over the weekend as he was visiting relatives down south but
he asked if I'd go with him to the cinema this coming
Saturday. He was sure that Steve would be happy to make up a
foursome again if you wanted to join us.'

Viv left it at that, scared she might have crossed the
line again. She glanced at the clock and got her coat from the
hallstand, buttoning it up and pulling on her gloves.

'What are you going to see?'

Surprised by Maddie's question, Viv decided she
might be interested in Steve after all. 'At first we thought we'd
go to a cinema in the city centre but we've decided instead to
go to the Grand Central here in Rutherglen.'

Seeing a flicker of interest in Maddie's eyes, she
continued. 'There's a Jeff Chandler film on at the Grand
Central and he's Dave's favourite actor. I can't remember the

title of the film but I know the second feature's called 'Street Corner' with Anne Crawford and Peggy Cummins. It finishes on Saturday.' The programme in most cinemas changed mid-week. Films that were shown on Monday, Tuesday and Wednesday were different to the ones shown on Thursday, Friday and Saturday. This allowed patrons to go to the same cinema twice in the one week.

'Right, I'll love you and leave you,' she said to Maddie, who was still in her dressing gown while she ate some breakfast.

'Okay,' Maddie called to her retreating form.

Shortly afterwards, still undecided about the cinema, Maddie roused herself and got ready for work. She came out of the close in time to see her usual tramcar move away from its stop. The next tram wouldn't be for about ten or fifteen minutes. Cursing under her breath, she hurried along to the bus stop in front of the opticians to wait for the No 22. Five minutes later, when the bus still hadn't arrived, she ran round to Victoria Street and went into Rutherglen railway station.

A race along the tunnel walkway over the tracks and down the stairs to the ticket office left her slightly out of breath, reinforcing what she already knew, that she needed to lose some weight. She joined the ticket queue and asked for the price of a return ticket to Glasgow Central. 'We have a special cheap day return, 1/- for first class or 8d. for second class,' the bespectacled man behind the glass told her, 'or you can have a weekly pass which works out cheaper.'

'A cheap day second class return,' she told him, pushing eight pennies through the slot. A shilling for the first class was much too extravagant for her limited budget.

'Have you been out singing?' The man picked up the eight coins and laughed at his own joke. Maddie said nothing but contented herself with a grimace.

She exited from Central Station on to Gordon Street, throbbing with humanity at this time of morning. Further along that street she turned right into Buchanan Street, which led her down to Argyle Street. She crossed to the other side of the road and almost collided with Helen coming out of St

Enoch Underground Station.

'Hello, Helen,' she smiled, 'I'm surprised to see you here, I thought you came into town by bus.'

'I usually do as there's a bus stop outside our house but I was running late this morning and the subway from Govan was quicker.'

Maddie smiled again. She herself called it the Underground but Glaswegians always referred to it as 'the subway'.

'My mother doesn't keep well and I need to help her with washing and breakfast before I come to work. The alarm didn't go off this morning and we slept in,' Helen explained.

Maddie felt sorry for Helen, with all her own health problems and having to look after her mother too. Helen didn't seem to mind though and, when Maddie thought about her own mother, she knew she would have been happy to do the same.

'Did you go to the staff dance on Friday night?' Helen asked, as they neared the store.

'Yes, Viv and I went together.'

'Who were your partners?'

Sure that Helen wasn't the type to gossip, Maddie said, 'Viv went with Dave Tucker from the carpet department and my partner was Steve Dixon from the warehouse.'

'That's great. And are they your steady boyfriends?'

'No, it was just a one night stand, so we could all go to the dance? The decorations are lovely, aren't they?' she added as they went through the swing door into the shop entrance.

'Gorgeous.' The two girls stood in the foyer for a few minutes to admire all the tinsel and glitter that adorned their store. To the left of the entrance door stood a 6' tall tree, its branches full of Christmas ornaments and lovely red velvet bows. Helen looked over at it. 'It's like the ones you see in these American films, isn't it?'

Maddie nodded. 'Your decorations in the canteen are lovely too.'

'Yes, we all stayed late one night to put them up.' The

pride was evident in Helen's voice.

'Let's go,' Maddie said as she saw the lift doors opening and the two of them made a dash to get in before they closed again.

Chapter Twenty-Five

December 1957

'Oh my God, how awful,' Viv said as she was reading the Reformer after dinner.

Maddie looked up from the library book she was reading. 'What's wrong?'

'Last Saturday there was a tragedy at a Clyde v Celtic football match at Shawfield stadium, when a wall collapsed on top of spectators. It says here that one boy was killed and forty eight others were injured. I didn't hear anything about it on the radio.'

'Neither did I, but it might only have been reported in the local paper. How awful for the families concerned, especially at Christmas time. Honestly, what is the world coming to; between accidents and murders, it's all you seem to read about in the papers nowadays.'

'Oh no,' Viv said, this time pointing to a piece at the bottom of the page she was reading. 'GRAND CENTRAL TO CLOSE' she read out. 'Says here the cinema is closing after thirty three years because of competition from the cinemas that use a wide screen. The Grand Central only has a normal sized screen and they're finding it hard to obtain films that suit so they're closing down. The Manager, who's worked there for twenty seven years, says that more people are buying television sets these days and not going to the cinema. How sad, I'm going to miss it.'

'Yes, it's very handy for us,' Maddie agreed.

'Never mind, at least we're lucky to have other cinemas in Rutherglen that we can use. The Odeon on Main Street, the Rio in Glasgow Road and Green's on East Main

Street,' Viv counted them off on her fingers, 'and there's also the Rhul at Burnside.'

'Yes, it's only a couple of bus stops away,' Maddie said. 'And don't forget that cinema in Kings Park.'

'Of course, the State cinema, I'd forgotten about that one. But out of them all the Grand Central was my favourite.'

Maddie shrugged. 'That's just because it's so near us. Anyway, can't be helped, Viv, just one of these things. Can't believe we'll be having Christmas at Fairfields in a few days' time. I always love being with your family.'

'Yes, it's such a happy time. That reminds me, we must get our gifts wrapped soon.' Viv's disappointment at the closure of the cinema was banished to the recesses of her mind as she anticipated Christmas day.

*

The twins were watching out for Viv and Maddie when they got to Fairfields on Christmas Eve. As usual, the girls had stopped early that day when the store closed to customers. They'd had their overnight cases packed in readiness for the bus trip to Annbank. Charlie had arranged to pick them up there and save them the long walk to the farm in darkness.

As soon as they saw the headlights coming up the drive, Elizabeth rushed outside, with Aileen at her heels. Elizabeth pulled at Maddie's arm. 'Come and see the new decorations on the Christmas tree.'

The tree, twinkling with decorations, stood in its usual place in the corner between the china cabinet and the settee. 'We've got some new Christmas bells,' Elizabeth ran over to the tree and swung one of the gold bells back and forward. 'And do you like these?' she asked Maddie, touching one of the red velvet bows which were attached here and there on the green branches.

'They're gorgeous,' Maddie smiled, finding Elizabeth's excitement infectious.

'Careful, Zeus,' Elizabeth cautioned, as the German Shepherd ran over to the tree and pushed one of the baubles with his nose, almost knocking the tree over. As it was, the fairy on the top was left hanging at a precarious angle.

'You're a vandal aren't you, Zeus?' Aileen rushed forward and grabbed him away from the tree. She threw her arms around his neck and lay her face against his fur. The dog twisted himself out of her grasp and jumped up to lick her cheek.

'Will you two give Maddie and Viv time to get their coats off before you start bombarding them with the new decorations,' Sheena called from the kitchen. 'Dinner will be ready in about fifteen minutes,' she announced, and began to hum 'Jingle Bells' as the twins helped her to lay out the table settings.

Chapter Twenty-Six

February 1958

Despite the keen wind, the day was bright and sunny, which lifted the spirits of the mourners a little. The cremation service was held in Kilmarnock, close to Grandad's flat. The crematorium was set in magnificent grounds which also helped to soften the bitterness of their pain.

'You've all done very well,' Maddie whispered to Sheena, when she carried some used plates into the farmhouse kitchen after the mourners had been fed. 'I'm really proud of you all.'

From her usual place between the cooker and the sink, Sheena turned round slowly to face Maddie. She gave her a sad smile and sniffed back the tears. 'Dad would have wanted everyone to remember him back here, rather than a formal affair in a hotel.'

Hearing the catch in her voice, Maddie opened her arms and cuddled Sheena, aware that the floodgates were at bursting point. She said no more but slipped away, allowing Sheena time to compose herself before returning to their guests.

Maddie fully understood the emotion Sheena was experiencing. The service had moved her too, grief at the memory of her own mum's funeral crashing in. But she didn't allow herself to dwell on her late mother too long, afraid that **his** face would come into the mix.

Folk were milling around the living room, some spilling out into the hallway, where Charlie had laid out some chairs. Most of the mourners were extended Kingston family members but many of the neighbouring farmers and their wives had joined the gathering too.

A number of Grandad's friends from Kilmarnock had attended the service but declined Sheena and Charlie's warm invitation to come back to Fairfields for something to eat and drink. Their reasons were varied but a common theme was age, mobility and lack of transport. They were all content with having paid their respects to Sheena's late father at the service and said how much they would miss him for his cheery smile and sense of humour.

Maddie had adored Viv's grandad in the fourteen months since she'd first met him at Christmas 1956. She felt privileged to have known him. Back in the living room, she felt a pull on her arm. She turned round to find Elizabeth staring up at her.

'Maddie, do you want to see Daisy's kittens? There are five and they're only two days old. Just this size,' the little girl said, holding her hands out, palms facing inwards, a short distance apart to give Maddie an idea of how tiny they were.

'I'd love to.' Maddie was keen to get away from thoughts of death into new life.

'Wait for me,' Aileen called, and followed them out of the back door.

They put on welly boots from the selection that always sat at the side of the door and, properly shod, they made their way through the barn, empty of cattle at this time of day. At the rear end of the barn, near the door into the cold room, Maddie saw the kittens. They were snug and warm in a basket filled with straw and more straw was piled up in a wall surrounding the basket.

Daisy was lying close by, her back paws against the basket, protecting her new-borns from harm. The cat eyed Maddie suspiciously as she peeped into the basket. 'Aw,' she murmured, drawing her finger along one kitten's back. Its fur felt like soft down.

This kitten was the only one of the five who was awake. The others were a very pale cream shade, minus Daisy's stripes as yet, but the kitten she stroked was a darker shade, more coffee coloured, making him or her stand out from its siblings.

'There were six altogether but one died,' Aileen told her. 'These ones are doing well.'

'You can lift him if you want?' Elizabeth's eyes were sparkling with excitement.

'No, I'll not disturb him, he looks too cosy. What sex are the other kittens?'

Aileen lifted the kitten up and petted him. He purred happily in her arms. 'One of the lighter coloured kittens is also a boy and the other three are girls.'

'We won't keep them all,' Elizabeth explained to Maddie. 'Maybe just a couple to help catch mice, but we'll find good homes for the rest.'

Aileen looked at Maddie. 'You and Viv could have one at the flat.'

Maddie shook her head. 'It's a lovely idea, Aileen, but Viv and I are out at work all day and it wouldn't be fair to the wee mite.'

Elizabeth caught her hand. 'But Maddie, cats are easier to look after than dogs. Dogs need walking but cats are more independent.'

'I know that but a top storey tenement flat is unsuitable for an animal and anyway our factor doesn't allow tenants to keep pets.' She didn't give her other reason that she doubted if she and Viv could afford to feed an animal as they had a struggle to meet bills as it was.

'Hello-oo,' Viv's voice reached them from outside and next minute her head appeared in the doorway.

'Aileen, Elizabeth, Auntie Pearl and Uncle Archie are leaving and want to say cheerio to you both.'

The kittens forgotten for the moment, the twins ran off to see their relatives, leaving Viv and Maddie to cross the field, arm in arm, at a more leisurely pace.

Chapter Twenty-Seven

March 1958

'I think I could discharge you from my clinic now,' Dr Hepworth said to Maddie, when she attended her appointment that Monday morning.

'But what if I start to have suicidal feelings again?'

He gave her an understanding smile. 'The medicine you're taking will keep such feelings away. But if any dark feelings should re-surface in the future, then you can ring Brian for a chat or ask your GP to refer you back to my clinic.'

'Fine,' she said 'and thanks for all you've done for me, Dr Hepworth.'

'You're welcome. I'm pleased to see you so well.' The psychiatrist got to his feet and shook hands with Maddie before opening his consulting room door for her.

She was coming out of the hospital's main door when she heard someone calling her name. She looked round to see Helen running towards her. 'Hello, Maddie, have you been to see Dr Hepworth?'

'Yes, and he's discharged me from his clinic.'

'That's great Maddie,' Helen said as they came through the hospital gates on to the main road. 'Will you still be attending Brian's group?'

'No, not unless I have any future problems. You're doing really well too, aren't you, Helen?'

'A lot of my improvement is thanks to you Maddie, for getting me the job in Marshall's canteen.' She linked arms with Maddie as they walked down towards Glasgow Cross.

'No, I only told you about the job, you got it for yourself, Helen. How's your mother keeping these days?'

'She's fairly well at the moment, thanks. In fact, she says she's well enough for me to go out at night now and again and leave her alone in the house. Maybe sometime you and I could go to the cinema or have a high tea somewhere. I would enjoy having someone to serve me for a change.'

'Why don't we go to Sloan's in the Argyle Arcade for a high tea on Friday after work? Viv is going to a reunion night out with her old school friends.'

'Great, Maddie, I'll look forward to that,' Helen said, as they parted company in Marshall's.

*

She does go on, Benson thought, unable to get a word in during his conversation with the landlady. Once she'd finally stopped chattering, Benson paid her a week's rent and shut his door firmly, listening to her footsteps going downstairs.

She had the rooms on the ground floor of the red sandstone house in Hamilton Road, Rutherglen, while the two upstairs bedrooms were his, having been turned into a bedroom and a living room with a scullery in it. The only place he had to share with Mrs Martin was the bathroom which was located downstairs. The landlady's son had done the conversion following the death of his father, with the idea of giving his widowed mother an income.

Benson had been unwilling to give up his tenancy in Bonnycross when he got the job at Bruce's Engineering Company in Farme Cross, near Rutherglen, before making sure the job worked out for him. Following his redundancy, he'd been unsuccessful in getting another job in Bonnycross and it was the chap in the Buroo who'd found this one for him. The pay was much less than he'd previously earned but at least it was a job. He was planning to stay in Rutherglen during the week and return home at the weekend. He wasn't starting in his job until tomorrow, Tuesday, but had travelled through to Rutherglen today to get himself settled into the digs.

Once he'd sorted out his belongings, he went down to the bathroom to spruce himself up a bit after travelling. Mrs Martin had left him bread, butter, milk and a packet of tea in the cupboard in the scullery but hunger began to gnaw at him and he felt in need of something more substantial. From his bedroom window he could see the trees swaying violently in the stiff wind, so he put his trench coat on over his sports jacket and made his way down Fraser Avenue to East Main Street. He walked past Green's cinema on one side of the road and the Rutherglen Repertory Theatre directly opposite. He crossed Farmeloan Road and went into Chapman's, the pub he'd seen from the bus when he first arrived in Rutherglen earlier in the day.

Chapman's had very little grub on offer but the barmaid, a sexily dressed brunette, managed to rustle up a hot pie, chips and baked beans, which she served him at the counter, along with his pint of heavy.

She introduced herself as Nancy and chatted to him while he was eating, or flirted might have been a truer word, showing an interest in his job at Bruce's Engineering and hearing about his life in Bonnycross.

When some more customers came into the pub, Nancy moved away to serve them and shortly afterwards, when he began to yawn, Benson left Chapman's and returned to his digs.

*

When Steve got off the bus in Duke Street after work that Monday night, he didn't go straight home but went to visit his friendly bookie's runner in Foundry Lane. He'd had another tip off for Saturday's big race.

'Hello, Stevie,' Pete greeted him. 'How's life treating you?'

'As lousy as ever. But I want to place a bet for Saturday, Pete. I'll put a fiver both ways on Malachy.'

'Had another tip off, Stevie?' Pete asked, grinning as he wrote out a betting slip.

'Yep, and I know it's going to do it for me,' Steve said, seeing the pound signs flash in front of his eyes as he handed over the money.

'Right pal, good luck for Saturday's race.' Pete winked at him before turning to another punter arriving to place a bet.

Feeling lucky and on an impulse Steve decided not to go home yet. Ma would only moan at him for gambling. He jumped on a No 40 bus to take him to the dog racing track at Shawfield, where he could spend a couple of hours with some of the lads he knew there.

Around ten o'clock he returned to Duke Street, minus a few more pounds in his pocket, and walked home from there. When he arrived at the council house he lived in with his mother, he used his key to let himself in, hoping that Ma was in bed and asleep so that she wouldn't get on to him for his bad habits. He couldn't help that he liked a flutter on the gee-gees and the greyhounds from time to time.

The house was in darkness when he went in and he was surprised when he switched on the light in the living room to find that the curtains had not been drawn and the fire had gone out.

Steve went into his bedroom to put his coat in the wardrobe, all the time expecting to hear Ma calling to him from her bedroom overlooking the back garden. But all was silent so she must be asleep. For no obvious reason, Steve began to feel a bit edgy and went to Ma's bedroom to check if she was still awake but he couldn't get the door to open. He pushed harder and eventually the door gave way a bit but there was something stopping it from opening fully.

His hand flew up to his mouth when he saw in the light from the hallway Ma's foot sticking out from behind the door. He squeezed himself around the half-opened door and stumbled over Ma's body lying behind it. His hand went to the light switch and he knew immediately he looked down that she was dead. She was wearing her nightclothes but the bed hadn't been slept in so she must have fallen on her way into bed.

'Oh Ma, I'm sorry, I didn't mean to let you down, you knew that, didn't you?' he asked his deceased mother, tears streaming down his face. He sat beside her for a long time, holding her ice cold hands in his. Eventually he roused himself and went out to find a phone box and summon help.

Chapter Twenty-Eight

'Molly was telling me today that Steve Dixon's mother had died,' Helen said on Friday night once she and Maddie had placed their order with the waitress in Sloan's restaurant. 'Molly said he found her lying behind the back of the door one night when he got home from work.'

'I heard a different story,' Maddie replied, twirling her fork around in her fingers as she was speaking, 'Viv told me she'd heard that he'd been at the dogs that evening and didn't find her until he went home late at night. I understand he's been given time off until after the funeral.'

'Well, either way, it's a horrible thing to happen. I dread anything like that happening to my mother.' Tears glinted in Helen's eyes as she looked across the table at Maddie. 'Will you go to the funeral tomorrow?'

Maddie shook her head. 'I didn't know his mother. For that matter I don't really know Steve very well and anyway I hate funerals as they always remind me of my mother's death.'

'Of course, Maddie. I'm sorry for being so insensitive,' Helen apologised.

Maddie was spared from replying when the waitress arrived with their fried haddock and chips, accompanied by bread and butter. The pieces of fish were so big they were almost falling off the sides of the plates.

'Oh my goodness, if I eat all this, I don't think I'll eat again for a week,' Maddie joked, knowing that with her healthy appetite she'd be looking for some more food by bedtime.

'I'm going to enjoy this because I've had no hand in the cooking.'

They chatted on while they were eating, the

conversation mainly centred round their work in Marshall's and their attendance at Brian's counselling group. Although Maddie had left the group, Helen still attended on a regular basis.

The waitress cleared away their used plates and returned shortly afterwards with a huge pot of tea and she placed a three tier cake stand on the centre of the table. The top plate held scones, pancakes were piled high on the middle one, with sponge cakes arranged around the bottom plate. 'I think we'll have to ask for a doggy bag,' Maddie said, when she saw the feast laid before them.

'My auntie was on holiday in America last summer and she said that's what they do over there. They always serve up far more than you need and then offer to put the remains in a box for you to take home. Seems a bit of a waste to me.'

'They'd be better to serve less and charge less. Mind you, this is a good deal that Sloan's do for the high tea.'

'I can hardly believe that all this only costs three shillings and nine pence each. Hope that's right and we don't discover it's double that price,' Helen whispered, checking round to see that no-one from another table was listening.

Maddie shrugged. 'Well if we've made a mistake in the price then they'll just have to let us wash the dishes. I wonder if anyone has actually had to do that.' They both started giggling at the thought but calmed down when they saw people at the next table looking over at them.

'What a great time we've had,' Helen said when the two of them left the restaurant arm in arm and walked out to the bus stop on Argyle Street. 'I hope Viv has had a good time with her friends.'

'I'm sure she would as they've all been friends since schooldays. I think they have a reunion once or twice a year and, from Viv's account, it's usually quite a riotous evening. Oh, here's your bus coming Helen,' Maddie said as the No 23 slowed down near the bus stop.

'Will you be alright on your own?'

'Sure, mine will be here in a few minutes. See you on Monday,' she called and waved as Helen got on to the bus.

Chapter Twenty-Nine

July 1958

Maddie wakened with a start when the alarm rang on the clock at the side of her bed. It was half past six and the early morning sun was streaming in through the window. She turned sleepily on to her other side to look at the view. She felt very much at home here in Fairfields and the family regarded this room as hers. Instead of looking at the back of the tenement buildings in King Street, as she did from her bed in the flat, from here she could gaze out over the trees and fields to the hills beyond.

It was at Easter when the girls were visiting the farm that Sheena had invited Maddie to go on holiday to North Berwick in July with her, Viv and the twins.

'Charlie will stay at home to look after the farm,' Sheena said.

'It's a holiday for me to get rid of a' you bossy females for a wee while,' he'd told Maddie, laughing as he spoke.

'Charlie can collect you two the night before we go and you can sleep here,' Sheena went on. 'That way you won't have to lug your cases on the bus.'

'Will Dad drive us all the way to North Berwick?' Aileen asked.

'No, Love, it would be too long to leave the animals if he did that but he'll take us into Queen Street Station in Glasgow and then come home again. We can travel the rest of the way by train. We can get a porter to help us with our luggage.'

'Goody,' Elizabeth smiled. 'I love going on the train.'

That had all seemed like yesterday, yet here they were ready to set off to North Berwick this morning. Maddie hadn't ever been in the seaside resort but Viv said it was a beautiful place.

Excitement coursed through her as she washed and dressed in a go-ray pleated skirt and a cotton blouse. She would carry a long-sleeved cardigan on the journey in case it turned cold.

'Breakfast ready, girls,' she heard Sheena calling and made her way through to the kitchen and the welcome smell of bacon, sausage and egg. This was accompanied by some of Sheena's delicious home-made crusty bread and freshly churned butter.

By eight o'clock they were ready to leave. The road was quiet and Charlie parked near the entrance to Queen Street Station. He found a porter and enlisted his help to carry their luggage on to the Edinburgh train standing on Platform 4. Sheena handed over their tickets to the official on duty and they followed Charlie and the porter on to the train.

Charlie tipped the porter, who doffed his railway cap and left them to it.

'Right, let's get you all into a seat.' Charlie escorted Sheena and the girls along the corridor until he found an empty compartment. 'You might be lucky to get the compartment to yourselves,' he said and put their cases up on the luggage rack above the seats. There were two large cases; Sheena and the twins had packed their clothes in one and the second one had been shared by Viv and Maddie. Each case had a tennis racket strapped to the top. One was Viv's and the other was Sheena's which she'd lent to Maddie for the holiday.

'You could ask the guard to get the cases down for you,' Charlie suggested.

Viv shook her head. 'We can manage them ourselves, can't we Maddie?'

'Of course.'

Aileen rushed over to one of the window seats. 'I'm going to sit here.'

'And I'll sit on this side,' Elizabeth skipped over to the seat facing her twin.

Maddie settled down beside Aileen, with Viv in the seat next to the door. Sheena faced Maddie, leaving an empty seat on her side.

'Have a nice holiday, girls,' Charlie gave each of them a kiss on the cheek, 'and you two do what Mum tells you,' he warned the twins.

He stood in the compartment doorway. 'Bye then,' he said, looking mainly at Maddie. 'If I don't see ye' through the week, I'll see ye' through the window.'

Maddie was the only one who laughed. 'That's a new one on me.'

Viv groaned and shook her head. 'Not for us it isn't.'

'Dad always tells corny jokes,' Elizabeth complained.

'And he tells the same ones all the time,' Aileen added.

Sheena laughed. 'You're all lucky. I've got to put up with his crummy jokes all the time. At least you lot get away from them some of the time.'

Charlie pretended to look crestfallen. 'None of you appreciate my talents. Except for Maddie, that is. Thank goodness for you, Maddie.'

Still laughing, Sheena walked with him out into the corridor. Watching them embrace, Maddie felt a sensation of happiness at their obvious affection for one another coupled with a twinge of jealousy.

Charlie stood on the platform and waved them off.

Very soon afterwards, due to their early rise, they all began to snooze. When they wakened, they were at Haymarket Station on the outskirts of Edinburgh.

'Think we'd better get the cases down now,' Sheena suggested, 'we'll be in Waverley Station in about five minutes.'

Maddie and Viv sprang into action and they alighted, complete with luggage, seconds after the train drew to a halt at the side of the platform.

'Take hands now, girls,' Sheena instructed the twins,

'this is a very busy station and we don't want anyone getting lost.'

'We still have another two trains to get,' Elizabeth informed Maddie as she held the older girl's hand tightly on their way across the main concourse.

Once on the second train, the twins' excitement mounted, especially when they began to see the magnificent white beaches they were chugging past. The gorgeous orange-coloured poppies, which grew in such profusion in East Lothian, waved their heads at the train passengers from the fields and railway embankments.

Before they knew it, the train was pulling into Drem Junction. 'Okay, girls, this is where we change for the North Berwick train. Make sure we don't leave anything behind.' Sheena's eyes scoured the compartment before she led her flock towards the exit door. During the ten minute wait at Drem Junction the twins chased one another along the platform and into the ticket office and waiting room, with strict instructions from Sheena to stay well away from the railway track.

They climbed aboard the North Berwick train when it steamed into the station, its horn tooting and smoke belching out of its funnel. From the train window, Maddie could see the red pantile roofs of the houses, typical of the east coast towns.

Sheena hailed a taxi at North Berwick station to take them to their digs at 75 Bridgehouse Road. 'We've come to these digs for years now,' she explained to Maddie when they were in the cab. 'The owners, Mr and Mrs Armstrong, live in one of the villas down at the beach but they were left the house in Bridgehouse Road when Mr Armstrong's father passed away and now they earn an income from summer letting. I always get the keys from Mrs Kirk at No 77.'

The taxi driver left their cases sitting at the gate of No 75, while Viv rang the doorbell of No 77.

Mrs Kirk opened the door, the keys in her hand. 'Hello, Viv, I was expecting you. How are you?' she asked Sheena and, without waiting for an answer, she beamed at the twins. 'My, how you two girls have grown in a year.'

'This is Maddie,' Viv introduced her friend.

'Hello,' the elderly lady smiled at Maddie before turning again to Sheena. 'Your hamper arrived yesterday and the men left it in the house.'

'Oh great.' Sheena had explained to Maddie earlier that they had to provide their own bed linen and towels. They were packed into a wicker hamper and sent on the day before the holiday by British Railways.

'Once you get unpacked and make up the beds, come into me for a cuppa before you go out. I've made your favourite salmon sandwiches,' Mrs Kirk winked at the twins.

'Thanks, Mrs Kirk,' Sheena said, glad she'd remembered to bring a couple of her home-baked fruit loaves for the old lady.

Chapter Thirty

On the first day of the holidays the family decided to go to the swimming pool. They took a short cut through the glen, which ran downhill from Bridgehouse Road to bring them out on the prom. It was a pleasant walk, shaded by a roof of bushes and trees and the tinkling sound of rivulets running over the stony surfaces on either side of the well-worn path.

'It's called the Fairy Glen,' Elizabeth told Maddie, holding her hand as they clambered down a particularly stony part of the path.

'What you mean is you and Aileen call it the Fairy Glen,' Viv laughed. 'They've decided that there are fairies and elves living in the bushes,' she said to Maddie.

'But there are fairies,' Aileen said emphatically. 'I've seen them washing themselves in the water.'

'If you say so,' Viv sighed and threw her arm round her sister's shoulder but Aileen shrugged it off again.

'Let's be quiet and listen for the fairies,' Maddie suggested and the twins spent the rest of the way down to the prom in silence in case any fairy folk appeared.

Situated down by the harbour, North Berwick's pool was overlooked by a steep rocky incline, inhabited by a multitude of sea birds, their raucous shrieks reaching the swimmers down below. This was in competition with the yells of kids already in the pool, together with the occasional splash as some brave soul jumped from the diving board positioned at the deep end.

As she undressed in the changing box, Maddie's heart sang at how lucky she was to have been adopted into Viv's family and enjoy a holiday at the seaside with them. She quickly donned her black and green swimsuit, one that she'd got cheaply from Marshall's by using her staff discount card.

While the four girls were in the water, Sheena sat on the spectators' bench with her knitting, sheltered from any wind by the overhanging rocks above her. She was making a jumper for Aileen, one with a cable stitch pattern on the body and also down the sleeves. She had bought sufficient balls of the lilac wool to do one for Elizabeth too. Usually they hated being dressed the same but they both seemed happy to have a matching lilac jumper.

The pool was unheated and swimmers needed to use energy to keep warm. Elizabeth was the first to come out, her red elasticated bathing costume weighed down with water. Her knees knocked together, and her teeth chattered.

Taking her purse out of her knitting bag, Sheena left the half-knitted jumper front lying on her seat and accompanied Elizabeth to buy Bovril from the mobile van at the pool entrance. 'One for me too,' Aileen shouted, climbing out of the pool, her long pleats pushed inside a bright yellow swimming cap, which complimented her yellow and brown elasticated costume. When Sheena and Elizabeth came back, Sheena was carrying Aileen's mug. The twins sat down on the concrete, wrapped in beach towels, and leaned back against their mother's legs.

Maddie's arms were covered in goose pimples when she hauled herself up out of the pool a short time later. Resting her elbows on the ledge, she pushed up further and swivelled round on to her stomach, her legs waving in the air. She stood for a few minutes in the sunshine, planting the soles of her feet firmly on the warm concrete.

'You girls get yourselves a mug of Bovril, too,' Sheena said once Viv left the water, handing over the money she had ready for this. She always brought a bag of loose change with her to North Berwick for just such expenses. Draping themselves in a towel, Maddie and Viv joined the queue that had formed at the van. By the time they returned, the twins had gone to get dressed again, and they sat beside Sheena on the bench. Maddie held the mug between her hands, savouring the comforting warmth. 'It's gorgeous,' she said, and slowly sipped the hot liquid, feeling it radiate through her body. 'I didn't realise how cold the water was until I came out.'

'Don't forget we're on the east coast,' Sheena reminded her. 'That's the North Sea out there,' she pointed to the cliff behind them, with a narrow path spiralling all the way to the top.

The twins came back, fully dressed once more. 'What will we do now?' Aileen asked, ever keen to try new things.

Before answering, Sheena finished her row of knitting to ensure she kept to her pattern. Then she looked up at the twins and smiled. 'I thought once Maddie and Viv are dressed again, we could go back to the house and make some sandwiches. Then we could take a picnic with us and climb the Law hill.'

'Yes,' Elizabeth clapped her hands. 'And we can climb right up to the top and get our picture taken standing beside the whalebone.'

Sheena looked at the two older girls and raised her eyebrows. 'I guess that's it decided then,' she laughed, and stuffed her knitting into its bag once more.

*

The midday sun was at its height when they started their ascent of the Law hill.

Viv and the twins had been up on numerous occasions and they knew every foothold on the way up. Maddie enjoyed the challenge, slipping from time to time on the shale scattered around, but she felt exhilarated by the time they reached the whalebone at the summit.

The whalebone was enclosed within some railings but you could stretch through the railings and touch it. The view over the Firth of Forth towards the Bass Rock was superb and from up here the players on the golf course looked in miniature. One man stood out from his companions because his jersey was a canary yellow colour.

A few feet from the whalebone they found a dip in the ground, almost like a small cave, where they settled down to enjoy their picnic, shaded from the hot afternoon sun. Sheena had put some orange juice and a bottle of lemonade into the picnic basket and a rug for them to sit on.

The food consumed, one by one they all dozed off and when they wakened it was well after three and much cooler. Another drink of lemonade and they were ready to set off downhill, sliding a bit on the shale but getting down to the bottom all in one piece.

Chapter Thirty-One

'Will we have our last game of tennis before we go home?' Viv asked Maddie on their last evening in North Berwick.

'Yes, let's. I've enjoyed playing again. It's the first time since I was at secondary school and our gym teacher, Miss Walker, gave us tennis lessons.'

'We could play back home too, there are public courts in Overtoun Park. Or there's a private club in Burnside. We'd learn a lot more about the rules there and maybe play in competitions too.'

'But joining a private club means spending money we don't have.' Maddie was aware she'd been more used to lack of money when she was growing up than Viv. 'There's no harm in enquiring though,' she added, when she saw the look of disappointment passing over her friend's face.

'We'll do that. And Mum says you can keep her tennis racket as she doesn't think she'll be using it again.'

'Is that someone taking my name in vain?' Sheena laughed as she came into the kitchen.

'I was telling Maddie that she could keep your tennis racket. In case we join the Burnside Tennis Club when we get home.'

'I think we might need to use the public courts in Rutherglen. They wouldn't cost so much,' Maddie said to Sheena.

'It might not cost as much as you think to join a tennis club, Maddie,' Sheena replied. 'And club memberships often include good social events too which would save you money for the cinema or dances.' She broke off when she heard the twins coming downstairs. 'Do you two want to go to the tennis courts with Viv and Maddie? I'll stay here and get the packing organised for us leaving tomorrow, and then I'll come down to the tennis courts and join you all.'

The twins skipped into the kitchen. 'Can we play tennis?' Aileen asked.

Sheena fetched her purse which was lying on the table. 'Hire a couple of rackets,' she said, handing her daughter a ten shilling note. 'And I want some change back,' she warned. 'Play on a different court and don't annoy Viv and Maddie as they want to stick to the rules.'

In the event they did use two courts at first but, by the time Sheena arrived, they'd moved on to one court to play doubles, with the older girls allowing the twins to cheat like mad.

'Will we walk down to Quality Street for a fish supper?' Sheena asked, when their time on the court was up and the lady in the pay booth was taking in her price board ready to close. During the two weeks in North Berwick, they'd bought fish suppers most nights; the shop in Quality Street was usually queued out with holidaymakers, all of them having the same idea. Her suggestion was taken up immediately and a short time later they sat down at the shore eating their fish and chips while they watched the sun go down over the Bass Rock.

'It always tastes so much better out of the newspaper than on a plate,' Maddie said, as she popped the last chip into her mouth and screwed the vinegar-soaked newspaper into a ball and threw it into the nearby litter bin.

'I'm going to miss my fish suppers when we get home,' Viv said as they made their way up the hill past the tennis courts again.

'Just as well tonight's was the last one,' Sheena replied as they turned into Bridgehouse Road once more. 'Or I'd be like the side of a house before long.'

With the light fading fast, Sheena drew all the curtains when they got into No 75. 'Right, girls, I think there's enough left in our tin of drinking chocolate to make us a hot drink before bed.'

*

'Heck, I've suddenly realised how quiet it was with you lot away in North Berwick.' Charlie beamed at them from his armchair, unable to keep the pleasure out of his voice at seeing his family again, even though Maddie and Viv would only stay overnight and return to Rutherglen.

'Did you miss us, Dad?' Elizabeth climbed up on to his knee and gave him a cuddle.

'I missed all the noise,' he told her, pulling his fingers gently through her curly hair. 'But yes, I did miss you, all of you, lots.'

'I think Zeus and Holly are glad to have us back, and Daisy too,' Aileen told him. As if he understood every word, Zeus came over to her to have his head and back patted and fondled.

'Will we let the girls see your trick, Zeus?' Charlie asked the dog, standing Elizabeth down off his knee while he got to his feet and left the room, followed by Zeus.

'This sounds interesting,' Sheena said to the girls, from her armchair where she was knitting. She was singing along to Frank Sinatra's 'I Left My Heart in San Francisco' on the record player when Charlie returned carrying Zeus' blue rubber ball.

'Wait till you see this,' he smiled at them all in turn and opened the little drawer on the side of the heavy oak wood coffee table which stood in the middle of the room. He put the ball into the drawer and closed it again, Zeus following his every move.

'Sit Zeus,' he instructed, raising his hand in the air, and the dog obeyed, his eyes fixed on Charlie's hand.

The instant Charlie's hand dropped to his side, the dog sprang into action. He placed his right paw on the top of the table, then used his left one to pull at the handle a few times until he opened the drawer. He picked up the ball in his mouth and ran out of the room with it, accompanied by a round of applause.

'That's amazing,' Maddie said when the noise had died down.

'German Shepherds are a most intelligent breed,'

Charlie boasted as Zeus re-appeared. He dropped the ball at Charlie's feet, then sat down to await his expected treat.

Chapter Thirty-Two

December 1958

'More coffee, Dave?' Sheena offered, lifting the pot ready to
fill up his cup.

'No thanks, Mrs Kingston,' he said, 'I've really
enjoyed the meal. Thank you for inviting me.' Dave had
joined the family at Fairfields for Christmas dinner, Sheena
and Charlie having met him for the first time a few weeks ago
when Viv took him home to meet her parents.

'We're happy to have you with us,' Sheena smiled.
'And forget the Mrs Kingston, just call us Sheena and
Charlie.'

'And I'm over the moon to have you here to rescue
me from all these females,' Charlie joked, and offered his
cigarette packet to their guest. Dave took one, then leaned
across the table as Charlie held out his lighter. Viv shook her
head when Charlie held out the packet to her; she'd recently
given up cigarettes and was proud of having gone for six
weeks now without a fag.

The two men sat back, the ends of their cigarettes
glowing red as they took a draw and exhaled smoke rings into
the air above them. Sheena pushed an ashtray along the table
to sit between them.

'Will you play snap with us, Maddie?' Aileen asked.
By now the twins looked on her as a big sister.

'Sure,' Maddie smiled. 'What about you, Viv?' she
looked over at her flatmate.

'I will play but before that,' Viv moved nearer to
Dave, rubbing her shoulder against his arm. 'Dave and I have
something to tell you all, don't we?' she smiled up at him.

Dave flicked the ash from his cigarette into the ashtray and squeezed her hand which was lying on the table. 'It's more like I have something to ask,' he said, looking from Charlie to Sheena, 'Viv and I would like to become engaged and we hope you don't have any objection.'

'Can we be bridesmaids?' Elizabeth asked before her parents had replied.

Viv smiled at the twins. 'Flower girls, you're too young to be bridesmaids.'

Charlie was first to find his voice. 'Well you certainly aren't letting the grass grow under your feet,' he turned to his elder daughter.

'I know Dad, but I love Dave and want to marry him.'

Charlie turned to Dave. 'I know you're a hard worker, Son, so you have my blessing. Have you told your own parents?'

'Not officially. I did tell them Viv and I were serious and wanted to be married and they were delighted as they like Viv. But I wanted to ask you first before I tell them it's definite.'

Sheena got up and kissed each of them in turn. 'I'm very happy for you both. I felt you were right for one another but just didn't expect an engagement so soon.'

'I didn't buy Viv an engagement ring until we'd spoken to you both, but we're planning to go into town next week so she can choose one.'

Maddie hadn't spoken since the announcement although no one appeared to have noticed. Her first reaction was hurt that Viv hadn't told her of the plans, then she began to feel ashamed of the surge of jealousy that coursed through her at the news.

Maddie didn't dislike Dave but was afraid he would spoil her friendship with Viv. She also worried about his involvement with the Kingstons; a family she looked on as her own. She knew her thinking was like that of a spoilt child but she so loved being part of this family, a family she'd never had before, that the thought of anything or anyone upsetting things filled her with anxiety, bordering on anger.

Before becoming part of the family at Fairfields, the only person she'd ever been so close to was her mother. She wiped away the tears that always threatened when she thought of her mum's sad end and the big hole she'd left in her daughter's life.

'Will you be my bridesmaid, Maddie?' Viv smiled at her across the table.

Maddie swallowed deeply and nodded. 'Of course I will,' she agreed, forcing herself to return Viv's smile. She then turned her attention to Zeus, when the dog laid his chin on her knee and stared up at her, his look saying 'don't forget I'm still here'.

'Oh, goody,' Elizabeth giggled, 'then we can walk down the aisle behind you, Maddie.'

There and then Maddie made a silent vow that she'd do everything in her power to hide her true feelings about the engagement from Viv, even though she was sure that Dave sensed the resentment she bore him.

At that moment she loathed herself for her feelings. Why shouldn't Viv meet and marry Dave? She knew it was her own vulnerability that made her resent Viv's love for him.

'How long an engagement do you want to have?' Sheena asked the happy couple.

'I'd really like to be married in June, Mum,' Viv told her. 'Ever since I saw the film Seven Brides for Seven Brothers I've always wanted to have a June wedding.'

'And where will you live?' Charlie asked.

'No problem there,' Dave answered. 'My parents said that their gift to us would be a deposit on a house, probably somewhere near them in the Giffnock or Clarkston area of Glasgow.'

'That's very generous of them,' Charlie said. 'We'll need to have them here to meet us.'

'Oh well, Charlie,' Sheena winked at her husband, 'I guess we'd better start saving for the wedding. Who will you have as a best man?' she asked her prospective son-in-law.

'I'm going to ask my friend Steve from Marshall's.'

'Oh, the chap **you've** been out with Maddie. That's a

lovely idea.'

Maddie managed to stifle the words, 'oh no, not him.' Although she'd been out with Steve when they'd made up a foursome, she didn't think she could ever love him.

After the dinner dishes were washed up, Maddie and Viv played a couple of games of snap with the twins, leaving Sheena and the two men to listen to a play on the radio.

When Dave left around half past ten, Maddie found herself relaxing once more. Over a mug of drinking chocolate, some further discussion took place about the forthcoming wedding and, despite her earlier feelings, Maddie was excited about being Viv's bridesmaid. It was after midnight when she slipped in between the sheets of her bed at Fairfields.

Chapter Thirty-Three

June 1959

'Make sure you don't trip up on Maddie's dress,' Sheena whispered to the twins, who were standing one on either side of Maddie in the vestibule of St Mark's in Kilmarnock, Grandad's church. Viv had asked to be married here. 'It will make me feel as if Grandad is with me on my wedding day,' she'd told Maddie.

'You all look lovely, girls,' Sheena smiled at them encouragingly, feeling justifiably proud of her work on the dresses. She kissed the three girls on the cheek, and straightened the band of flowers on Elizabeth's hair. Then, looking regal in her own peach outfit, she was escorted to her seat by the usher. She couldn't remember the lad's name but knew he was a workmate of Dave's.

Dave and his best man, Steve, sat on the pew in front of her, with Dave looking round from time to time to see if his bride had arrived yet. He caught Sheena's eye on one occasion and gave her a nervous smile. In return she winked and gave him a thumbs up.

The organist, who'd been playing Handel's Largo as the guests assembled, drew to a stop. Next minute the first stirrings of Mendelsohn's Wedding March took over. Dave and Steve got to their feet. Glancing round, Dave saw Viv standing at the back door, her hand on Charlie's arm. He turned round to face the Minister again while the wedding party processed down the aisle, with Viv's bouquet of pink roses and freesia shaking as she walked.

There were oohs and aahs from the guests as Viv and Charlie swept past their pews, Viv's dress a froth of white tulle and sequins, with a long train running behind her over the royal blue carpet. Behind came Maddie, followed by the twins, their lilac ballerina-length dresses toning well with Maddie's deep purple one.

Dave beamed at Viv and stood very close to her as the service started. Maddie took Viv's bouquet while the couple made their vows and afterwards they went to the vestry to sign the register. 'You've all done really well,' Sheena congratulated them while they were in the vestry, 'and the service went without a hitch.'

One of Sheena's friends, the wife of a neighbouring farmer, sang 'I'll Walk Beside You' while the register was being signed.

'Ready?' Mr McKenzie, the minister, looked around them. Then, assured that they were indeed ready, he led the party out of the church by the opposite aisle.

*

When the tables at Lochside hotel had been cleared and moved away to leave an empty square in the centre of the floor, the band started playing.

'May I have this dance, Mrs Tucker?' Dave, relaxed now that the meal and the speeches were over, beamed at his new wife. He drew Viv into his arms and they glided over the dance floor to applause from their guests, Dave singing to his bride.

Around the world I've searched for you

I travelled on when hope was gone to keep a rendezvous

I knew somewhere, sometime, somehow

You'd look at me and I would see the smile you're smiling now.

A twinge of yearning surged through Maddie. If only she was able to feel about a man like that. But she knew such thoughts were pointless. Thanks to Benson, it was something she'd never experience. Her hatred of her stepfather surfaced and a shadow passed across her face.

Her thoughts were interrupted by a voice at her side and she remembered that Steve was standing beside her. 'I think it's our turn now,' he smiled and escorted her on to the dance floor. Immediately her whole body became tense and she held herself apart from him. 'Relax,' he said, as he had done that night at the Plaza, and with difficulty she managed to do that.

She and Steve were followed by the twins, who danced together. Then Charlie led Dave's mother on to the floor while his father danced with Sheena. Cheers went up from the guests watching the main party dancing and then they were invited by the band leader to join in. By the time that first tune was finished, the floor was quite crowded and Maddie was happy to merge into it.

Another popular song started playing and Steve began to sing quietly into Maddie's ear.

> *Heaven, I'm in Heaven*
> *And my heart beats so that I can hardly speak*
> *And I seem to find the happiness I seek*
> *When we're out together dancing cheek to cheek.*

As he sang, his cheek rubbed against hers and she prayed that the dance would end. After what seemed an eternity the music stopped and she immediately drew back from him and made her way towards the top table.

'Not so quick young lady,' Charlie said as she made to sit down. 'I think this is our dance,' he smiled and she willingly took his hand and let him lead her on to the dance floor.

Although Maddie had to endure dancing a few more times with Steve, during the evening she partnered many others, for which she was thankful.

Chapter Thirty-Four

December 1959

'Are you coming to the pub with us, Will?' Tom Jarvis asked that Friday, as Benson was gathering up his belongings after his shift in Bruce's Engineering Works.

'Aye, might as well,' he said, and walked up the road towards Rutherglen with the other engineers, the air soon becoming blue with the jokes they were cracking.

The engineers always drank in the Black Bull in Rutherglen and as they passed the registry office they noticed a crowd had gathered outside to watch a wedding group. His companions skirted round the crowd and carried on walking but Benson stopped and stared at the bridal couple who were having a picture taken. He looked closer at the bride, wearing a navy blue suit and a pink hat. Her hair was different but it was definitely her. Despite a large birthmark at the side of his eye, the groom was a handsome guy so it looked like she'd done alright for herself.

Benson was overcome by her beauty. His initial reaction was to go forward and speak to her but he sensed she wouldn't welcome that. He'd have to find a way to discover where she lived and pay her a visit. While he was considering this, he heard someone saying his name and turned round to see Matt Brown standing beside him. Matt had worked in Bruce's Engineering with him, before moving to another firm a few months back.

'Hello Matt,' he grinned, thumping him on the back, 'you scrub up well,' he added, noticing Matt was dressed for the wedding, with a flower in his buttonhole.

'Aye, the bridegroom Steve is my young cousin,' Matt said.

'Do the newlyweds live in Rutherglen?'

'Aye, they've a flat in Main Street. What about you and I having a jar together next Friday night, Will?'

Benson thought the bride had caught sight of him, although it might have been his imagination. Then he remembered Matt was waiting for an answer. 'That'll be great, Matt. I'll meet you in the Black Bull. I better go, my mates will be wondering where I've got to,' he said and hurried off in the direction of the pub.

*

Maddie turned to smile at the camera but when she caught sight of a face in the crowd the smile froze on her lips. Oh my God, not him. Her grip tightened on Steve's arm and she closed her eyes for a second but when she opened them again he was still there, as large as life, looking towards her. She shivered at the sight of the face that put dread into her very soul.

'Could you turn a little to the left and look at Steve?' the photographer asked her and, when he was satisfied he'd captured the right image, he pressed down the shutter.

By the time Maddie looked towards the crowd again, **his** face had disappeared and instead she saw Helen smiling and waving over to her, indicating that she wanted to take a photograph of the happy couple. Maddie whispered to Steve and they both turned towards Helen and smiled. Maddie had invited Helen's mum to the wedding but Mrs Ford was too unwell at the moment and Helen had arranged for a carer to sit with her mum while she was out of the house.

'Maddie, can we have our picture taken with you and Steve?'

The twins appeared at Maddie's side, looking so grown up in the calf length dresses Sheena had made for them. Aileen wore a deep turquoise shade while Elizabeth's was lemon. Sheena had made the dresses fairly plain, in keeping with the suits Maddie and Viv were wearing. Elizabeth's hair was curled softly around her face and Aileen's pleats had been cut and her hair fell, shiny and sleek, into a page boy style. Maddie found it hard to believe they were the same little girls she'd met at Fairfields that first Christmas. They were turning out to be real stunners.

'Of course you can.' Maddie gestured to the photographer, who came over and obliged. Eventually the photographer finished but, even once they were safely on their way to Fairfields for the reception, Maddie could still picture the face in the crowd with its leering smile.

Steve sat beside her in the car, his arm round her waist, nibbling at her ear lobe and rubbing his cheek against hers. Viv sat on Steve's other side, with Dave in the passenger seat beside Charlie. Poor Steve was in seventh Heaven to have Maddie as his wife while she felt so guilty, knowing what a fraud she was. She could never love him but he'd saved her from having to give up the flat. Once Viv had moved out to live with her new husband, it had been an almighty struggle for Maddie to pay the rent on her own and the little she'd managed to save in her bank account from her wages had very quickly been swallowed up. At one point she'd considered advertising for another female flatmate but decided against it, aware that she wasn't good at forming relationships. She did ask Helen but she wouldn't have been happy at leaving her mother and, although disappointed, Maddie fully understood her reasons.

Steve had persisted to ask her out until she finally gave in and began dating him. Following his mother's death, Steve had continued to live in his council house and, when he finally proposed to Maddie, he suggested that they share the cost of only one house.

She couldn't say yes to him straight away but agreed to consider his proposal. For Steve, besotted with her, this was enough to keep his hopes alive. Maddie experienced many sleepless nights, wrestling with the problem, and one afternoon when she and Viv were alone, she'd had a heart to heart chat with her best friend.

Viv was thrilled to hear that Steve had proposed and expressed surprise that Maddie was unable to make a decision.

'He's such a caring person and loves you so much Maddie. I'm sure he would be an excellent husband for you. Do you think you're just having collywobbles at the thought of marriage, rather than Steve himself?'

When Maddie didn't reply straight away, Viv went on. 'I know you've had problems during your childhood Maddie but you shouldn't let it waste the rest of your life, Love.'

Maddie smiled at her friend and grasped her hand. 'Yes, I'm sure you're right Viv, I analyse things too deeply.'

Over the next couple of weeks, the more Maddie thought about Steve's proposal, the more it seemed like the answer to her financial problems. She convinced herself that love for him would come once they were married.

When she finally told Steve that she would be his wife, he was overjoyed. Her family members at Fairfields were delighted for her and preparations for the wedding began. Maddie was excited about all the arrangements at first but as the months went by and the big day drew nearer she began to regret her decision. By then, however, Sheena was busy with all the preparations and Maddie felt she had to go through with it.

She came out of her reverie when the bridal car arrived back at the farm.

Charlie jumped out and unlocked the door for the newly-weds. Once inside the farmhouse, Maddie and Viv disappeared into Viv's old bedroom to freshen up. Shortly afterwards Sheena and the twins arrived, followed by the wedding guests. Everyone mingled well, most of the guests knowing one another, and champagne was brought out for the toast.

Sheena, with the help of some of her farming neighbours, had laid on a sumptuous feast which was served buffet style. An American idea, it was becoming more and more popular for social gatherings in Britain. Knowing Maddie and Steve couldn't afford a reception, Sheena had straightaway offered to do the catering. 'After all, Fairfields is your second home now, Maddie, and you and Steve are part of the family,' she assured them. They accepted her offer gratefully, the cost of which Sheena and Charlie insisted was their wedding gift to the couple

It was well after midnight when the last of the guests departed and Charlie drove the newly-weds to their overnight accommodation at the Maple Tree Hotel in Kilmarnock. It was a wedding gift from Viv and Dave, who'd been their matron of honour and best man.

*

Steve sat on the edge of the bed in Room 16 at the Maple Tree Hotel, waiting for Maddie to come out of the bathroom. She was taking an age to get undressed and into her night attire.

'Thought you'd fallen down the toilet pan,' he joked when she finally emerged, wearing a calf-length pink nightdress, through which in the light of the bedside lamp he could see the outline of her legs. Excited by the sight, he pulled the bedclothes aside to allow her to get into the double bed, then he slid in beside her. She allowed him to kiss her, moving from her lips down to her neck and shoulders, but when he started to pull up her nightie, she pushed his hand away.

'I'm tired, Steve, it's been a long day,' she protested, yawning, 'could you switch off the light please?' And without another word, she turned her back on him.

Wounded by her reaction to his attempt at lovemaking, he put out the lamp and lay in the darkness, trying to convince himself that Maddie was shy and things would be better tomorrow night. He loved her so much, in fact he was crazy about her, but she always seemed so distant. She'd been like this during the months they'd been dating but he'd hoped that she would change once they were married.

Frustrated and unhappy, he dropped his head further into the pillow and tried to sleep.

Chapter Thirty-Five

January 1960

She was coming towards him from Rutherglen Cross. Although desperate to speak to her, Benson hid in the grey evening gloom out of sight in the doorway of the jeweller's shop until she was safely past. The assistant inside peered out through the glass panel on the shop door, no doubt wondering if he was about to get a last minute customer before the shop closed at six o'clock.

'Sorry mate,' Benson muttered, exiting his hideout. With a safe distance between them, he crept his way along Main Street behind her, hugging the side of the buildings and glancing into a shop window if he felt she was about to turn round. But she didn't look back and he saw her cut into the tenement close beside Black's, the newsagents.

A couple of minutes later, keen not to lose his prey, Benson walked through the entrance of the tenement at No 197. He crept up the stairs in an effort not to alert Maddie that she was being followed. He could, of course, have asked Matt Brown in the pub the other night for his cousin's address but that would have aroused suspicion. Nor could he have told Matt the truth and said he wanted to stalk his cousin's new wife.

His rubber soled shoes made no sound on the stairway and Maddie had just turned the key in the lock when his giant hand covered hers and, with a strong push, Benson opened the door of the flat and followed her inside. He stood against the closed door blocking off Maddie's means of escape. 'Hello, Maddie,' he leered, his voice full of menace.

In silence she stared at him, unable to believe her eyes.

'What's wrong? Cat got your tongue? Aren't you going to ask me what I'm doing here?'

She suddenly came to life. 'Get out,' she ordered him, the cold calmness in her voice in sharp contrast to the fear lurking in her eyes.

'Oh don't be like that, Maddie. You weren't always so stand-offish, eh.' He placed his massive paws under her chin and raised her face to his, their lips almost touching.

She froze when his hand moved down the front of her body, then threw herself away from him and tried another tack. 'You'd better leave if you know what's good for you. My husband will be home soon and he is a very, very jealous man. I should warn you he is a boxer,' she threw in for good measure.

'Is that so?' He gave her the wide smile she remembered, showing his gums and decayed teeth. She shivered, for once praying that Steve would be home early from work.

Hearing footsteps coming upstairs, Benson moved back. 'I'll go this time but I warn you I'll be back and I won't be so accommodating then,' he threatened.

On his way downstairs he passed a young chap on the first floor landing. He recognised the birthmark. The younger man nodded at Benson as they passed one another. A boxer? The thought made Benson grin. In your dreams Maddie, that young buck wouldn't last two minutes in a boxing ring.

When Steve walked into the flat, Maddie was still standing in the lobby. 'What's wrong? You look as if you've seen a ghost.'

'I'm fine,' she stammered, 'we were busy today and I'm tired, that's all.'

'Who was the guy I passed on the stairs just now? Was he up here to visit you?'

'What guy? No, nobody's been here. Why do you say that?'

'I don't know why, Maddie. I don't know anything

anymore but you sure as hell don't ever seem pleased to see me. A month married and I've been living like a monk. What's wrong? Tell me, Maddie,' he pleaded, putting his arms around her. 'Is it something I've done?'

'Nothing's wrong?' she shrugged herself out of his embrace. 'Sorry, I've got a migraine coming on.'

'For God sake, Maddie, if you aren't too tired, you've got a headache. I'm getting fed up with all your excuses,' he yelled and stomped off to the bedroom to change out of his warehouse overalls. He came out again wearing his grey trousers and dark blue polo necked sweater.

Maddie still stood in the lobby. 'I'm sorry, Steve, but it's just me, I can't change myself,' she apologised. 'I'll go and put the potatoes on for the dinner.'

But Steve, his face like thunder, took his checked sports jacket down off the hallstand and pushed his arms into its sleeves. 'Don't bother cooking any for me, I'm going to Chapman's for some decent company. With any luck, I might meet a buxom blonde who finds me more interesting than my wife does.'

When the door closed behind him and his footsteps had descended the stairs, Maddie went into the kitchen and sat down at the table, her head resting on her folded arms. She couldn't let Benson worm his way back into her life; she couldn't. Her shoulders shook as the floodgates opened and even the loud ticking of the clock on the mantelpiece was obscured by the sound of her wracking sobs.

*

Benson had already downed a pint and was on to his second when he saw the young bridegroom come into the pub, his face like thunder. He sat on a bar stool, with his back to Benson, and ordered a whisky. He drank it in one go and asked for another.

Benson smirked; so the young lovers have had a tiff already. Swallowing the rest of his beer in one go, Benson slipped out the side door of the pub on to Farmeloan Road. He turned on to Main Street and went back to the tenement at No 197. It was a gloomy night and the street was deserted when

Benson walked into the close and climbed the stairs once more.

*

Maddie was still wide awake a few hours later when Steve arrived home. She knew he'd had a bucket-full when she heard him staggering around and cursing as he fell heavily against the bunker in the lobby. She remained mute, pushing her bruised, tear-stained face deep into the pillow, and prayed that he wouldn't come into the bedroom and try to get into bed with her. She relaxed a little when she heard the door to the front room open and the creaking of the settee as he made it into a bed. He'd slept on the bed settee on the last two occasions that she'd rejected his advances and thankfully hadn't forced her to have sex with him. Tonight of all nights, after her humiliation at the hands of Benson, that would have been the last straw.

After a time all became quiet and she guessed Steve had dropped off to sleep. Maddie lay there in the dark, unable to believe that Benson was back in her life after all this time. Would she never be rid of him?

Chapter Thirty-Six

March 1960

The sun shone brightly that Sunday morning, with the first signs of spring in the flower beds and trees down on Main Street. The ironing done, Maddie prepared tonight's dinner; a dinner which Steve may or may not eat. He hadn't come home last night so probably ate at the pub. It suited Maddie as she got the house to herself. But today she had other things on her mind.

Viv and Dave had a few social engagements this weekend and Maddie wasn't going to Fairfields as she often did on a Sunday because Sheena and Charlie and the twins were on a short holiday break. Charlie had a reciprocal arrangement with a neighbouring farmer to look after the animals in his absence.

Maddie got off the tram in the city centre and walked under the Hielanman's Umbrella, the local name for a railway bridge that spanned Argyle Street. It was leaving twenty five past eleven on her watch as she turned right into Hope Street. She hurried into the bus station and boarded the bus as it was about to leave. The red double decker drove out of its stance on to Waterloo Street and headed east.

It was after four o'clock when Maddie got back to Rutherglen. Steve was already in the flat, still pretty drunk but slightly less so than normal. And for once they didn't have a blazing row.

*

On Monday evening Maddie was reading her book in the armchair at the side of the fireplace when the doorbell rang. Having reached an exciting bit in the story, she ignored the second ring too, hoping the caller would think she was out and go away. It's probably Jehovah's Witnesses making a nuisance of themselves, she thought. She never invited them in and told them she was a member of the Church of Scotland.

This was only partly true as, although she'd joined the Parish Church when she and Viv moved to Rutherglen, she hadn't darkened its door for almost a year now and she and Steve had been married in the registry office. She had intended going to church but somehow life got in the way. Steve had never been a churchgoer and Maddie herself wasn't sure that she still had a faith.

When the bell rang a third time, she sighed and put her book down. Then she heard Steve plodding to the door. She'd forgotten he'd come home a short time ago, having worked on later in the warehouse once the shop was closed. It was surprising that he hadn't gone straight to the pub or to place a bet as was his habit so she guessed he was out of funds at the moment.

In the three months they'd been married their relationship had gone from bad to worse. She knew it was mainly her fault; her spurning of his sexual advances made him turn more and more for comfort in drinking and gambling. As he'd stopped trying to be intimate by now, she sometimes wondered if he met women in the pub who accommodated him but she was just happy to be left in peace. It's all Benson's fault, she thought bitterly, he ruined my life.

She and Steve had little communication and sat in different rooms. On his arrival home tonight, Steve had gone into the front room and switched on the little black and white television set Sheena and Charlie had bought them for Christmas. Maddie had heard him laughing at whatever programme he was watching, probably something smutty.

Her musings were halted when Steve ushered two policemen into the kitchen. The first one, a man who looked in his forties and of stocky build was dwarfed by his younger colleague, who, despite the high ceilings in the flat, had to lower his head when coming through the doorway.

'Good evening, Mrs Dixon, I'm Sergeant McLellan,' the older man introduced himself, 'and this is my colleague, Constable Duncan.' Maddie remained in her armchair while Steve directed the two policemen to a couple of easy chairs facing her.

The Sergeant took off his hat and balanced it on his knee, revealing his grey spiky hair, while the Constable took out his notebook.

'I'm sorry to trouble you, Mrs Dixon,' Sergeant McLellan began, 'but can you confirm that William Benson of 46 Rowan Avenue, Bonnycross, in West Lothian is your father?'

'Stepfather,' she corrected him while Steve, standing behind the police officer, stared at her in amazement.

'Right,' the Sergeant nodded. 'I'm afraid I have some bad news for you. Mr Benson was found dead in his house yesterday evening.'

Maddie continued to look at the policeman, no emotion visible in her face. 'What happened? Did he have a heart attack?'

'Mr Benson appears to have been gassed,' the Constable told her. 'His body was lying close to the gas oven which was switched on but unlit.' He let that sink in before continuing. 'We believe he died on Sunday, sometime between 1 and 2 pm. That evening a neighbour reported seeing the door lying open.'

Maddie shrugged. 'I always thought he'd die from drinking as he was an alcoholic. He must have forgotten in his drunken state that he'd switched on the gas cooker.' She stared into the fire for a moment. One large piece of coal fell down towards the front of the fire, leaving a gaping red hole where it had been. 'Apologies if I sound hard, but I can't say I'm sorry to hear he's dead. He wasn't my real father and we never got on. When my mother died in 1956 I was glad to leave Bonnycross and come to Glasgow.'

'And have you been in contact with Mr Benson since

then?' the Constable asked.

She shook her head. 'I've not seen him since the day I left Bonnycross. In fact, it was the day before as I packed my things while he was at work. I knew he wouldn't be able to trace me as I was eighteen at the time and a free agent so the police weren't likely to start a missing person enquiry.'

She could feel Steve's eyes questioning her. She'd not spoken to him about her stepfather, just saying that her parents were both dead. Which in a sense was true.

Sergeant McLellan got to his feet and nodded to the Constable, who closed his notebook and put it back into his pocket. The Sergeant cleared his throat. 'As Mr Benson's next of kin, the West Lothian police have requested that you go tomorrow to identify his body.'

'Do I have to?'

'You can refuse but we'd appreciate your help. We'll arrange transport for you.'

'O.K.,' Maddie agreed, and Steve showed the two officers out.

'Why didn't you tell me about your stepfather, Maddie?' Steve asked when he returned to the kitchen.

She was still sitting in the chair, staring into the fire. 'Didn't think it was important,' she said in a leaden voice, then looked up at him. 'He wasn't my real Dad; I hated him and was glad to come here to Glasgow and start a new life.'

Steve sighed deeply. 'I don't understand you, Maddie, and I wonder how many other secrets you've kept from me.'

Without replying, Maddie turned back to the fire.

When it was obvious she wasn't prepared to pursue the conversation, he left the room and a moment later he left the flat, banging the door behind him.

Chapter Thirty-Seven

July 1960

Afterwards Maddie always remembered the date the letter arrived. It was 26th July 1960 which would have been her mother's forty-third birthday. Mum had been almost thirty-nine when she died, far too young. She was only sixteen years older at the time of her death than I am now, Maddie sighed, plunged into deep sorrow as always when thinking about her mother's long painful illness and death.

Being Tuesday, Maddie had come home early but Steve was still at work. When she'd unlocked the door, the letter was lying, address facing up, on the lobby floor. She went into the kitchen and stood with her back to the window, staring at the brown envelope for a few minutes before she opened it. It looked official, with the sender's details franked on the front, Douglas, Maxwell and Sharp, 65 George Street, Edinburgh. It sounded like a legal company and letters from lawyers always made her nervous. With trembling hands she drew the thick vellum sheet out of its envelope and she gasped when she read the heading on the letter.

THE LATE MR WILLIAM BENTON – DECEASED 20th MARCH, 1960

She went over to the table and flopped down into a chair. The parchment shook in her hand as she held it. My God, she thought, is that monster going to haunt me forever? She moved the crystal vase holding the orange roses Steve had bought her in an attempt to soften her feelings for him, and laid the letter down. She flattened out the folds and scanned the words.

Monday, 25th July, 1960.

Mrs Madeleine Dixon
197 Main Street
Rutherglen
GLASGOW

Dear Mrs Dixon

We represent the late Mr William Benton, who has named you as sole beneficiary of his Estate. Before we proceed further, I would ask you to confirm that your maiden name is Granger and provide us with your date of birth. We also require you to furnish us with personal identification, such as a Birth Certificate.

I look forward to your reply and enclose a stamped, addressed envelope for your use.
Yours faithfully

George C. Douglas, Senior Partner
Encl.

Maddie gripped the edge of the table tightly, closing her eyes while she took in this information. Seeing her stepfather's hateful name on the page brought back her earlier torture at his hands. Why on earth would he leave her money? Was it to salve his conscience? Didn't he know she could never take anything from him? It would be like blood money.

She took deep breaths until she felt calmer. Over the last four years since she'd fled from Bonnycross, she'd convinced herself that the odious creature was out of her mind. But now the old pain and anger rose up, making her nauseous, just as it had done all those years ago and she laid her arms across the table and rested her head on them. All she could think of was that she hated him and was glad he was dead.

She lost all track of time and when she finally looked up, Steve was standing in the doorway, dressed in his overalls, staring at her. 'What's wrong? You look as though you're in a dream world.'

'More like a nightmare.'

He moved towards her and laid his hands on her shoulders, pleased when she didn't shake them off again. 'Can I help?'

Hearing his caring tone, something she hadn't heard for some time, tears began to run down her cheeks. She shook her head and gave him the letter to read.

'This is your stepfather, the one who was gassed,' he stated rather than asked. When she nodded, he took her hand, caressing her fingers with his. 'Maddie, I know you've had a difficult life but I can help you … if you'll let me.'

'No-one can help. He was my stepfather,' she said through gritted teeth, 'Mum's second husband. I hated him then and I hate him even more now.'

He stroked the back of her hand. 'But Maddie, why did you never tell me about him? I thought you'd been brought up by your mother single-handedly.'

'I let you think that as I've tried to erase him from my memory. Him, and the horrible things he made me do. He was always drunk and I nearly choked from the smell of alcohol on his breath.'

Steve gasped when he heard this. 'My God, I didn't realise … Maddie, is this why you won't let me near you?' She didn't answer. 'But where was your mother when all this was happening?' he asked, his voice taking on an angry tone.

'She was asleep in their bed across the hall.' Maddie stopped speaking to blow her nose. 'She was scared of him too and I used to see her taking tablets before going to bed. I realise now that they must have been sleeping tablets.'

'And did she know what was going on?'

She shook her head and took her hand away. 'No, or at least I don't think so. She never mentioned him to me and I was too scared to say anything.' She stopped speaking and dropped her head into her hands again.

Steve sat down beside Maddie and drew his fingers through her hair. 'Don't bother cooking tonight, Love. Instead you go and wash your face and we can go to the Cross café for something to eat. I got paid today for my extra overtime,' he said, caressing her with his voice.

She held his hand as she looked at him through her tears. 'Okay,' she nodded, even managing to give him a weak smile.

Half an hour later they sat at a table in the café, Maddie washed and changed into a fresh skirt and blouse.

'You look more like yourself, Maddie,' Steve smiled across at her as they studied the menu. 'Think I'll go for fish 'n chips. What about you?'

'Same for me,' she said, 'and I'll have a glass of milk with it.'

Steve got up to place their order at the counter and on his way back to the table he stopped at the juke box in the corner. He read through the songs that were available, then pressed some buttons and pushed a coin into the slot at the side of the machine. As he sat down again, the first strains started of Pat Boone singing 'Love Letters in the Sand'.

'Thanks,' Maddie said, 'that's one of my favourites.'

'I remembered,' he grinned, taking her hand as they listened to the velvety voice of the American crooner.

By the time they left the café and headed back to the flat, they were closer than they'd been for months. Steve almost dared to hope that Maddie might be more responsive to him tonight, now that she'd shared the problem with him, but he would certainly not force her. He wanted her to come to him willingly.

They turned on the radio to hear the news before bed. Maddie seemed comfortable to sit beside him on the settee with his arm around her shoulders. He was overjoyed when she snuggled closer to him and felt that the future looked rosier than he could have dreamed of only a few hours earlier.

It was in this relaxed mood that Steve made a fatal mistake. 'You'll need to reply to the lawyer's letter,' he said, 'some extra money will be welcome right now, won't it, Love?'

She raised her head from his shoulder and looked into his eyes. 'No, I don't want his money or anything to do with him.'

'But Maddie, don't you think you're being too hasty, Love. After all, nothing can change the past, but why should you miss out on some money that you deserve.'

'It would be like condoning what he did. Like offering him the forgiveness I don't have. Can't you understand?'

'Sort of, but I still think you're being selfish if you refuse to accept money that we badly need, just out of stupid pride.'

Maddie couldn't believe she was hearing correctly. After all she'd suffered and Steve thought she was being selfish. 'Yes, we need it for you to drink and gamble you mean,' she threw back at him. A moment ago she'd thought they were becoming closer but after his recent comment she knew they were as far apart as ever.

'I didn't mean it for me.'

'Oh didn't you. Are you sure about that?' she yelled at him, standing up and moving to the other side of the room.

He got up then too. 'Suit yourself,' he shouted back and stormed out of the house, the brief moment of warmth between them gone.

With only a lamp for illumination, Maddie rocked back and forward on her chair, wrestling with her situation.

A few hours later she was no nearer to arriving at a decision as to whether or not she'd accept Benson's money. It was pitch black outside and she got up and put on the light before going over to draw the curtains.

Chapter Thirty-Eight

August 1960

'Do you fancy a coffee in Luigi's after work today?' Viv asked, when she bumped into Maddie waiting for the lift up to the Counting House. Viv had recently been transferred from haberdashery to women's fashions on the second floor. 'Give us a chance for a blether.'

'That would be great, Viv, but would Dave not expect you to go home with him?'

'Dave's going straight from work to deliver some carpets to Lord Macfarlane's pad in Aberfoyle. At least six miles past Aberfoyle, a place called Kinlochard. Dave said you should see this house, it's huge, the last word in luxury.' Lord Macfarlane was one of Marshall's most prestigious customers and was always treated with kid gloves. 'When he delivers the carpets, Dave will have to arrange a suitable time with His Lordship for our carpet fitters to lay them. What about Steve?' she asked, as the lift arrived and the two girls got in, the only passengers.

'Don't worry about him, he'll be visiting his bookie pal as usual,' Maddie said, pressing the buttons for the second and fifth floors. Her voice was brittle and uncaring.

Viv was worried about Maddie. She was sure that things weren't good between her and Steve but she didn't want to interfere in matters that were between a husband and wife. She simply said, 'I'll see you tonight then,' and got out as the lift stopped at the second floor.

*

There was no sign of Maddie when Steve got home from work that night. She stopped earlier than he did but as far as he could make out she'd not been into the flat and no dinner had been prepared. Nothing new there, he thought; she did just as she wanted with no explanation of where she'd been or when she'd be home.

'Two can play at that game. If the bitch gets home soon and makes dinner, she can eat the lot herself for all I care,' he muttered, taking his jacket down from the hallstand and putting it on again. Then, banging the door behind him, he stomped down the stairs of the tenement.

He called in at the Black Bull first of all and gave himself some fuel. As he listened to the buzz of conversation around the bar, he tried not to think of gambling but, unhappy with the way Maddie was treating him, he succumbed soon afterwards. When he left the Black Bull to go to his favourite pub, Chapman's, he stopped off in the lane at the corner of the Bower Bar where Bernie White conducted his business. Even though it was after seven, Bernie was still there.

'Hi Steve,' Bernie greeted him, recognising a good customer. 'What can I do for you?'

'I want a two way bet on 'Shamus' Filly' running in the three o'clock tomorrow. I've got a good feeling about that mare,' he told Bernie.

'How much?'

Steve pulled two pound notes from his pocket. 'A pound each way.' When he opened out the money he discovered there were actually three notes folded together but he gave them all to the bookie. 'The third pound I'll use for ten shillings each way on 'Spirited Lad'. That way I'm bound to win,' he prophesied.

*

Viv was sitting in their usual booth in Luigi's when Maddie got to the café.

'Hi, Maddie,' Viv greeted her old flatmate. 'Didn't order until you got here.'

Maddie sat down facing her best friend. 'I'm going to have some fish and chips and mushy peas, it'll save cooking when I get back to the flat.' She didn't make any reference to where Steve was or when he'd get home and Viv left well alone.

'Think I'll join you with the fish and chips. I can always use the excuse I'm eating for two,' she grinned. Maddie had been delighted to hear Viv was pregnant, especially as she and Dave were eager to become parents.

'How's your bump doing?'

'Getting more obvious. I've had to start wearing maternity clothes.'

'How much longer will you be working?'

'About a couple of months. Janet in haberdashery returned to the store when her baby was a few months old but Dave and I are both agreed that I'll be a full time mum. It'll be a struggle financially but we'll get there.'

'For a start, you won't be going out as much socially so that will save you money.' Maddie stopped speaking when the waitress arrived and they gave her their meal orders, along with a pot of tea for two.

'I hope she won't bring the tea too early,' Maddie said, once the waitress was out of earshot. 'Otherwise it means the tea's stone cold by the time the food comes.'

Viv felt Maddie looked a bit tense. 'So, how're things with you?'

'At work fine, at home dreadful.'

'Oh dear, is Steve still betting on the horses?' Viv thanked her lucky stars that Dave had no interest in gambling and was a good saver.

Maddie looked down and drummed her fingers on the table, only the top of her head visible to Viv. 'Last week he sold some of our wedding gifts while I was out and spent the proceeds on his gambling.' With Maddie speaking to the table top, Viv had to listen carefully to hear what was unfolding. 'He bets on horses or dogs and then goes to the pub and blows whatever money he has left. Of course, if he does win on the horses, which is rarely, he drinks even more. Don't know how much more of it I can take, Viv.' When Maddie looked up, the tears were streaming down her cheeks.

'I didn't realise it was so bad,' Viv whispered, placing her hands over Maddie's.

'It's getting worse.'

Before Viv could reply, the waitress brought their meals to the table. 'Would you like some tartare sauce?' she asked.

'Yes please,' Viv replied.

The two girls remained silent until the waitress returned with a glass dish which she plonked down in the centre of the table. 'Anything else?' When they shook their heads, she moved over to a nearby table to clear it of used plates.

'Do you want to talk about things?' Viv asked Maddie, as she passed over the salt and pepper shakers.

Maddie sprinkled salt over her meal. Then she sniffed back the tears and smiled at her friend. 'Talking wouldn't help, Viv. I'd rather enjoy my meal and hear about what you and Dave have been up to.'

Happy to oblige, Viv told her, in between mouthfuls, that she and Dave had been at a party in Gerry and Sylvia Morgan's house on Friday night and had attended Dave's aunt and uncle's Silver Wedding on Saturday in Giffnock Bowling Club.

'Friday night was a casual affair but I wore a new dress for the Silver Wedding.'

'What was your dress like?' It crossed Maddie's mind that previously she'd have accompanied Viv to buy her dress.

As if Viv read her mind, she said, 'I didn't buy a new dress, Mum ran me one up on her sewing machine. It's a black cotton material with large pink flowers on it.'

'Sounds lovely.'

'Yes, I felt good in it. Mum made it slightly wider at the front to accommodate my bulge, and she can take it in again once the baby is born?'

'Did you have a good time at the Silver Wedding?'

'Yes, we did. Dave and I were saying we've only got another twenty-three years and ten months until our Silver Wedding.' Viv laughed as she said this, a blush of happiness spreading across her cheeks.

Once again Maddie felt that surge of jealousy when she saw the ecstasy on her friend's face every time she spoke about her beloved husband. But, caring for Viv as she did, she couldn't grudge her friend such happiness.

Chapter Thirty-Nine

February 1961

'I baptise you Peter Charles John Tucker,' Mr McKenzie said in his beautiful Highland lilt as he dipped his fingers into the water in the font and made the Sign of the Cross on the baby's forehead. Little Peter, unaware of his celebrity status today, slept in the minister's arms.

Having conducted Viv and Dave's marriage service here in St Mark's in Kilmarnock, Mr McKenzie had readily agreed to baptise their first born son. And so it was that on this cold and frosty morning in late February, the first five or six pews in the church were occupied by the couple's family members and close friends.

With Steve and Maddie standing on either side of them as Godparents, Viv and Dave made their vows to bring Peter up in a Christian home and to teach him the ways of the Lord. With the baptism over, Mr McKenzie handed the baby back to his mother and she in turn placed him into the waiting arms of Maddie, his Godmother. As the organ started up for the hymn of blessing, a sudden burst of winter sun shone through the nearby window, suffusing Maddie and Peter in light, reminding Viv of the Madonna and Child. As she stared down at Peter, Maddie's facial expression of love and wonder pulled at Viv's heartstrings and she prayed fervently that her dearest friend would soon experience the same joy of motherhood that she had.

The blessing over, Steve turned and led the four of them and the baby out through the side door of the church, while the remainder of the congregation stayed in their pews.

Dave drove them back to Fairfields to await the return

of the guests at the end of the service. Sheena had as always offered to hold the lunch at the farmhouse, since there wasn't enough room in Viv and Dave's small terraced house in Clarkston.

When she walked into the farmhouse kitchen, Maddie was almost knocked off her feet by a black ball of fur. 'Oh, this is Star,' Viv told her, as Zeus also came loping into the kitchen to greet them.

'So when did Star arrive?' A pair of eyes stared at Maddie through the fur and the dog's wet nose rubbed against her hand.

'He was abandoned by his owners and someone brought him here. You know what Mum and Dad are like about strays, they simply can't resist taking them in. You're a lucky dog, aren't you Star?' Viv said, bending a little with her son in her arms, to pat the German Shepherd's soft hair.

'He looks so small beside Zeus,' Maddie held out her hand to be licked by the larger dog.

'He's only a puppy, Dad reckons about four or five months old.'

They just had time to change Peter's nappy and down a quick cuppa when the back door opened and Sheena and Charlie and the twins came in.

'We left immediately after the service was over to let us get the kettles boiled before everyone else gets here,' Sheena explained. 'Aileen,' she said to the taller of her twin daughters, 'could you start putting milk and sugar out on the table please?'

'Sure Mum,' Aileen smiled, throwing her coat over the back of a kitchen chair and rolling her jumper sleeves up. At nearly 15, Aileen was almost as tall as her dad.

'So you've been introduced to Star,' Elizabeth said to Maddie when she came into the living room. Smaller in height than her twin sister, Elizabeth was turning into a most attractive young lady with her dimples showing each time she smiled.

To Maddie's eyes, Aileen and Elizabeth were both becoming real stunners as they got older and luckily they both had a good nature to accompany their looks.

'Star really introduced himself,' Maddie told her, and laughed as the puppy rolled around the carpet at her feet, enjoying having his tummy tickled.

Viv, who'd been playing with Zeus, got to her feet. 'Excuse me, Zeus, my services are required elsewhere,' she said to the dog when she heard the lusty cries of her son, who had wakened and wanted a feed.

*

'It's been a lovely day,' Maddie said later that afternoon, when she and Viv were sitting together in the living room once all the other guests had left.

'Yes, and I was so proud of Peter behaving so well in church. I was terrified he would bawl the place down if he was fractious.'

'He's really a very contented baby, isn't he?' Maddie looked down and smiled at the infant, gurgling happily in his carry cot sitting between the two women. The magnificent pale blue and white satin pillow his head rested on and the matching satin cover laid loosely over his legs had been made for him by his proud grandma.

Baby Peter looked at them both in turn, beaming widely when he saw his mother's familiar face. Viv stretched over and put her finger inside the baby's hand, tickling his palm.

He laughed and curled his tiny digits around her finger. 'We're so lucky to have you, aren't we, darling?' she cooed to her child, 'and when Aunt Maddie and Uncle Steve have a baby, you'll have a playmate won't you? Sorry, Maddie,' she stopped herself, 'I'm getting a bit carried away.'

Maddie shrugged. 'No problem, I'm sure you and Dave will have lots of kids and Peter will have plenty of playmates.' She said no more, leaving Viv afraid that she'd intruded too much into Maddie's business. Viv sighed; even after all these years, she still knew there was a wall between them at such times.

Chapter Forty

October 1961

It was almost six o'clock when Maddie and Helen came out of the main door of Marshall's that Saturday. They had arranged to have a high tea in Wendy's restaurant in West George Street before going on to the Odeon in Renfield Street to see 'The Guns of Navarone'.

'Did you read the book when it came out a few years ago?' Helen had asked, when they were arranging their outing a few days earlier.

'No but I remember it was written by Alistair MacLean. My downstairs neighbour was telling me that he was a pupil of MacLean's in the mid-fifties at Gallowflat School in Rutherglen.'

'Well I did read the book and I'm sure it will be a really exciting film. It has a great cast.' Helen took the newspaper cutting about the film out of her bag. 'Gregory Peck, David Niven, Anthony Quinn, Stanley Baker and Anthony Quayle. Need I say more?' she smiled.

Maddie shook her head. 'Let's go on Saturday evening.'

The film proved to be as exciting as Helen had predicted and the two women were engrossed from start to finish.

When Maddie got home around half past ten, there was no sign of Steve. No doubt in Chapman's as usual, she thought bitterly, trying not to let the picture of him arriving home, swearing and acting aggressively towards her, spoil her memory of the evening spent with Helen.

She made herself a mug of cocoa and sat down to

listen to the Saturday night serial on the radio. She usually enjoyed the serial but tonight she couldn't concentrate, her mind too much on Steve's behaviour, and after ten minutes she switched off. Yawning, she undressed and climbed into bed.

*

Having lost a massive amount on the horses that Saturday afternoon, Steve went on a pub crawl after work, using the remainder of the money from his weekly pay packet. He was roaring drunk by the time he came out of the last pub at closing time. Much better to get drunk, he thought, than go home to that torn-faced bitch he lived with. And to think they could have had the money Benson left her if she hadn't been so proud.

He stumbled along, stopping on a piece of spare ground beside a tenement to relieve himself. The flat was in darkness when he arrived home shortly after eleven o'clock. The drink he'd consumed had left him in an argumentative frame of mind.

Maddie had floated off into a lovely dream when all hell let loose. The bedroom door was flung open with a force that almost took it off its hinges and Steve lunged into the room. He staggered around and cursed loudly about her treatment of him.

'Who the hell do you think you are?' he yelled, in a voice loud enough to waken everyone in the tenement building. 'You're my wife but you treat me like dirt and I won't stand for it any longer. Do you hear me?' he shouted, even louder than before.

With all sleep now wiped away, Maddie stared up at him, open-mouthed. His thick dark, wavy hair that she'd admired a few years ago, was now in a sorry state; matted, tangled and unwashed, with some threads of grey visible.

His tie was half off and hanging loose and the front of his blue shirt was stained with beer. His fly was open and the tail of his shirt was hanging out of his trousers. The sight of his florid complexion and bloodshot eyes reminded her of Benson and a shiver ran down her spine.

It took all her courage to remain impassive and

disinterested. 'Get out of here, you drunken skunk,' she thundered back at him, pulling the blankets up at her chin, in case the sight of her off the shoulder nightdress fuelled his lust. 'You should be ashamed of yourself getting into such a state, you're a disgrace and I despise you. I wish I'd never married you.'

He staggered back, as though she'd punched him. 'The same goes for me. You're my wife and it's time you began acting like one instead of the … the frigid bitch that you are. Viv's lovely but you're nothing like her. In fact, you're not a proper woman at all,' he threw at her.

Beating her up could not have hurt more and Maddie shut her eyes to dull the pain of his words. When she opened them again, his eyes were standing out like doorstops and his hands were tightly clenched into fists. Sure that he was going to rape her, panic set in and her courage evaporated. Then, as though the air had been taken out of him, he turned his back on her and stumbled out of the bedroom, banging into the door frame as he did so.

'She's no wife, never has been and never will be,' Steve muttered as he opened a can of beer and threw himself down into the armchair to drink it.

Maddie heard him in the kitchen, muttering and cursing, for some time. Then, when silence came, she plunged her head into the pillow and sobbed herself to sleep.

Steve eventually fell asleep in the chair and a couple of hours later wakened up feeling stiff and cold. He staggered through to the front room and dropped down on the settee, not bothering to open it out into a bed as he usually did.

He could have exerted his strength and power over Maddie to make her succumb to his sexual demands but he didn't want that. He'd never wanted that. From the first moment he'd set eyes on her, he'd wanted her to come to him willingly but, by now, he knew that was never going to happen.

It was with this thought in mind that Steve finally fell into a proper sleep, to waken up the following morning with a gigantic hangover.

Chapter Forty-One

December 1962

Just like in previous years, Maddie and Steve spent Christmas day at Fairfields, enjoying the usual merriment in the bosom of the Kingston family. Ever since his marriage to Maddie, Steve had been welcomed into their midst and Charlie and Sheena treated both him and Dave like the sons they'd never had.

Peter had been too young to be aware of Christmas last year but by now, at almost two, he knew that Santa Claus had come down the chimney and left lots of presents. Steve had become the toddler's favourite uncle and Peter insisted on his high chair being placed beside Steve's chair at the table. Seeing the delight on Peter's face as he pulled the first cracker with Uncle Steve, Maddie was riddled with guilt, aware of how much Steve would have loved to be a father to their kids. Once again she silently cursed Benson for rendering her unable to be a proper wife to Steve.

'You sit down and relax Sheena and Viv and I will do the dishes,' Maddie said, once everyone had risen from the table after their sumptuous feast.

'No, leave them girls and come and sit on the settee. I'll deal with the dishes later.'

'We'll do no such thing, Mum,' Viv agreed with Maddie. 'You've been working hard all day so the least we can do is the washing up.'

'Leave them to it,' Charlie said. 'Then they can blether away in the kitchen undisturbed.'

'Okay, girls, thanks,' Sheena shrugged, knowing she was outnumbered.

Viv closed over the kitchen door so as not to disturb the family and began to stack up the coffee cups and saucers at the side of the sink. 'Are you alright Maddie? You seemed very quiet at dinner.'

Maddie emptied all the remains left on the dinner plates into the dustbin before she answered. 'No point in trying to lie to you Viv,' she said as she poured boiling water into the basin and added a squirt of washing up liquid, 'Steve and I had another blazing row before we left the flat today.' She started washing the cutlery before doing the crockery. 'He threatened not to come today but I told him it would be discourteous to your mum and dad so he changed his mind at the last minute.'

'Oh Maddie, I'm so sorry that things haven't got any better between you,' Viv said, her eyes filling up at the plight of her friend's marriage. She lifted some knives and forks from the cutlery section on the dish rack and began drying them. 'I've been so worried about you, in case Steve becomes violent towards you. He isn't violent, is he?' she asked hesitantly, as she laid the dry cutlery on to the kitchen table.

'No, after a row, he always storms out of the door. He usually takes himself off either to place a bet or to the pub to drown his sorrows.'

'What are the rows about?' Viv asked, even though by now she had a fair idea of the problem.

Maddie grimaced. 'He feels I'm neglecting him and accuses me of not being a good wife to him.' She turned to Viv and sniffed back the tears. 'But I can't seem to let him near me Viv. I let him go so far and then I freeze. No wonder he calls me frigid,' she said bitterly.

Viv put her arm around Maddie's shoulder and kissed her cheek. 'I wish there was something I could do to help, Love. Do you think it would do any good if I asked Dave to have a word with Steve?'

Maddie shook her head vigorously. 'No, because it isn't Steve's fault, it's mine. I can't be what he wants me to be and it's getting worse as time goes by,' she sobbed silently.

'Hurry up, you two.' Aileen came into the kitchen and interrupted their conversation. 'We want to play a game.'

'We're nearly finished,' Viv told her, while Maddie turned away from Aileen's line of vision and wiped her eyes with the tea towel. 'Just give us another five minutes.'

'Okay,' Aileen sighed, 'we'll set up the board until you're ready.'

Chapter Forty-Two

March 1964

Maddie's birthday fell on Good Friday that year. After work on Friday, Helen treated her to high tea at Sloane's and they went on to a dance in the Highlander's Institute in Elmbank Street. There was no birthday card or gift from Steve but that was of no surprise as nowadays they were married in name only. On Saturday evening Maddie was invited to Clarkston and Viv made her a cake; a Happy Birthday cake little Peter called it. She enjoyed herself very much and Dave drove her home around ten o'clock to her empty flat.

In the fifteen months that had elapsed since she and Viv had discussed Maddie's marital problems, Viv hadn't mentioned them again but Maddie knew that her friend was concerned about her and Steve. Although it was over two years since the night that Steve had first accused her of not being a proper woman, the thought had preyed on Maddie's mind. An uneasy truce had begun where they each lived their own life but under the one roof. It was Maddie who kept that roof over their heads as Steve drank most of what he earned. Maddie often considered throwing him out on to the street; the main reason she didn't was because of what other people might think rather than any sympathy for him.

She undressed and drank a cup of tea before bed. She looked at the clock; almost chucking out time. She knew he'd come in roaring drunk as usual, causing a disturbance both to her and their neighbours in the tenement.

It was only a few weeks ago that Maddie had overheard her downstairs neighbour, Mr Trotter, telling another of the neighbours how he'd often seen Steve staggering along King Street at chucking out time, before going up the lane that led from there into Main Street. 'Don't know how his poor wife stands for it,' Mr Trotter had finished.

She began to imagine Steve in Chapman's right now, flirting with one of the barmaids. The more she thought about his behaviour, the more her anger rose. Suddenly something inside Maddie snapped and she put on her shoes and flung a coat over her nightdress.

*

Steve had made a killing that Saturday, with two of his horses romping home in first place. His pub crawl of some City Centre haunts started just after six. Many hours later, after making his drunken way back to Rutherglen by bus, he decided to have a wee nightcap in Chapman's before going home.

Steve was there until throwing out time and Nancy, his favourite barmaid, helped him to his feet. 'Come on now Stevie it's time to go. We need to get cleared up and get home. I need my beauty sleep after all,' she nudged him and winked.

'You're beautiful enough, darlin'.' Steve slurred the compliment, wishing he was going home to Nancy instead of the frigid bitch he was married to.

'Flattery gets you everywhere,' Nancy laughed, 'but tonight that's going to be outside to let me get the place locked up. Goodnight Stevie, safe home,' she said, propping him up outside the pub, before she closed the side doors and bolted them from inside. Unwilling to go home to Maddie just yet, Steve sat on the pavement for a wee while, singing loudly and out of key.

When he began to feel chilled, he tried to stand up again. On his third attempt, he finally made it on to his feet, wobbled about a bit, then headed towards King Street at the rear of the pub where he relieved himself against a wall.

After swaying his way up the dark lane, Steve blinked when he saw the street lights on Main Street. Entering his tenement close, he clambered his way upstairs, leaning heavily on the banister. Some of the stair lights had gone out and it took a fair time for him to reach even the middle landing. In the semi-darkness he didn't notice the figure standing quietly on the landing. Reaching the top step, he felt a push, which propelled him backwards down the flight he had just climbed. He didn't even have time to cry out and a minute later his body lay awkwardly on the concrete landing below.

*

Maddie climbed into bed and lay wide awake in the darkness, staring up at the ceiling. There would be no sleep for her tonight she knew. Yet inside she felt very calm.

After hours of wakefulness, Maddie did eventually drift off for a time but she was wakened by a loud knocking on her door. She rubbed her eyes and yawned. The alarm clock, its digits giving off a greenish glow in the darkness, showed the time to be ten past five. She sat on the edge of the bed for a moment, the carpet pile caressing the soles of her feet. As she switched on the bedside lamp, the bell rang again, for a much longer time. Pushing her feet into her warm, wool-lined slippers, she threw her dressing gown on top of her nightdress and tied its belt as she made her way out into the lobby.

She opened the door to two uniformed police officers, one male and one female, standing on her doormat.

'Mrs Dixon?' the male officer asked and Maddie nodded. 'I'm sorry to disturb you at such an unearthly hour. I'm Sergeant Walter McInnes and this is Constable Wendy Marshall. We're from Rutherglen Police Station and I'm afraid we have some bad news for you.'

'Can we speak inside?' Constable Marshall's voice was a whisper.

Maddie opened the door a bit further and stood back to let the officers in. She ushered them into the kitchen, where a warmth still lingered from the long gone out coal fire. 'Take a seat.' She pointed to the two armchairs, one on either side of the fireplace.

'You have an armchair, Mrs Dixon,' the Sergeant instructed, removing his hat and gloves. 'I'll use this one,' he said, bringing a dining chair over from the recessed area of the room, while Constable Marshall sat in the armchair facing Maddie. 'It's about your husband, Steve Dixon,' the Sergeant explained, once they were all settled.

Maddie shook her head and sighed. 'What's he been up to now? Drunk and disorderly no doubt and sleeping it off in a cell.'

'I'm afraid it's a bit more serious than that. There's been an accident. It would appear that Mr Dixon fell down your tenement stairs at some time during the night. Mr Trotter in the flat below found him when he was going out to start his shift on the trams this morning.'

Maddie gasped and rubbed her hand across her forehead. 'Which hospital is he in?'

'Unfortunately Mr Dixon was dead by the time Mr Trotter found him.'

'I take it he was drunk when it happened.'

The Sergeant nodded. 'It would appear so.'

Constable Marshall got to her feet. 'Can I make you a cup of tea?' she asked Maddie, concern evident in her voice.

Maddie remained silent as she watched the minute hand go round on the clock sitting on the mantelpiece. Then, remembering the officers were there, she looked up at the Constable.

'You'll get the tea and sugar in the cupboard, but I don't think there's much milk left.' The conversation stopped while the young Constable made three mugs of tea, putting plenty of sugar in Maddie's. Once she'd handed round the mugs, she sat down again.

Maddie spoke again, almost to herself this time. 'I knew something would happen to him. His drinking has increased, especially when he's had some big losses on the horses.'

'Did Mr Dixon drink every night?' the Sergeant asked her.

Maddie held the pottery mug between her hands, warming them. 'Most nights yes, but especially on Saturday nights. I never see him on a Saturday. He places some bets straight after work and spends the rest of the evening doing a pub crawl.' She stopped to drink some more tea, then continued, without any interruption from the officers. 'He drinks even more when he loses but even when his horse comes in, he either places the winnings on another race or spends it on booze. I certainly don't see any of the money,' she finished with a brittle laugh.

'Didn't you miss him not coming home tonight?' the Constable asked, putting her mug down on the hearth while she wrote in her notebook.

Tears glistened in Maddie's eyes. 'He doesn't always come home. Sometimes sleeps on a mate's sofa or perhaps sleeps rough for all I know.' She looked directly at the Constable. 'We haven't shared a bed for years now so I don't always hear him come in.'

'Is there anyone we can contact for you, Mrs Dixon. A relative or a friend perhaps?'

'My best friend is Viv. I spent the evening with her and her husband and their young son, Peter.' Maddie's knuckles were white with clenching them. 'It's my birthday you see and they had me over to their house for dinner. Viv's husband ran me home about ten o'clock.'

'Will we contact your friend for you?' the Constable asked.

Maddie shook her head. 'It's too early. With running after young Peter all day, poor Viv needs her sleep. I'll contact her myself later.'

'I'm sorry to have brought bad news, Mrs Dixon.' The Sergeant got up and put his mug into the sink. 'It would be most helpful if on Monday you could identify your husband's body.'

Maddie sighed. 'If I have to.'

The Constable stood up and laid her hand on Maddie's arm. 'I'll have someone pick you up on Monday morning and take you to the police mortuary. Would ten o'clock suit?'

Maddie nodded but stayed in her chair.

'We'll see ourselves out.' The Sergeant gave Maddie's shoulder a gentle squeeze and he followed his female colleague out of the kitchen.

'She took that pretty calmly,' Sergeant McInnes said

quietly as they got to the front door.

'Yes, but obviously he led her a dog's life ...' his
Constable shrugged, as she followed him out on to the landing.

From the kitchen Maddie heard the front door close
but remained where she was, staring into the grey ashes, the
remnants of the fire.

Chapter Forty-Three

June 1964

'You know you can stay here any night, if you're feeling lonely,' Viv said, as she laid Peter's dinner plate on the table in front of him, pulling his chair further under the table and placing another cushion under him to raise him up a bit. 'You won't sit on your high chair any longer, will you, darling?' she said, beaming at her son. 'Think you're too old for that now.'

'Of course you're too old for a high chair. You're three and a half after all,' Maddie smiled at the little boy, who lifted his knife and fork, holding them in the wrong hands. 'It's good that he's doing so much for himself as he'll be able to help you when the baby comes.'

'That's true,' Viv agreed, running her hands across the six month bulge on her stomach. 'It'll be strange having a young baby to work with again. Peter's quite determined that he's going to have a wee sister so hope he isn't disappointed.'

'You'll be a lovely big brother, Peter, whether you have a sister or a brother, won't you?' Maddie changed his knife and fork around for him.

'Mummy and Daddy are going to buy me a wee sister,' Peter told her.

'Will I cut your meat for you?' she offered, saying no more about the new baby's gender. 'Yes, please.' Peter's speech was very clear. He was big for his age, a most independent little boy, often appearing older than his years.

'Okay,' Maddie said, once she'd cut everything on the plate into small, manageable pieces, then sat back to let him feed himself as he preferred.

Viv had suggested that she give Peter his dinner now

and then Dave, Maddie and she could enjoy their meal in peace once Peter was in bed.

'He usually ends up with more food on the floor and on his clothes than in his mouth,' Viv complained, as she dried the items lying on the dish rack.

'No, I don't,' the little boy said, his mouth full of mashed potato.

'That's me told,' Viv giggled. 'As I was saying, Maddie, you can stay here anytime.'

'Thanks, Viv, I appreciate that but I'm fine, honestly. I'm used to being on my own. Half the time Steve stayed out all night anyway when he was on a drinking binge.'

Viv sighed and shook her head. 'You've not had it easy, Love,' she said to her friend, putting the clean glasses back into the cupboard. Viv knew that Maddie and Steve hadn't had a good marriage and she always thanked her lucky stars for her life with Dave. 'I don't know how you've coped, Maddie, but you've done really well. I don't think I could be as strong as you. No, keep the food on your plate, Peter. There's a good boy,' she congratulated him, sitting beside his chair and helping him to finish the remains on his plate.

'What a clever boy you are, eating up all your dinner,' Maddie smiled at him, wiping away the food around his mouth with a serviette. 'I wonder what Mummy has for you now?'

'Look what I've got for you,' Viv said in a singsong voice, as she put a little tub of ice cream in front of her son. 'It's your favourite strawberry ice cream, darling.'

'Mmm,' he said, his eyes wide with pleasure, as he took the plastic spoon from his mum.

While he was eating, Viv continued the previous conversation. 'But as I was saying, Maddie, I'm full of admiration for how well you coped with Steve's death.'

Maddie shrugged. 'You don't have any choice, Viv, just have to get on with it. I'm so lucky to have you and Dave as friends and also Helen to go out with at times.'

'And we all just want to help you, Love. Right, let's move into the living room for a wee while. Dave won't be home for over an hour yet.'

They chatted for a time while Peter played with some of his toys on the floor beside them. 'Have you had any word about the compensation payment?' Viv asked.

'Not yet but at least I've got the money due from Marshall's. It's very little as Steve only paid into the pension fund for a few years but it's better than nothing at all.'

'Are you managing alright with your rent?'

'Yes, it's good that I'll be getting my incremental rise at work at the end of the year. Between that and the small pension I get from Marshall's I should manage to pay the bills.'

'Do you not get a Widow's Pension?'

'No, I'm too young for that. I think you've to be forty-eight or over to be entitled to a Widow's Pension. Still at least I'm lucky I've got a job and can earn some money. And I've been told I should get something from his life insurance through his pension.'

'Well, that should be a help to you.' Viv changed the subject. 'Would you like to bath this little man before his dad gets home?

'Sure thing.' Maddie held out her arms and Peter came into them happily.

'What do you say Peter, if we give you a bath and afterwards we could read your book about penguins, the one you got last week?'

'Yes, please. Let's go,' he laughed and jumped off Maddie's knee and pulled on her arm until she got up and followed him into the bathroom.

'I'll come up and say goodnight once Aunt Maddie has read your story,' his mum called after him.

*

The post arrived next morning as Maddie was leaving for work. She stuffed the envelopes into her bag and headed for the station. She boarded her usual train at Rutherglen station, which as ever was jam packed, but she managed to get the last remaining vacant seat in the compartment. A pleasant change from her normal stand in the doorway, all the way into the Central Station.

Taking out her mail, she slit the envelopes open with the tail of her metal comb. Three of the envelopes contained bills but inside the last one was a sizeable cheque from the insurance company.

During her lunch hour Maddie deposited the cheque into her bank account. Together with Benson's legacy, it made her account look very healthy. Because Steve didn't know that she'd accepted Benson's money, it was still in her account, gaining interest. If Steve had got his hands on the money, it would have gone into the coffers of the nearest betting shop.

Chapter Forty-Four

September 1964

Dropping her book on to the chair, Maddie dived out into the lobby when she heard the phone ringing. She grabbed the receiver off its cradle. 'Hello, Rutherglen 2811,' she said breathlessly, playing with the phone cord as she did so. When she'd had the telephone installed earlier in the year, she could only get a party line and shared it with old Mrs Thomson in the ground floor flat. The old lady always seemed to be on the phone to her sister but fortunately the line had been free for Dave's call from the Southern General Hospital. Sheena and Charlie were looking after Peter at Fairfields.

'Maddie,' Dave shouted in his excitement, 'it's a girl. She's fifteen minutes old and weighs seven and a half pounds.'

Maddie leaned back against the bunker, a sigh of relief washing over her. The last few weeks, since Viv had been told the baby was lying in a breech position, had been fraught for them all, especially Viv and Dave.

'Maddie, are you still there?'

'Yes … yes, it's fantastic news. And how's Viv, and the baby of course.'

'They're both fine, thank God.'

'And did Viv need a Caesarean?'

'No, the baby turned at the last minute so she was able to have a normal delivery. It was a very long labour, poor lamb, and Viv's blood pressure shot up.'

'She's alright though?'

'She's fine now but I was worried sick about her. I'm so glad they are both safe.'

Maddie thought again what a caring man Dave was.

No wonder he and Viv had such a happy marriage as they each thought of the other before themselves. 'And what's the name?' Dave seemed not to have heard her, so Maddie prompted him again. 'The baby's name. What's it to be?'

'Oh yes, we're going to call her Sara,' he said and Maddie could almost hear the smile in his voice. 'Sara Elizabeth Aileen to be exact. Peter's delighted of course as he wanted a baby sister from the start.'

'Yes, he told me. Have you phoned Fairfields?'

'I phoned them first before I rang you and I could hear Peter's screams of joy over the line. I tried to speak to him but he was too excited to answer me so I'm going to the farm to collect him and bring him to the hospital to visit his new sister.'

'That's great. And what about your own parents, Dave?'

'I tried them but they were out so I'll give them a ring now.'

'Will it be alright for me to pop into the ward tomorrow to see Viv and the baby?'

'Yes, the afternoon visiting is between three and four and at night it's between seven and eight. But phone the hospital before you go in case they move her to another ward.'

'Will do, Dave, and many congratulations,' she finished but he'd already hung up.

*

The next afternoon when Maddie walked into Ward 7 of the Maternity Department, Viv was sitting in a chair at the side of her bed cradling her daughter. Viv looked the picture of health after her ordeal the previous day and was a marvellous advert for motherhood.

Maddie sat down on the edge of Viv's bed and peeped in at the tiny face nestling inside the white lacy shawl that Sheena had knitted for her. 'She's gorgeous, Viv,' she said, and placed her lips gently on the brow of the newborn.

'Do you want to hold her?' Viv offered.

Maddie took the infant from her mother. 'Gosh it feels strange to hold a tiny baby again,' she said, drawing the tip of her finger along the perfect line of the baby's eyebrows.

'I felt that too the first time I held her. Of course, Peter wanted to hold her when Dave brought him in yesterday but I sat him on my knee and we held her together. That seemed to satisfy him, didn't it, Sara?' she said, smiling up at her daughter lying in Maddie's arms.

Maddie took the tiny hand in hers and stroked the little fingers. 'Look, I think she's smiling or is she in fact filling her nappy?'

'She's good at that.' Viv laughed and took the child back. She sniffed for a minute and grimaced. 'You're right, Maddie, she needs her nappy changed again.'

Once Sara had been changed, she promptly fell asleep in her mother's arms, leaving Viv and Maddie the chance for a chat, which only finished once the bell rang to herald the end of visiting.

Chapter Forty-Five

September 1966

'Happy birthday to you, happy birthday to you,
    happy birthday, dear Sara, happy birthday to you.'
    The family members all sang heartily to Sara on her second birthday, the most noise coming from her big brother, Peter. 'Blow out your candles, Sara,' he instructed her.
    'Sara's a bit young to blow out the candles on her own, Darling, so you'll have help her,' Viv told him.
    Peter obliged and beamed as everyone applauded.
    Sheena got to her feet and lifted the birthday cake, decorated with pink fairies and satin ribbon, off the table. 'I'll go and cut the cake Peter, and maybe afterwards you could pass round the plate for me?' she said to her grandson.
    At nearly six, Peter was tall for his age and very articulate. Because of this he'd started at primary school at four and a half and was now in Primary 2. From the reports his parents had received from Peter's teacher, he was clever and hard-working and didn't appear to create any problems. He was a really friendly child too, so didn't lack for company either.
    'How's work going?' Charlie asked Maddie, once the excitement of the cake was over.
    'Not bad Charlie. The girls in the typing pool are a good bunch and I get on well with my boss, Miss Edwards. She's known as a bit of a tartar but as long as you work hard and get in on time in the morning she's alright.'
    'That's great, lass. I'm sure you're a good worker so you won't get into her bad books.'
    'Is everything fine on the farm too, Charlie?' she enquired.

'Yep, I've no complaints. There's been enough rain recently to provide good grazing for the cows and the milk return's been plentiful.' Little Sara and Daisy the cat both appeared at Charlie's feet at the same time so he lifted Sara on to one knee and Daisy on the other.

'Pussy cat,' Sara almost said the words as she stretched out her delicate arm and stroked Daisy's head. Daisy purred happily.

'Say Daisy,' Charlie said and Sara smiled at him and the word came out like 'Baysey.'

'Clever girl,' her proud grandfather smiled at his little princess and cuddled her closer.

'What are the twins going to do for their twenty-first next April?' Maddie asked Viv.

'I'm not sure. Mum and Dad wondered about a party in the Co-operative Hall in Kilmarnock but it depends what Aileen and Elizabeth want themselves. By the way the twins asked me to say goodbye to you as they are out on a double date tonight with their two current boyfriends. You were in the toilet when the boys arrived for them.'

'I wondered where they'd vanished to,' Maddie smiled.

Viv took Sara from Charlie as the toddler was becoming fractious. Viv cradled her, rocking her gently to and fro, in the hope that she'd fall asleep. 'I can hardly believe they're nearly twenty-one,' she said to Maddie.

Maddie nodded. 'It seems like yesterday that I first came to Fairfields just before the twins' eleventh birthday and here they're almost twenty-one. Where have the years gone?'

'Time passes so quickly,' Viv agreed. 'That's why it's so important to enjoy every minute we have. I think she's nearly off,' her voice dropped to a whisper, and she carried her daughter slowly out of the room to put her into the cot Sheena kept in the spare bedroom.

'That should be her for the next couple of hours,' Viv said on her return to the living room. 'Now what about we have a coffee and a blether,' she suggested, receiving a thumbs up from Maddie.

Chapter Forty-Six

April 1967

'Charlie and I wanted to have a party for the girls in a hall or a hotel but they insisted on having it here,' Sheena said as she gave plates of food to Maddie and Viv to leave on the buffet table in the front room. At Fairfields they very rarely used the front room as the family always liked to congregate in the living room, to be able to speak through to Sheena if she was working in the kitchen. But with the number of guests invited to the twins' twenty-first Party, they needed to utilise the front room space for the buffet.

'I can understand the way Aileen and Elizabeth feel.' Maddie continued her conversation with Sheena on her return to collect some more plates laden with goodies. 'Fairfields has been so much a part of their lives and we've enjoyed so many lovely times here.'

'I suppose so. Anyway as long as the girls have a great time, that's all that matters.'

The twins had turned into delightful young ladies. Having been born non-identical twins, their ambitions and personalities were quite different but thankfully the strong bond they'd had in childhood had remained and their loyalty to one another was obvious. Aileen had taken an office job on leaving school and a couple of years later had joined the police force, doing very well in her exams. Elizabeth had followed the ambition she'd harboured as a child and had entered the nursing profession, a job she was eminently suited for. Both girls were doing well with their careers and, like Viv, Maddie was proud of them.

She was just sorry that the girls weren't always at

home when she visited Fairfields, due to the odd hours both had to work. Aileen had met her boyfriend Drew, also a police officer, when she was on her course at Tullyallan Police College. Viv and Maddie were convinced the romance would lead to wedding bells. Elizabeth was going out with Kenneth, one of the physiotherapists attached to her ward in Mearnskirk Hospital.

'And where are the birthday girls?' Maddie asked Sheena on one of her many trips to the kitchen. She picked up a tea towel and began to dry the items draining on the dish rack.

Sheena shrugged and smiled. 'Somewhere in Ayr, I think. Drew and Kenneth have taken the two of them out for the day. I told them to make sure they were home before the guests arrived for the party.' As if on cue, the back door opened and the four young people came in, followed by the usual menagerie of Zeus, Holly, Star and Daisy.

When the twins went off to change for the party, Charlie invited the two lads to join him in a wee snifter. 'I've just come in from milking,' he told them, 'and I always look forward to a wee nip afterwards.'

'Don't forget you have to change your clothes before our guests come,' Sheena reminded him.

'I'll do that once I've had my wee noggin,' he said, squeezing his wife's hand as she passed by his armchair.

*

An hour later the house was bursting at the seams with the party in full swing.

The joint birthday cake was brought out after everyone had eaten their fill from the buffet. Charlie, slightly merry by this time, got to his feet and gave a very moving speech about the joy Aileen and Elizabeth had brought to him and Sheena and how proud they were of their daughters.

Maddie's eyes filled up and as ever she thought how lucky she was to have been accepted into this wonderfully caring family. When she looked around, she couldn't see a dry eye in the house. But they were tears of joy and the evening went on in that happy vein until well into the wee small hours.

Chapter Forty-Seven

May 1967

When Maddie went into the Board Room for her half past eleven interview that day, three of Marshall's Directors plus the store manager, Eric Chalmers, were seated at the table, their backs to the window. She was invited to take a seat on the opposite side of the table, facing them.

'Could the curtains be drawn behind you please?' She directed her question to Mr Chalmers, one hand shielding her eyes from the fierce May sunshine that flooded into the room.

'Of course.' He got up from his seat and drew the curtains halfway over. 'Is that better?'

'Yes, thanks,' she nodded and watched him return to his seat. With his upright frame and the gentlemanly behaviour he displayed at all times Maddie found it hard to believe that he was conducting a fling with Patricia Harper behind his wife's back. She had a fleeting vision of the two in bed and then pulled herself back to the present when she realised that Mr McLaughlin, the Senior Director of the firm, had spoken to her.

'Pardon,' she apologised.

'I see from your application form Miss Granger that you have been with us now for over ten years working in the typing pool,' he repeated, giving her an encouraging smile.

'Yes. Ten years past last December.' She'd gone back to her maiden name after Steve's death.

He nodded and wrote something on the paper in front of him.

Maddie hadn't told any other members of the Counting House staff that she'd applied to be Miss Edwards' replacement following her retirement last month. Only Viv and Helen knew and they'd encouraged her to go for it. Due to her relationship with Mr Chalmers, Maddie felt sure that Patricia would know that she'd applied but Patricia hadn't said anything to Maddie. Patricia's behaviour was always very professional, something Maddie admired about her.

Poor Miss Edwards hadn't planned to retire until her birthday in December but when she was discovered to have a stomach ulcer, she'd had to undergo emergency surgery. After discussion with the management, Miss Edwards had decided to take her retirement forthwith.

'And what makes you think you are a good candidate to step into Miss Edwards' shoes?' was Mr McLaughlin's next question.

Maddie had been expecting this type of question, aware that many of the other girls in the typing pool had been with Marshall's much longer. However, she'd overheard Julie and some of the others saying that they weren't interested in the Manager's job, much preferring the camaraderie of the typing pool. She cleared her throat before she replied, trying to keep her hands on her lap and not wave them about as she was inclined to do when she was nervous.

'I'm aware that Miss Edwards is a hard act to follow,' she began, looking first at Mr McLaughlin and then to the other members of the interview panel, 'but I am someone who enjoys a challenge. I think I have enough knowledge of the working of the Counting House by now to be able to handle the duties of Manager.' Other panel members fired questions at her and Maddie, warmed to the task by now, was happy with the answers she offered.

The interview lasted a little more than half an hour and, overall, Maddie thought she'd made a reasonable impression on the panel although she wouldn't get a result until the other candidates were interviewed. As far as she was aware, she was the only person from Marshall's current staff who was being interviewed and the other applicants were from outside the store.

When she emerged from the Board Room, it was time

for her lunch so, instead of returning to the typing pool, she went directly to the staff canteen.

'How did it go?' Helen asked her quietly, as she was dishing up the steak pie and potatoes that Maddie had chosen from the menu.

'I think I did quite well, although I won't know until later today or tomorrow once the other candidates have been seen.'

'Let me know,' Helen smiled at her, as Maddie moved on to the drinks cabinet and Helen attended to the next member of staff waiting to be served.

*

It was after four o'clock when Maddie was called to Mr Chalmers' office to be told she'd been successful in getting the post of Counting House Manager.

'Congratulations, Miss Granger,' he smiled at her. 'I'm pleased to offer you the post, to take effect as from next week at the salary that was discussed at the interview this morning.'

'Thank you very much, Mr Chalmers. I'm happy to accept.'

'Patricia Harper will be working as your secretary as she did for Miss Edwards,' he said, and Maddie noticed his face flush slightly as he mentioned Patricia's name.

'That's good, Mr Chalmers. Patricia and I get on well together.'

'Excellent,' he said and ushered her out of his office again.

Maddie could hardly wait to get to Fairfields after work and tell them the good news. Sheena had invited her for dinner and to let her see the pictures from the twins' 21st party.

Viv and the kids were already at the farm when she arrived, with Dave due to come later when he'd finished work. The twins were also there, having managed to get the same day off for once. Star and Holly were stretched out on the kitchen floor, with Zeus in his favourite place, lying across the doorway between the kitchen and the living room. Daisy was nowhere to be seen, most likely snoozing on top of Sheena and

Charlie's bed.

Viv threw her hands out and hugged Maddie as soon as she walked in the back door. 'You got it.'

'How did you know?'

'Oh Maddie, it's written all over your face,' Viv said, giving her friend another hug. 'Not that I expected anything else as I know Miss Edwards recommended you for her post.'

'Who said that?' As ever, Maddie was amazed at how much Viv seemed to hear about Marshall's even though she no longer worked there.

'You know Dave and I meet Tommy Barrett and his wife socially and the other night, once he'd had a few, Tommy told me that Miss Edwards thought you would be the ideal person to take over from her.'

Maddie smiled. Tommy Barrett was one of the people on the interview panel. 'I'm glad you didn't tell me that before the interview as I'd probably have been even more nervous in case I let Miss Edwards down.'

'But you didn't,' Sheena said, coming through from the bedroom to congratulate Maddie. 'And now we have something to celebrate. Maddie got the job as Counting House Manager,' she called to Charlie, who came in from the barn at that moment.

'Fantastic, Maddie. We must have a bottle of something with our dinner tonight to celebrate your success, lass,' he said, hugging her. She smiled happily, used by now to the smell of the farm that always came from his clothes.

'Do you want to see the pictures, Maddie?' Elizabeth asked.

'Oh yes, I've been looking forward to seeing them.'

She stretched out her hand for the packet of pictures and sat down to look through them. 'What a gorgeous picture,' she said, holding up a photograph of the twins with Sheena and Charlie at the 21st party.

Aileen laughed. 'Yes, and for once Mum actually likes herself in a photograph.'

Sheena, who'd been listening to the radio while mashing the potatoes, peered round the kitchen door. 'Well,

I'm usually mucking about or doing something daft like closing my eyes or making a face. It's a change to see one in which I'm looking pretty decent.'

'Glad you've brought the photos at last,' Charlie said to Aileen when he sat down on the settee between his twin daughters to look at the pictures.

'It was difficult as every time one of us has been here the other had the pictures at work to show to colleagues,' Elizabeth told him, throwing an arm around his shoulders and cuddling against him.

'Anyway, better late than never,' Aileen said, handing her dad the pile of photos.

When the six o'clock news started, Charlie moved over to the armchair in the corner. With Holly at his feet, he stared at the black and white picture on the screen of their new television set. 'I know that woman's face, who is she again?'

Maddie went over and sat on the arm of his seat. 'That's Winnie Ewing, the SNP candidate who won the seat in Hamilton last week,' she said looking at the woman speaking animatedly to a reporter about what she hoped to achieve for her constituents.

'I thought I knew her face. These Scottish Nationalists are real troublemakers,' he said. 'God help us if they ever get into power, they'll ruin the country in five minutes.'

Sheena called out from the kitchen. 'If that's you off your soap box now, you'll be pleased to know it's your favourite dinner tonight.'

Charlie's face broke into a beaming smile. 'Good old mince and tatties,' he said, winking at Maddie, 'you can't beat it. Keep all your fancy food and give me mince and tatties any day.'

Chapter Forty-Eight

June 1967

Coming to the end of her chapter, Maddie closed the paperback, inserting her bookmark in at her place. She'd read Nevil Shute's 'A Town Like Alice' before and seen the film too but she was enjoying reading it again. She'd finished reading at the bit where Joe had been crucified by the Japanese guards and she was glad she knew that he survived so that he and Jean could meet again after the war. She'd enjoyed all Nevil Shute's novels but this one was definitely her favourite. Although she knew only too well it wasn't always the way in the real world, she liked a happy ending in a book.

She stretched and yawned, through the train window watching the rural scene that they were whizzing past. She loved the bright yellow colour of the rape seed in the fields. It seemed ages since she'd boarded the train in Queen Street Station this morning and she'd read for most of the journey so far. Now they were in the heart of Perthshire, the county of trees as her mother had always described it. The thought of her mother brought a smile to Maddie's face.

She'd normally be working on a Friday but she'd taken Friday, Saturday and Monday as holidays so that she could enjoy a long weekend break from work. Maddie thought how lucky she was with her friends; Helen and her mum and Viv and the family. And of course her adopted parents at Fairfields. She was so grateful to have them all in her life. Good friends like them were a real treasure.

Viv always found time for her, despite having such a busy life. And both Viv and Dave were keen for Maddie to have lots of contact with the kids, who seemed to be growing by the minute. Peter was due to move into Primary 3 at Carolside Primary in August, not far from their home in Clarkston. He'd grown so much in the past year that Viv had to buy him a complete new uniform in a bigger size.

Maddie's thoughts went back to Peter's first day at school. He'd looked so smart, with his grey short trousers and grey top hose, a white shirt and his green and grey striped tie. On the pocket of his dark green blazer Viv had sewn the badge with a picture of the school on it. Maddie had enjoyed buying his school bag for him, and picking pencils, a ruler and an eraser for the bag.

Sara was now almost three and a pretty wee thing with a gorgeous smile, although the same little madam could lead her mother a merry dance at times with her temper tantrums. The kids were spoiled by so many people; their doting parents and grandparents, Maddie herself and of course their beloved twin aunts.

The chap sitting on the other side of the table caught Maddie's eye and smiled. She smiled back. Although he'd been opposite her since they left Queen Street Station in Glasgow, they hadn't spoken. She wondered if he, like her, was getting off in Arbroath or if he was going all the way to Aberdeen, where the train would terminate.

She went to the toilet, glad of the exercise after sitting so long in the one place. After using the facilities, she re-applied her lipstick and combed her hair. Her long pony tail had been gone for a few years now and she preferred her hair in this sleek page boy style. Going into the next compartment where the shop was located, she bought a ham sandwich, a packet of cheese and onion crisps and a cup of coffee.

She carried her lunch back to her seat, carefully holding the coffee cup out from her body to avoid spilling any due to the occasional lurching of the train. Back in her seat, she took the sandwich out of its packet and ripped open her crisps. As the coffee was piping hot, she'd let it cool a little before she drank it.

As she was munching quietly on her ham sandwich, the chap opposite lay his folded Glasgow Herald down on the table and smiled at her again. 'I'm stuck with the last two cryptic clues in the crossword,' he said.

She liked his deep, rich-sounding voice. 'Can't you cheat and check the answers?'

'Unfortunately I'll need to wait until tomorrow as the answers won't be in the paper till then. One way, I suppose, to make sure you buy the paper each day.' He laughed and his bright blue eyes crinkled at the sides when he did so.

He's one handsome guy, she thought, surprising herself as she was usually fairly immune to male charms. 'Would you like some crisps?' She held out the packet towards him.

'No thanks, I'm only going as far as Dundee. That's where I live and I'll get lunch when I get home.'

'I've never been in Dundee. Is it a large town?'

'It's a city actually and yes quite large. About the fourth biggest in Scotland, after Glasgow, Edinburgh and Aberdeen. Is it Aberdeen you're going to?'

'No I'm getting off at Arbroath. My friend Helen and her mother have rented a holiday house there and they invited me to come up for the weekend to join them.'

'That sounds nice. You'll need to have a walk along the cliff path while you're there.'

'Yes, Helen mentioned that to me. Her mother isn't very fit but she says she'd be happy to sit in the sun and watch the world go by while we tackle the cliff path.'

'Sounds like a good plan, providing the sunshine plays along,' he said, and laughed again. He had what she'd call an infectious laugh.

'Helen was saying there's a part on the cliff path that's quite dangerous.'

'It is a bit, you have to be careful. The view over the cliffs, with all the sea birds, is stunning. Excuse me,' he said a few minutes later, easing himself out of the seat and walking off in the direction of the toilet sign. On his return, he took his brief case down from the luggage rack. 'Would you like me to bring your case down to save you when you get to Arbroath?'

'Oh, yes please.'

He lifted Maddie's case down and laid it on the spare seat beside her.

'It's been lovely to meet you,' the young man said as the train was approaching Dundee railway station. He raked his hand through his thick fair hair and Maddie noticed that he wasn't wearing a ring. 'The name's Len Singleton,' he added, holding his hand out.

Maddie took his hand, warm to the touch, but dry. She hated folk with sweaty hands. 'Nice to meet you too. I'm Maddie Granger.'

'I hope we'll meet again sometime, Maddie. Meantime, look after yourself.' He beamed at her as he left and once on the platform, he turned round and gave her a wave before making his way towards the station exit.

*

Helen was waiting for Maddie on the platform at Arbroath.

'Great to have you with us, Maddie,' she said, giving her friend a warm hug.

'Good to be here.' Maddie let Helen take her vanity case with her toiletries, leaving her with the larger case.

Helen guided her towards the main exit. 'How was your journey?' she asked as she hailed a taxi outside the station. 'It's too far to walk with the luggage,' she explained.

'Birch House, at Harbour Row,' Helen said to the driver, then turned to Maddie. 'Seems the wrong name for a place near the harbour, doesn't it? It should be Seagull House or Swan House or something,' she suggested as the cab pulled away from the station entrance. 'So, your journey, how was it?'

'Very relaxing. I'm almost three quarters way through my book.' Maddie didn't say anything about her meeting with Len Singleton, preferring to keep that to herself.

'And are you hungry?'

'No, I had a sandwich on the train. How is your mother enjoying her holiday?'

'Very much and her legs haven't been too painful which is great. Her arthritis seems to have died down a bit at the moment, thank goodness. I think Mum's glad you've come to give me some company. Poor Mum always worries that I'm bored with just the two of us.'

'It's great you have such a good relationship with your mother, Helen.'

'You miss your mother, don't you, Maddie?' And seeing the shadow that passed across her friend's face at the memory of her mother, Helen dropped the subject. 'Here we are, home sweet home,' she said as the taxi drew up in front of Birch House.

Chapter Forty-Nine

'Will your mum be alright?' Maddie asked, as she followed Helen up the cliff path at Arbroath on Saturday afternoon. Helen's sturdy walking boots left patterned prints on the earthen path, softened by the recent rain.

Pulling her bag further up on to her shoulder, Helen turned round to her friend. 'She'll be fine. Mum will enjoy people watching while she has her tea and scone and she'll likely be on to her second or third pot of tea by the time we get back.'

'Then let's hope there's a toilet in the café.'

The girls had left Mrs Ford at a window table in the Harbour Café to enjoy one of the freshly baked scones on offer. From the café window Helen's mum could see the colourful craft bobbing up and down in the water, accompanied by the raucous chorus of seagulls circling around in search of tasty tit-bits dropped by holidaymakers. The gulls were especially fond of raking in the empty papers stuffed into the litter bins for any leftovers from fish suppers.

They'd only gone a short distance along the headland when Maddie stopped at the edge of the path. 'Look at the sheer drop down there,' she said, pointing down the almost perpendicular cliff below them.

Helen looked back. 'Don't get too close to the edge, Maddie,' she cautioned. 'This path is known to be dangerous in parts and the Council have put up notices warning people to take care.'

'I can see why. Anyone falling down there wouldn't stand a chance of survival.'

Maddie looked down the cliff face and shivered. The ground down at water level was spiked by sharp rocks. A fall down there would be fatal.

The girls walked on for about twenty minutes before resting on a seat that looked down over the cliff to the little cove at the bottom. They sat in companionable silence, enjoying the call of the birds and the sound of the water crashing in over the rocks.

After about ten minutes, Maddie glanced at her watch. 'I think we should turn back now. Your mum will be getting a bit bored in the café.'

'Yes, you're right, there's a limit to how many cups of tea even my mum can drink.'

Helen led the way back to the harbour area once more. They walked in single file, both enjoying the stillness and the scenery. Although still quite bright, some nasty looking grey clouds had descended, ready to drop their load at any minute.

'Are these thistles?' Maddie asked when she caught up with Helen, who was down on her knees inspecting some wild flowers growing at the edge of the path.

'I'm not sure but they certainly look like miniature thistles, don't they?' Helen hunched down further and took a pair of nail scissors out of her bag. 'I'll take a bit of this so that I can use it at the art class.' Helen had recently joined a painting class in her local community centre and was proving to be a very proficient artist.

'Got you,' she said as she cut off two of the thistle-like flowers and straightened up to put her scissors back into her bag.

'Careful,' Maddie yelled as Helen tottered slightly on a slippery bit of gravel and her left foot dropped over the cliff edge, the scissors hurtling down to the foot of the cliff.

Maddie rushed towards her and grabbed Helen just in time, the two of them landing down heavily on the path.

'Are you alright?' Maddie was breathless from the weight of Helen lying on top of her.

'I think so.' Helen placed her hands on the ground and pushed herself on to her feet. She winced as she tried to put weight on her ankle. 'Think I've twisted my ankle.'

Maddie picked up Helen's bag and put it over her

arm, along with her own bag. Then she held out her free arm. 'Hold on to me,' she said and the two of them slowly continued along the path, much of the time with Helen hopping on one foot.

When the girls finally reached the Harbour Café, Maddie helped Helen down into a seat beside her mother, with her foot up on another chair. Then Maddie asked if a member of staff could phone for an ambulance.

'Would you like a cup of sweet tea?' the café owner asked Helen. 'It's good for shock.'

'You do need something, Love. Are you in a lot of pain?' Mrs Ford asked, holding Helen's hand tightly.

'It's not too bad,' a white-faced Helen said, then winced again as she tried to move her foot to another position.

'I think it might be better if my friend didn't eat or drink anything,' Maddie suggested to the café owner. 'In case she needs an anaesthetic.'

The man nodded. 'You're right, I hadn't thought of that. I'll go and bring you some ice to keep your friend's leg from swelling and then we'll just let her rest until the ambulance comes.'

*

The Accident and Emergency Department at Dundee Royal Infirmary was extremely busy when Helen arrived there at about two o'clock. She was accompanied by her mother and Maddie, both of whom had been allowed to ride in the ambulance with her. The ambulance driver got her into a wheelchair, which he pushed along the corridor to the reception desk, with Maddie and Mrs Ford walking one on either side of the chair.

'I think we might be here some time, going by the number of people waiting to be seen,' Maddie said to the other two, once Helen had been checked in at the reception desk. The cubicles in the department were all full, with patients lying on trolleys in the corridors waiting for a bed.

Doctors and nurses seemed to be dashing about all over the place, as the three of them sat listening to young children crying over their injuries. The patients were taken in order of seriousness, so they expected to be waiting quite a long time. It was after four o'clock when a nurse came to escort Helen into a bay, where she'd be seen by a doctor. 'If you and your friend wait here,' the nurse said, smiling at Helen's mum, 'your daughter's injury will be looked at.'

Maddie sat crossing and uncrossing her legs while she waited. Beside her, Mrs Ford's foot tapped constantly on the floor.

About an hour later, the same nurse returned. 'If you ladies would come with me, doctor would like to speak to you,' she informed them.

They followed her into a cubicle, where Helen was lying on a bed.

'Oh, Mum, they want to keep me in. They might need to operate on my ankle,' she burst out, holding her mother's hand tightly, concern written all over her face.

'Don't fret so, I'll manage until you're better.' Mrs Ford smiled and planted a kiss on her daughter's forehead. 'It'll only be for a few days,' she soothed, making light of the situation they'd found themselves in.

'Hello,' the young doctor smiled, as he came into the cubicle behind the two women. To Maddie he seemed vaguely familiar but the penny dropped when he said, 'I'm Dr Singleton.' Of course, she thought, it's the chap from the train yesterday and she was surprised to find her heart beating faster.

He looked even more handsome today wearing his white coat, his stethoscope hanging out of the pocket and his eyes even bluer than she remembered. She got the distinct impression he recognised her too although he said nothing.

'Are you Helen's mother?' He looked at Mrs Ford as he was speaking and she nodded. 'The x-ray shows that Helen has broken her ankle in the fall but she may not need an operation. We'll admit her for a day or two for observation and further x-rays. After that, we can decide if we need to insert a metal plate into it. Meantime, we've given Helen an injection of morphine which will help ease her pain.' He turned and smiled at his patient. 'I've already explained this to

Helen herself.'

'Can we visit Helen each day until the decision is made?' Mrs Ford asked him.

'Of course. Helen will be going to Ward 15 where the visiting hours are displayed.'

'Don't worry Helen, we'll get you sorted,' he assured her, as he moved over to examine the patient in the opposite cubicle.

'How are we going to manage, Mum?' Helen asked when he had gone. 'And I'm so sorry Maddie that your weekend visit has proved such a disaster.'

'No, it hasn't. Look, I'm going to stay on here to help your mum.'

'But what about your work?'

'I'll contact Marshall's and tell them I'll take the two weeks' holiday due to me.'

The cubicle curtain was pulled aside and a young nurse appeared. 'Hello, I'm Nurse Anderson. I'm just going to check your blood pressure,' she said to Helen.

'You two go to the canteen,' Helen said to her mother and friend, as the nurse started to place the cuff round her arm. 'I know you had a scone, Mum, but Maddie hasn't had anything since breakfast. I'll be well looked after here, won't I, nurse?'

'You will indeed,' the nurse agreed and turned to Mrs Ford and Maddie. 'It's probably best that you go to the canteen as Helen will be some time yet before she goes to Ward 15.' She glanced at the clock. 'If you come to the ward around eight o'clock you could see her for a few minutes before we settle her down to sleep.'

The two women nodded and did as she suggested, turning as they left the cubicle to blow Helen a kiss.

Chapter Fifty

On Monday morning Maddie used the telephone box near the house to make two important calls. She had to let her office know she would be taking the two weeks' holiday due to her and also needed to tell Viv that she couldn't be at Clarkston after work on Tuesday as normal.

She always had dinner with Viv and the family on a Tuesday, which also allowed her to spend time with Peter and Sara. She loved these kids like they were her own and she selfishly guarded her time with them. Of course Viv always accused her of spoiling them but deep down Maddie knew her best friend was delighted about her close affection for the children.

Armed with lots of loose change, Maddie dialled Marshall's number first, twisting the phone cord in her fingers as she waited for a reply. When Nell, the store's senior telephonist, spoke, Maddie pressed button A and explained the situation. Nell transferred the call directly to the Counting House. After a few rings, Julie from the typing pool answered.

'Hello Julie, Maddie Granger speaking. Is Patricia around?' Maddie had come to rely a great deal on Patricia, who'd proved to be a most efficient secretary. Together she and Patricia made a good team.

'Hello Maddie.' Patricia's chirpy tones rang out across the line.

'Bit of an emergency here, Patricia. I'm in Arbroath with Helen Ford and her mother and I was due to come home today.'

'Yes, you're due back at work tomorrow.'

'Well now I won't be. Poor Helen had a tumble when we were walking on the cliff path. She's broken her ankle and is in hospital in Dundee.'

'Oh, that's awful,' Patricia managed to get in, as Maddie's money ran out. She quickly pushed a two shilling coin, a florin, into the slot before the call was disconnected.

'I'm going to take the two weeks' holiday that's owed to me and stay up here to give Mrs Ford some support. Could you tell everyone who needs to know, Patricia?'

'No problem, Maddie, I'm on to it,' Patricia promised.

'I'm also going to miss the next monthly management meeting. Could you put my apologies in for that too? And will you also give a proxy vote of yes for me about the new work rotas the Directors have proposed?'

'Of course. I'll be there to take the Minutes and will let you know everything that is decided. Don't you worry about anything Maddie, just concentrate on Helen and Mrs Ford.'

'Thanks, Patricia, you're a treasure,' Maddie said, meaning every word. Patricia Harper was someone Maddie knew she could totally depend on to keep things going during her absence in Arbroath. 'And could you let Molly in the canteen know what's happened to Helen? She'll be submitting medical certificates once her holiday period is up.'

'That's fine. Keep me informed of how Helen goes, won't you?'

'Of course I will Patricia. Thanks a lot, bye.'

'Bye,' Patricia replied.

Maddie pressed button B and collected the coins left from that phone call before she dialled Viv's number in Clarkston.

'Oh, hi, Maddie,' Viv said when she heard the familiar voice, 'how was your weekend in Arbroath?'

'I'm still in Arbroath,' Maddie replied and proceeded to repeat the story to Viv.

'I'm sorry we won't see you tomorrow night, Maddie,' Viv said when Maddie drew to a halt, 'but I'm even sorrier for poor Helen and her mum. It's good you'll be there for Mrs Ford. Please give them my best wishes.'

'Will do. Are the kids alright?'

'Yes, growing by the minute and noisy as ever. Peter fell in Rouken Glen yesterday and grazed his knee. He let me clean and dress his wound without crying and I praised him for being a brave soldier. Think he was quite proud of himself.'

The pips sounded again and Maddie shoved her last sixpence into the slot. 'And so he should, brave boy that he is. Tell the kids I'll look forward to seeing them when I get home.'

'They'll be sorry not to see you tomorrow but they can save up all their stories until we see you again.'

'Great. Love to you all.'

Mrs Ford came into the hallway as Maddie returned to the house. 'Have you finished your phone calls, my dear?'

'I have and everything is sorted out so there's no need to worry,' she said to the dear old soul with the snow white hair and lined face. 'We won't be able to visit Helen until this afternoon so what do you say to a stroll into town to the nearest teashop?'

Mrs Ford's face brightened up immediately. 'What a great idea, Maddie. Lead on Macduff,' she said.

*

On Tuesday evening when Mrs Ford and Maddie walked into Ward 15 at visiting time, they were pleasantly surprised to find Helen wide awake after her operation to have a pin inserted earlier in the afternoon. The x-rays had shown that this was necessary and she'd been put on that day's list for surgery.

'Hello,' she waved cheerily from her bed, which was on the right hand side of the ward, the bed nearest the door.

It was a large ward, the walls painted in a soft green shade, the ceiling in white. There were about twelve beds running along both sides of the ward, with the nurses' station to the left of the entrance. As they crossed over to Helen's bed, their shoes squeaked on the dark green linoleum, polished until you could almost see your reflection in it.

Maddie smiled at her friend and kissed her cheek. 'When we phoned they told us your operation had been a success but we certainly didn't expect you to be so wide awake.' She was pleased to see that the sick bowl sitting on the bedside cabinet hadn't been used. Maddie lifted the bedclothes a little and saw Helen's leg was in a plaster cast from her toes up to almost her knee.

'Great to see you awake, Love.' Mrs Ford leaned over and kissed her daughter, holding her hand. 'Are you in any pain?'

'No pain at all,' Helen assured them, 'mind you, I probably still have some anaesthetic in my system.'

'Yes,' Maddie nodded, 'and they'll likely give you some painkillers later to help you sleep.'

'The nurse said that. I'll get them with my cup of tea after visiting is over. Can you pour me some water please, Mum?'

Mrs Ford half-filled the tumbler sitting beside the water jug and Maddie raised Helen's head up off the pillow while the old lady held the glass to her daughter's lips.

Helen took a few sips and sank back down again into her pillow.

Maddie turned her head slightly when she heard a familiar voice coming from the bed directly opposite Helen's, which had the screens closed around it.

'OK Mrs Frame, could you stretch out your arm please? Good,' the voice said encouragingly, 'now will you lay your arm like this? That's great.' She could hear the sound of him squeezing the pump on the blood pressure monitor. 'Good, that's much better this time. We'll check it again in the morning, Mrs Frame.'

Maddie could imagine him smiling at his patient as he spoke. 'Sorry, I was miles away,' she apologised when she realised Mrs Ford had been speaking to her.

'I could see that. I was telling Helen that we found yet another lovely teashop today.'

'Yes. The teacloths on the table were all beautifully hand-embroidered and there was a great variety on the menu. We can take you there once you leave hospital, Helen.'

'The nurse said tomorrow I should be able to sit up in a chair at the side of my bed.'

The screens around Mrs Frame's bed opened and Len

Singleton emerged from behind them. He caught Maddie's glance and she was sure she saw a look of pleasure flicker in his eyes although of course he didn't make it obvious. She liked how professional he was at all times.

'Doctor, do you know when my daughter will be allowed home?' Mrs Ford waylaid him as he was going towards the door.

'If Helen makes a good recovery from her operation, and so far she appears to be doing that, then she could be home by tomorrow. She will need to attend for physiotherapy at some stage though.' He smiled at the old lady and at Helen but didn't turn to Maddie again. 'Now you must excuse me,' he said, patting Mrs Ford's shoulder, 'I've got some other patients to see.'

Chapter Fifty-One

'Helen's boots are safe,' Maddie called to Mrs Ford on Wednesday afternoon when she came up the path. The old lady had been standing at the open door of Birch House while Maddie had gone down to the phone box.

'I asked about Helen's boots and they've been put into the Sister's room.' They'd only discovered the boots had been left behind in Ward 15 an hour after Helen's return to Birch House. Their absence hadn't been noticed earlier because Helen had worn a slipper on her uninjured foot, with the plastered one in a sling contraption given to her by the hospital staff.

'That's great news.' Mrs Ford stood back to let Maddie enter the house before her. 'Helen had to save hard to buy those boots.'

'I told the nurse I spoke to that I'd come to the hospital to collect them.'

'Thanks a lot, Maddie, I don't know what I'd have done without you these past few days. I'll make you a sandwich before you go for the bus.'

'Thanks. I'll pop upstairs to see if Helen is awake so I can give her the good news,' Maddie called back, as she climbed stairs to Helen's bedroom.

*

When Maddie got off the bus outside Dundee Royal Infirmary that afternoon, she took the lift up to Ward 15, where she approached a young student nurse in the entrance hallway to explain her purpose in returning to the ward.

'If you wait here, I'll get the boots from Sister's office for you.' The girl, wearing the pink and white dress that identified her rank, scurried away and returned a few minutes later carrying the boots in a plastic bag. 'I will need to ask you to sign for them.'

'No problem,' Maddie smiled, and duly signed her name against the item on the sheet the nurse produced. She emerged from the ward and made her way along the corridor towards the lifts. She was passing the entrance to Ward 14 on her left when a doctor emerged, reading a set of patient case notes.

The two almost collided. The doctor said 'sorry' absentmindedly and then looked straight at Maddie. Her heart almost stopped; it was Len Singleton.

'Hello again,' he smiled at Maddie, his blush matching her own. 'I hope your friend is alright.'

'Oh she is, thanks, but her boots were left behind when she went home this afternoon,' she said, holding up the plastic bag.

'I do hope she will make progress,' he went on as the two fell into step. 'Are you staying on in Arbroath a bit longer?'

'Yes, I've taken two weeks' holiday from work so that I can help Helen's mum.'

'That's great.' By this time they'd reached the lift Maddie was going to use to go down to the main exit.

'Would you like to go out one night? Maybe to a film or out for a meal?' he said suddenly, taking her by surprise.

'That … that would be lovely,' she stammered, sure that her heart was going to jump right out of her body. She'd never felt like this before.

He beamed at her. 'I wanted to ask you before but it would have been unprofessional while your friend was my patient. I finish early tomorrow so how would tomorrow night suit?'

'That's fine,' she said, smiling at the handsome figure looking down on her from his six foot plus height.

'I could pick you up about seven if you give me your address in Arbroath', he said, taking his diary and pen out of the top pocket of his white coat. 'I could get it from Helen's case notes but it's easier to jot it down now.'

'It's Birch House, Shore Road, Arbroath.'

He wrote it down and put the diary back into his pocket. 'OK, see you tomorrow,' he said, giving her another dazzling smile. 'Sorry I've got to dash now,' he apologised as he vanished around the corner.

As she waited for the lift to arrive, Maddie tried to convince herself that she hadn't dreamed all that happened in the past few minutes.

Chapter Fifty-Two

Maddie could barely conceal her excitement from Helen and her mother as seven o'clock drew near on Thursday evening. They had both been delighted to hear about her date. She'd been trying to keep it low key but, despite her best efforts, she failed to hide her nervous tension.

She spent time over what she'd wear for her date. She rejected a couple of different outfits before plumping for a red flowery cotton skirt and a white gypsy style blouse, its collar and sleeves edged with lace. She wore a set of red glass beads and matching earrings and finished the outfit with medium heeled red sandals and a little red clutch bag. Since moving into Miss Edwards' job in Marshalls, her increase in salary had allowed her more cash to splash out on clothes from the ladies department on the second floor.

'Oh you do look lovely, my dear,' Mrs Ford told her when she went downstairs to the front room to join Helen and her mum. Helen sat in an armchair near the window with her plastered leg resting of a stool. She smiled in admiration when she saw Maddie. 'Wow, you're really going to sweep him off his feet in that outfit Maddie.'

'It isn't too much is it?' Maddie asked anxiously.

'No,' they said in unison.

Mrs Ford caught hold of Maddie's arm. 'It's just right for a lovely summer's night like this. Oh, here's Dr Singleton now,' she said as a car drew up outside the house.

'What a swish car,' Mrs Ford said, looking in awe at the pale blue Ford Anglia.

After a quick farewell to Helen and her mum, Maddie climbed into the passenger seat, while Len held open the door like a true gentleman. 'What a lovely car,' she said, once she was settled inside the vehicle.

'Of course I'd prefer a Merc,' he said, as he got in on the driver's side, 'but this is as much as I can afford on a junior doctor's salary. When it's raining heavily water gets in through the door and I get wet feet. You're all right,' he told Maddie, 'it's my side that leaks.' He held out her seatbelt. 'These belts are optional but, having seen the result of injured people who didn't wear one, I think it's better to use them.'

She clicked her belt into place and turned to wave at Mrs Ford who was still standing at the front door. Len followed the coast road in the direction of Dundee. 'Would you like to go to the cinema or for something to eat?'

'I don't mind,' she said, realising the minute she'd uttered the words what an unhelpful answer it was. But nerves were making her mute. She knew how useless she was at forming relationships and she didn't want to jeopardise this one before it had even started.

'The Sound of Music is showing at the Regal in Broughty Ferry. Have you seen it?'

'No,' she shook her head.

'Neither have I, even although it's been out for a couple of years. But I've heard good reports from friends who've seen it.'

'That sounds good,' was the best she could come up with.

She cursed silently for her short answers, which must sound so feeble to Len. The cinema would be better than a meal she thought. There wouldn't be the need for much conversation at the cinema, unlike if they were sitting together across a table at a fancy restaurant, with her desperately trying to keep his interest with stimulating chat. Also, if it was an up-market type of place, she'd have problems understanding the menu, especially if it was in French, and knowing which cutlery to use. Yes, the cinema was definitely the better option.

'The film doesn't start until half past eight,' his voice broke into her train of thoughts, 'and I know a café quite close to the Regal where we could get a coffee and something to eat. Would a sandwich be sufficient for you?'

'Yes, it would be fine,' she replied, not mentioning that she'd had no dinner before she left and really needed more than that to eat. But a sandwich would be enough to stave off her hunger she decided.

Arriving in Broughty Ferry, he parked at the kerb outside 'The Ferry Café' situated just a few hundred yards from the Regal cinema, which stood on a corner site overlooking the water. 'We could leave the car here after we've eaten and walk along to the Regal,' he suggested.

The café was bright and airy, with the large windows affording a delightful view over the water to Fife. On such a glorious summer evening as this, the visibility was good enough to see the bridges at Dundee in the distance. The original rail bridge over the Tay was the one that she'd read about in John Prebble's book 'The High Girders'; she remembered crying while reading of all the people who lost their lives when the bridge collapsed in stormy conditions.

Quite close to the rail bridge was the recently constructed road bridge, which had been opened last summer by Queen Elizabeth, the Queen Mother. Having been brought up at Glamis Castle, the people of Angus had a real soft spot for the Queen Mum and she was always welcomed to this part of the world.

There were chintz covers on the tables in the café and a single rose vase sat in the centre of each table. The curtains had been pulled back to let the sunlight into the café.

In the event Maddie didn't have to go to the cinema hungry after all. The waitress brought them a massive plateful of sandwiches with various fillings and once they'd scoffed the lot Len ordered them each a portion of home-make apple pie and custard. By the time she was finished, Maddie was full to burst.

Len was very relaxed to be with and Maddie quickly found herself more at ease in his company, allowing the conversation to flow naturally and smoothly, with no awkward silences. Unlike most men she'd known, Len didn't constantly speak about his work and football but discussed lots of other subjects. He had a knowledge of many things and she soaked up all the interesting things he told her. They discovered they had many common interests, including music, walking, swimming and tennis.

She told Len about leaving Bonnycross for Glasgow and how she'd been adopted into Viv's family. Len told her about his home and family in Peebles, near the Scottish borders, and of attending college in Dundee before taking up his present post in Dundee Royal.

'I didn't know there was a University in Dundee.'

'There wasn't when I first came up here. I was enrolled in St Andrew's University but the medical school was in Dundee. But with Dundee University now built, from here on Degrees will be from Dundee. I'm happy though as it's good to have a Degree from St Andrew's on my C.V.'

'And do you like living in Dundee?'

'I do and that's why, once I qualified, I applied for a post in Dundee Royal.' He looked at his watch. 'We better make a move as we still have to buy the cinema tickets,' he said and signalled to the waitress to bring the bill.

The Sound of Music was a long film, based on the life of the von Trapp family from Austria during the Second World War. When Len put his arm round her at one stage and pulled her closer to him, she laid her head against his shoulder, enjoying the contact with him. She also liked the smell of his aftershave, a spicy perfume. She couldn't believe she'd only know him for less than a week; it felt as though he'd been part of her life forever.

'The hills are alive with the sound of music' she sang as they were walking back to the car. 'Sorry,' she apologised, aware of what a tuneless singer she was.

'No need for apologies,' he smiled, as he unlocked the car door for her, 'it's hard to get the tunes out of your head, isn't it?'

The sun was setting by the time they came out of the cinema and by mutual consent Len drove the car down on to the beach, where they sat together in companionable silence to watch the sun finally disappear. They drove back to Arbroath in moonlight. Stopping outside Birch House, Len lowered his lips to Maddie's and she responded immediately. She was breathless when they drew apart and wanted a repeat performance. This is how Viv must have felt when she first met Dave, she thought, and decided the experience had been worth waiting for.

'I'm doing long shifts over the next couple of days but I wondered if you were free on Sunday so that we could make a day of it?'

'Sunday would be alright,' she said, delighted that he wanted to see her again.

'That's great,' he said, treating her to another beaming smile. 'I thought, since we both enjoy walking, we could drive out to the Glens of Angus and walk part of Jock's road.'

'Sounds intriguing. Who was Jock?'

He laughed. 'I don't have a clue but the walk I can recommend.'

'Will I make us up a picnic?'

'Excellent,' he said, 'and I'll treat you to dinner on the way home at a wee hotel I know.'

She smiled, no fears now of menus or cutlery, she thought.

They shared another farewell kiss, then Len waited until Maddie opened the door of Birch House before he turned on the ignition. She waved until the car was out of sight.

The house was in darkness and she crept upstairs, keen not to waken Helen or Mrs Ford. As she undressed for bed, she felt an inner glow. The treatment she'd received at the hands of Benson and all the problems of Steve's addictions receded into the back of her mind. She knew that for the first time in her life she had found true love.

Chapter Fifty-Three

On Sunday morning Maddie wakened to a bright blue sky and barely no wind, an ideal day for walking.

'Can I help you, Mrs Ford?' she asked, when she went into the kitchen to the smell of bacon cooking on the stove and the table laid for breakfast.

'It's all under control thanks, Maddie,' the old lady told her, 'but you could make up your picnic until Helen gets downstairs.'

'Fine, she's combing her hair so she shouldn't be long.' Maddie hummed along to the songs of Oscar and Hammerstein that were playing on the radio while she spread some bread and cheese to sustain Len and her on their walk. She took a couple of Golden Delicious apples and two oranges from the fruit bowl and packed them all into the little picnic basket Helen had brought with them on holiday.

'Make sure you take plenty to drink, Maddie,' Mrs Ford reminded her, 'walking in the countryside can be thirsty work.'

'Will do.' Maddie put a couple of small bottles of apple juice into the basket and filled two plastic containers with water direct from the tap. 'Think this should do us,' she said, closing down the lid of the basket firmly. She left it in the hallway, ready to put into Len's car.

'Good morning,' Helen said, as she came into the kitchen on her crutches. 'What a lovely day you're getting for your walk, Maddie. Just wish I was coming with you.'

'It's such a shame that you can't get out walking, Helen. Such rotten luck too that it happened so early on in the holiday.'

Mrs Ford pulled a chair out from the table for her

daughter. 'Still, in another way, isn't it good that you have some time to recuperate up here, where you can sit outside the house and enjoy the sea air?'

'That's true,' Helen agreed, while her mother walked round to the opposite side of the table and positioned a chair where Helen could rest her plastered foot.

Breakfast over, Maddie and Mrs Ford did the washing up while Helen sat at the table and chatted. Maddie ran upstairs to get a jacket in case the weather turned cooler and she'd barely come down again when there was a toot from the road outside.

'It's Dr Singleton,' Mrs Ford told her, looking out of the window. 'He's certainly a good timekeeper.'

'Have a great time, Maddie,' Helen called after her disappearing figure.

'Thanks, see you later.' And with that, she was gone.

When she got out to the car, Len took the picnic basket from her. 'Probably best we divide the food into our rucksacks so that we can have our picnic up on the moor instead of waiting until we come down to the car again.'

'Good idea,' she said, unzipping her rucksack, 'saves lugging a basket around with us.' As they were doing this, she threw a couple of furtive glances at Len, finding it hard to believe that this handsome, intelligent man was happy to spend time with her. Even once they were on the journey, she still felt she wanted to pinch herself to believe that she wasn't dreaming.

When they arrived at Glen Clova, they left the Ford Anglia in the car park there and set off in glorious sunshine. Hand in hand, they strolled along a tree-lined path, happy to be in one another's company. There was no need for conversation, they just enjoyed being together.

The river coursed its way playfully over the rocky bed at their side, with the bright June sun piercing its way through the trees and casting their shadows before them.

When they reached the entrance to Glen Doll, Maddie held her breath, sure she'd stepped into a picture postcard. Although the heather was not yet in bloom, in another three months the moorland around them would be a blaze of colour. Standing amongst the patchy tufts of grass, Maddie stared wordlessly at the waterfall above them. Appropriately named the White Water, it cascaded down from a cleft in the hills, lathering its forceful way to where they were standing.

Maddie was pulled out of her reverie when Len pointed to a high hill ahead of them. 'That's the track we'll follow,' he said, opening up his map that hung in a plastic bag around his neck. On the map he drew his finger along the route they would take; up the hill, over the top and back down into the valley on the other side.

Maddie turned her amazed eyes on to his beaming face. 'You do realise that the hill we are about to tackle is to me like what Everest must have been to Sir Edmund.'

'Rubbish,' he grinned, 'it'll be like a stroll in the park.'

'If you say so,' she replied, steeling herself for the upward slog.

With Len taking the lead, Maddie clambered behind him over the boulders, often sliding on shale, until near the top her efforts were rewarded when they saw a stag standing erect and regal on the ridge above them.

Len managed to get a photograph of the magnificent creature before it loped away. A minute later a couple of kestrel hawks flew over their heads to descend across the gorge towards the river. Maddie scrambled up to the top, accepting Len's offer of a heave up and they greedily drank from their water containers.

Sitting on the moorland shelf, Maddie stared in wonderment at the sheer drop beneath them, trying to believe they'd really climbed it.

'It was worth the effort for the view, wasn't it?' Len murmured in her ear. She nodded and leaned her head against his shoulder. Her action was spontaneous and Len didn't show any objection to it.

'Is your foot sore?' he asked when she started to untie the lace of her boot.

'It's my toe, I could feel the boot rubbing against it as

I climbed up.' She removed the boot and her socks to reveal her big toe, red and raw.

'Think you need that covered, it's going to bleed if left unprotected,' Len said and took a first aid kit out of his rucksack. He applied some cream to the affected area and placed a plaster over it. 'That should help.'

'Thank you, doctor,' Maddie smiled at him and put her boot on again.

She gazed at the vast heathery wilderness ahead of them. 'I'm looking forward to our trek across the moor. What's that building over there?' she pointed across the gorge to the shelf on the opposite side of the river.

'It's a little bothy that was built following a fatal accident up here back in the late fifties. I can remember reading about the accident in the newspapers at the time.'

'What happened?'

'A group of university students from Glasgow were in this area one New Year. They lost their way in bad weather and died up there in deep snowdrifts. The bothy was built to assist any future walkers who got into trouble.'

'What a sad story,' she mused. 'Are there other bothies?'

'There are bothies in many remote parts of the country. They range from very basic to some that have heaters for warmth and to boil water.'

Maddie hung on Len's words. She loved the sound of his voice; he was so knowledgeable, yet not in a patronising way.

'At least we're lucky with the weather today,' his voice broke into her thoughts. 'I think we should move on though as we have quite a long way to go,' he said, getting to his feet and pulling on his rucksack once more.

They started out across the moorland and after about an hour they stopped in a sheltered spot to eat their sandwiches. They spread a rug on the heather to sit on as the ground was still slightly damp from the previous few days of rain. They luxuriated in the peace and tranquillity around them. Not even a bird disturbed their idyll and Maddie dropped off for a short nap.

When she wakened, Len was lying on the rug beside her, turned on his side, looking down at her. He smiled. 'You look lovely when you are asleep, so peaceful and content.'

She smiled up at him. 'Couldn't be anything else in a place like this.'

He lowered his head and their lips met. Once again Maddie's heart seemed to explode and she curled herself into the fold of his arms.

They lay together like that for ages before Len glanced up at a black cloud that had appeared within the past few minutes. 'Let's go, in case the weather changes.'

As she followed Len across the moor, Maddie tried to drink in the scenery, wishing she could bottle it and take it home with her for future viewing. Lulled into a false sense of security, she allowed a gap to widen between them, although she still had Len in her sights when the accident happened.

Not looking where she was walking, she failed to see the large hole ahead until she plunged right into it. It was full of mud from the previous days' rain and she was sucked down until only her head and shoulders were visible above ground. She clung to the sides of the hole, and yelled Len's name. She prayed she hadn't fallen into quicksand. She was sure quicksand was only found in low-lying marshy ground but her hysteria was such that she couldn't even have been sure of her own name.

By the time Len raced back to her, she was still thrashing about unsuccessfully to throw herself out of the hole. Immediately he removed her mud-encrusted backpack and then grabbed her under the armpits, positioning himself feet apart near the edge of the hole. Her muddy jacket made it difficult to grip her and he hauled for some minutes to no avail. He was panting and out of breath when, with a sucking sound, her feet were at last released from the mud and she was wrenched free to land on top of him at the edge of the hole.

They clung together in total silence until, as one, relief made them burst into laughter. Maddie was in a sorry state; there was mud clinging to the soles of her boots and her trousers were encased in the stuff. But, thankfully, she was otherwise intact. Len cleaned her down as well as he could with the towels they had in their packs.

But it was an impossible task and eventually she had to continue walking as she was. The mud on the soles of her boots made the going slippery for Maddie and she held on to Len's hand for support on their way downhill again. Their descent followed a line of larch trees and she grabbed hold of their thin barks where she could for added support. They both cheered when they caught sight of the Ford Anglia waiting for them in the car park. Maddie slipped her feet out of her muddy boots and took off her waterproof trousers and jacket before getting into the car.

'Just as well I didn't book our table at the hotel until eight o'clock,' Len said as they drove away from Glen Clova. 'We'll have time to get back to Birch House so you can have a bath and a change of clothes.'

'Yes, I certainly couldn't go into a hotel in this state.'

Back at Birch House, Mrs Ford made some tea for Len and he told her and Helen about their exploits while Maddie cleaned herself up.

Helen giggled when Maddie appeared downstairs again, bathed and changed into clean clothes. 'Keep out of mud this time, Maddie.'

'I'll do my best,' Maddie replied, taking Len's arm as the two of them headed off to dinner.

Chapter Fifty-Four

October 1967

The autumn colours were superb when Len and Maddie drove
into Moffat that afternoon, on their way to Peebles to stay with
the Singleton family for the weekend. It was to be Maddie's
first meeting with Len's parents and his sister, Rose, and she
prayed that they'd like her. Whether they did or not wouldn't
make any difference to her feelings for Len, or his for her, but
she'd feel much happier if they accepted her into their midst.

'I love the ram,' she said, looking up at the statue
gracing the main street, looming tall over the cars parked on
either side of it.

'Yes, Moffat is famous for the ram statue, as well as
for Moffat toffee, of course,' Len told her as he drew into a
space being vacated by another driver. 'Let's stop here for a
drink,' he said, switching off the engine.

'It'll be good for you to have a rest from driving too,'
she agreed, as she clambered out of the Ford Anglia, which
she now knew Len had christened Hilda. 'What on earth made
you call it Hilda?' she'd asked, when he first told her.

'No real reason,' he'd shrugged. 'I did once have an
English teacher called Hilda Colquhoun. She was a real
inspiration and I liked her so, since I also like my car, I
decided to call it Hilda.'

'As good a reason as any I suppose.'

Leaving Hilda parked a few cars along from the ram
statue, they found a little café near the Moffat Post Office
where they ordered some coffee and shortbread. 'Delicious,'
was Maddie's verdict on tasting the shortbread.

Afterwards they wandered along both sides of the

street to let Maddie see what shops Moffat had to offer. 'There's a woollen mill that sells tartan goods. It attracts a lot of tourists from down south and from America,' Len told her. 'Next time we're here, if we have more time to spare, we could have a look round the mill if you'd like. I think you can watch some of the staff working at the looms.'

'That would be interesting,' she said, happy to hear Len speak about next time, in a way that assured her theirs was a lasting relationship. 'Maybe I could buy your mother some of the Moffat toffee you mentioned.'

'Oh, she'd love that. Mum has a real sweet tooth.'

They crossed the road to the Moffat Toffee shop to make their purchase before getting back into Hilda, and following the road to Peebles.

'What a lovely town,' Maddie said as they drove straight ahead at the roundabout in Peebles, with the town centre to their left and a large church on their right.

'Yes, I'm biased of course but Peebles is a pretty place to live,' Len agreed as they crossed a bridge over the River Tweed. Leaning forward, Maddie caught her breath at the sight of the trees along the riverbank to her right. A sweep of colour reflecting on the water, the trees multi coloured in their autumn finery.

'Autumn's my favourite season, but I've never before seen such a blaze of colour.'

'It's a popular place for fishermen and photographers. And lots of artists sit down there, working at their easels. You often see that view on calendars too,' Len said, as he turned left and drove along on the opposite side of the river. Further along on the right stood his parents' home. Len reversed up the driveway, with the car facing the river.

'What a view.' Winding down the car window, Maddie gazed at the scene in front of her. The river stretched for miles to her left and right, with a number of exquisitely designed, white painted bridges spanning the River Tweed. On the opposite side of the river was the town with quite a number of church spires pointing up to the blue sky above them. The hills behind the town were clothed in their autumn best and a large building was visible through the trees on the hillside. 'What's that large white building?'

'That's Peebles Hydro Hotel,' a voice said and Maddie turned round in her seat to find Len's mother standing at the front door of the villa, which was appropriately named 'Riverview'. Getting out of the car, Maddie walked towards the older lady, who was wearing a smart pleated tartan skirt and a white blouse with three quarter length sleeves. Her greying hair had been treated to a blue rinse.

'Mum, this is Maddie,' Len said and the two women shook hands.

As Maddie looked into Mrs Singleton's smiling face, her fears disappeared. This woman reminded her of Sheena and immediately made Maddie feel welcome.

'Lovely to meet you, Maddie. Len's told us lots about you. All good,' she smiled, seeing the serious look that passed across her visitor's face. 'You get Maddie's case out of the car, Len, and I'll put on the kettle for a cup of tea. I bet you could do with a drink, Maddie.'

'We stopped in Moffat for a coffee,' she told Mrs Singleton as the older woman stood aside to let Maddie enter the house first. 'But I'll still enjoy a cup of tea now.' She handed her hostess the box of Moffat toffee. 'Len told me you like this toffee, Mrs Singleton.'

'Thank you, Maddie, I love Moffat toffee. And the name's Myra.'

Len appeared in the wide entrance hall behind them, carrying their luggage. 'Put the luggage into your rooms, Len, and Maddie can have a seat in the lounge until I fetch the tea tray,' his mother instructed, before bustling away towards the back of the house.

Maddie wandered into the lounge, a huge room with comfortable brown leather settees and armchairs placed around a beautiful marble fireplace. A grand piano stood at the far corner of the room with silver framed photographs sitting on it; one of them Len at his Graduation. The curtains were the last word in luxury. Maddie moved over to the large picture window, her feet sinking into the deep carpet pile as she did so, to gaze yet again at the view over the river to the hills behind the town.

'Dad always says that view would sell this house.' When she turned round, Len was standing behind her. He folded her into his arms, rubbing his cheek against hers. When Myra came into the room Maddie moved to a seat while Len helped his mother with the tray.

'Dad and Rose are playing golf this afternoon but they're looking forward to meeting Maddie on their return,' Myra told them as the three of them were enjoying a cup of tea and some of her home-made gingerbread.

'Is Rose staying all weekend?' Len asked, passing the crystal butter dish to Maddie.

'No, she'll stay for dinner and then head home for her swimming competition tomorrow.'

Myra stirred a spoonful of sugar into her tea as she was speaking. Maddie noticed the sugar spoon had a crest on it and looked like solid silver in contrast to the crested ones that her mum used to buy on her occasional trips to the seaside. She pulled herself back to the present when she heard Myra speaking to her. 'My daughter is a keen swimmer and trains hard in the hope that she might be able to compete in next year's Olympics in Mexico.'

'Even if Rose doesn't make it to Mexico,' Len said, 'she should be able to compete in the Commonwealth Games in Edinburgh in 1970.'

'Len was telling me that Rose lives in Edinburgh,' Maddie said to Myra.

'Yes, she's a lawyer in the Capital. It took up a lot of time travelling back and forward to work from here so she bought a flat in Morningside six months ago.'

Maddie was helping to clear away the tea things, when there was a crunching of tyres on the driveway. 'That'll be the golfers back,' Myra said, and took the tray away.

Maddie was standing beside Len near the window when Mr Singleton came into the hallway, lugging his bag containing his golf clubs. From her place near the window Maddie saw Rose stow her clubs into the back of her

Volkswagen fastback.

'That's Rose's new car,' Len said at her side, 'I'm hoping to afford a similar car one of these days. Meantime, Hilda does fine.'

'She sure does, I've become really fond of Hilda,' she told him, then looked towards the door as Mr Singleton came into the room.

'Pleased to meet you, my dear,' he said, shaking her hand warmly. 'Len's been keeping you a secret for too long.'

'Nice to meet you too, Mr Singleton.'

'Norman's the name,' he said. 'Let's not stand on ceremony.'

'Well, I guess this is Maddie we're meeting at last,' Rose's voice boomed out loudly as she followed her father into the sitting room. She shook hands with Maddie and smiled at her pleasantly but Maddie had the distinct impression that Rose was taking in every detail of her appearance. Perhaps she's deciding if I'm good enough for her wee brother, she thought.

'How did the game go?' Len asked.

Rose slapped her brother on the back in a rather masculine way. 'I won of course but Dad accepted defeat well, especially when we got to the nineteenth hole.'

Maddie was about to say she thought there were only eighteen holes on a golf course when she remembered Charlie once telling her that the nineteenth hole meant the bar at the end of the game. Thank goodness she'd remembered in time and hadn't made a fool of herself.

On the whole, the evening went well and after dinner they had a game of cards before Rose took herself off back to Edinburgh. She and Len seemed to get on quite well although Maddie didn't feel that, as siblings, they shared a lot in common.

On Sunday morning she and Len went to church with his parents. It was the church at the roundabout that Maddie had noticed when they'd first arrived in Peebles.

She enjoyed the hymn singing and got a lot out of the minister's sermon. The service reminded her of how far she'd drifted away from organised religion, although she still classed herself as a believer. After a light lunch at 'Riverview', she and Len took themselves off for a drive so that he could show her some of his old haunts.

When they returned about five o'clock, Myra had dinner prepared. The four of them shared some pleasant conversation over the meal, after which Maddie and Len set off so that he could drop Maddie off at her flat in Rutherglen before driving back to Dundee.

'I've had a lovely time and it was good to meet your parents,' she told Len on their homeward journey.

'Yes, you all seemed to get on well, Maddie. I'm pleased about that,' he said, lifting his hand off the steering wheel for a moment to lay it over hers. 'How did you get on with dear old Rose?'

'I found her a bit difficult to talk to but I guess things were alright between us.'

'Don't worry about her, she takes a bit of getting used to. You'll have guessed that she's a lesbian. She prefers women to men,' he explained when Maddie looked at him blankly. Maddie blushed, feeling foolish; she'd known about men called homosexuals but hadn't been aware until now that there were women attracted to their own sex too.

'Rose is a bit of a snob,' Len continued, once he'd given Maddie time to digest what he'd just told her, 'but she's got a kind heart and is very loyal once she gets to know you.' He squeezed Maddie's hand, then put his own hand back on the steering wheel as he came to a junction where he needed to change gear.

They sat quietly for the rest of the journey, each happy with their own thoughts. Maddie now and again turned her head to look at her beloved Len's profile, trying to believe that this fantastic man really did love her, Maddie Granger. She smiled to herself at the irony of the situation. She, who had always ridiculed the notion of love at first sight, had now done just that.

At that moment, sitting there in the fast descending darkness, with the car radio playing softly, Maddie admitted to herself that Len Singleton was the man she wanted to spend the rest of her life with.

Chapter Fifty-Five

April 1968

Everything happened quickly once Maddie and Len discovered they were in love and by Christmas they were engaged. Thinking of that wonderful day, Maddie held out her left hand to watch the emerald and two diamond stones on her engagement ring sparkle in the sunlight pouring through her bedroom window at Fairfields. The ring had cost practically all of Len's savings but he'd insisted on buying it. He was keen that she get the ring she preferred to all the others they looked at.

And now, four months on, it was their wedding day. She felt so different about today's wedding compared to the charade she'd gone through with Steve. Marriage to him had taught her one thing; never again would she marry without love. But this time it was for keeps; she couldn't imagine not having Len in her life and knew he felt the same about her.

The Singletons would have liked a big, expensive do, which they'd offered to pay for. Maddie and Len had different ideas though and they were determined to have the small, personal wedding that they both craved. At two o'clock, therefore, she and Len would be in St Luke's Church to be declared husband and wife together by the same minister who'd officiated at Viv and Dave's wedding. The party afterwards would be held here at Fairfields, the place where Maddie had spent the happiest times of her life.

Sheena and Charlie had done all the arranging, although Sheena had consulted Myra Stapleton over the catering, to which she and Norman had generously contributed.

Maddie would wear the ivory coloured calf-length dress Sheena had made for her. The dress was in a classical A-style design and enhanced her figure. A sprig of orange blossom would decorate her hair. Maddie's three adopted sisters were her attendants; Viv in a lilac dress, while the twins had chosen a deep pink shade for theirs. The stars of the show, however, were definitely going to be young Peter and Sara. Peter would be wearing a Royal Stewart kilt as page boy and flower girl Sara had insisted on having an ivory coloured dress, the same as Auntie Maddie's. Len had asked his old school friend, Tom, to be his best man and they too would be dressed in kilts.

Maddie and Len had kept the guest list short. Six people were coming from the Singleton side, including Rose and her friend/partner, Stella. Half a dozen of Sheena and Charlie's close friends were included and Len had invited four of his colleagues from work. Maddie had asked Helen and her mum and Patricia Harper with her latest boyfriend, Trevor. Maddie had heard on the Marshall's grapevine that Patricia had by now broken off her affair with Eric Chalmers, the store manager, although she and Patricia had never discussed it directly.

Still seated on the bed, Maddie glanced at the clock on the bedside table. Len would be leaving Peebles about now with his parents and Tom. She jumped up, aware that she'd better get her skates on if she wanted to arrive at the church on time. She was singing 'Get me to the church on time' when Viv called to her from the hallway. 'Maddie, do you want some help in there?'

'Yes please.'

'Right, be in a mo.'

Maddie slipped out of her towelling dressing gown, which she'd donned after her bath, and began to put on her new satin underwear. Over the last few months she'd cut down on her portion sizes at meals in an attempt to shed a few extra pounds. She stood now and admired her new shape, dressed in satin briefs and bra, in front of the full-length mirror. Yes, missing out on all these cakes and biscuits in between meals had certainly paid off and she patted her slimmed down stomach.

Viv came into the bedroom and stopped short when she saw Maddie standing in front of the mirror. 'Wow, love the sexy undies.' Her eyebrows arched in approval.

'As long as Len appreciates them too,' Maddie said, as she wriggled into her tights.

Viv put on her pretend 'I am shocked' face, then burst out laughing.

'What are you two up to in there?' Charlie called as he passed the bedroom. 'Come and share the joke with the rest of us.'

Viv opened the door a crack and peered out. 'Sorry Dad,' she winked at him, 'you're too young to understand.'

'Can you help me with my underskirt?' Maddie asked, once her giggles had subsided.

Taking care not to disturb Maddie's hairdo, Viv dropped the satin underskirt over her shoulders. 'Now for the dress,' she said, and handed Maddie a chiffon scarf to lay over her hair, while the dress was being pulled on. Then Viv stood back to admire the picture Maddie made once the dress was on and zipped up.

'Fantastic, he'll be bowled over.'

Lastly Viv handed Maddie her posy of delicate shaded roses. The bridesmaids had similar posies and young Sara had a smaller version.

When the cars arrived, the wedding party departed in stages, with Charlie and Maddie travelling in the last car.

*

It was just after eight when the happy couple arrived at their honeymoon destination, Ailean Chraggan Hotel at Weem, near Aberfeldy. Perthshire was looking its best in the spring evening sunshine when they drove into the hotel car park. The white-washed hotel, standing up on a little hillock off the road, was small and intimate. Mrs Morrison, the hotel owner, greeted them in the hallway and, after they signed the register, she showed them to their room. It was a bright and airy front-facing room and looked towards Poplar Avenue, a tree lined road which stretched for almost a mile towards the neighbouring, larger town of Aberfeldy.

'I've given you our best room, with the most attractive view,' Mrs Morrison said, smiling at them both in turn. 'Now can I offer you something to eat and drink after your journey?'

'No, thank you,' they said in unison.

'We ate on the way here,' Len lied, hoping he sounded convincing.

'Fine, if you're sure,' she said and turned towards the door. Then she stopped for a moment, with her hand on the doorknob. 'I'll wish you goodnight then and breakfast is served in the dining room downstairs between half past seven and nine o'clock.'

'Thank you.' They again spoke in unison and as soon as Mrs Morrison had gone, they fell on to the bed laughing.

'I wanted to say to her forget the food, missus, we just want to get into bed,' Len said when his laughter had subsided. He kissed Maddie's neck and his lips made their way down towards her cleavage, his passion at boiling point.

'You randy devil,' she murmured, undoing his tie and starting to open his shirt buttons. 'If you'd said that you might have given poor Mrs Morrison a heart attack. Then you'd have needed to give her mouth to mouth resuscitation and I'd have been jealous.'

She stopped speaking when her new husband found his way into her satin underwear, undoing her bra at the back. Seconds later they were as naked as the day they were born. Over the past few months, they'd both been fired up on many occasions but had managed to keep a lid on their desires, keen to make their wedding night special. Now that night was here and they were relishing every second of it.

'Was it alright for you, Darling?' Len asked, once their union had been consummated and his breathing was steady once more.

'Wonderful. But I'm like Oliver Twist, I want more,' she whispered, her eyes aglow as she played with the hair at the back of his neck.

'Don't know if I have the energy, but I'm willing to

have a damned good try,' he said and began to caress her once more.

*

After a hearty Scottish breakfast, they went, on Mrs Morrison's recommendation, to the Birks o' Aberfeldy. 'There's a bench overlooking the waterfall where Rabbie Burns is said to have composed one of his most famous works,' she told them proudly.

Part way up the forest track, their path was blocked by a fallen tree trunk. Len's long legs climbed easily over the gnarled old trunk and he held out his hand to his new wife.

'Give me your hand, Darling,' he said, and he grasped Maddie's hand firmly, his other hand under her elbow as he helped her over the obstacle. 'Let's rest here and have a drink,' he suggested, noticing Maddie's cheeks were flushed with the effort of clambering up the Birks.

Using the tree trunk as a bench seat, they gulped some water from their flasks. Because it was such a hot day, they'd removed their anoraks at the start of their climb and tied them round their waists so the jackets now afforded them some padding from the rough knots in the trunk.

'Glad we took Mrs Morrison's advice about coming here,' Len said, looking up at the huge trees above their heads, so tall you had to crane your neck to see their tops.

'It's magnificent, and so quiet, although I wouldn't like to fall down there.' Maddie's gaze fell on the steep gorge to their left down to the valley.

'No, wouldn't fancy your chances of surviving that,' Len agreed, throwing his arm protectively around Maddie's waist.

'I'm sure Mrs Morrison knows we're just married,' Maddie remarked, once she'd satisfied her thirst and put her flask back into her rucksack. She leaned her head on Len's shoulder and closed her eyes, drinking in the forest sounds and smells around her.

Len didn't reply immediately, content to sit and draw his fingers through her fringe. 'I think the fact that we looked at one another when she asked if we drank tea or coffee at breakfast was a dead giveaway. As an old married couple we'd have known what we each preferred.'

'Mind you,' she reminded him, 'the confetti that fell out of your trouser turn-ups was probably more revealing. I bet you left a trail of confetti across the hallway last night.'

'Och, she'll be used to honeymooners at the hotel. It's a perfect little place off the beaten track as a honeymoon hideaway.' They sat together in silence for some time, each content to be so close to the other and to drink in the beauty around them.

Len was first to break their idyll. 'It's such a beautiful spot,' he sighed, 'see the way the trees are forming an arch above us, looks as though we are about to walk through a green tunnel.' He got to his feet, pulling Maddie up beside him and kissed her. 'Come on, lazy bones, race you to the top,' he challenged and by the time they reached the top of the Birks they were both panting for breath.

They dropped on to a grassy spot under the trees and lay there until their breathing became more even. 'I love you, Len Singleton,' she turned and smiled at him.

'And I'm crazy for you, Maddie Singleton, and I want to make mad, passionate love to you right this minute.'

She sniggered. 'Well that's one idea you can forget about, lover boy, I like my comfort don't forget.'

'Right,' he grinned and pulled her to her feet. 'There's only one thing for it. We need to get down to Hilda again tout suite and head back to the hotel so that I can have my evil way with you missus.'

Chapter Fifty-Six

June 1968

His soft tones drifting through from the kitchen radio, Jim
Reeves serenaded Maddie with 'Welcome to My World' as
she placed the stepladders close to the bay window to hang her
new curtains. With today being her day off, she'd taken the
opportunity to get things done in this new home she and Len
had purchased a few weeks before their wedding in April.
She'd bought the curtains in Marshall's sale and they were the
finest quality Sanderson in gold and pale green shades. Once
they were hooked up under the pelmet and she'd sorted them
out to her satisfaction, Maddie stood back in the middle of the
room. Yes, they looked good against the heavily embossed
cream wallpaper they'd chosen. Deciding now was a good
time for a break, she made a milky coffee and cut a slice of
Sheena's home-made fruit bread, then returned to the front
room to admire her curtains while she drank her coffee.

Following their engagement last Christmas, they'd
made no firm decision about where to live after their marriage
but it was made for them early in the New Year, when Len
was offered a more senior post in general surgery at the
Victoria Infirmary in Glasgow. Maddie was overjoyed as,
although she liked Dundee well enough, she felt the people
that mattered in her life all lived in the Glasgow area. It also
meant she didn't have to give up her work in Marshall's, a job
she really enjoyed, so that was another plus.

Then had come their hunt for a suitable house. In
February they'd seen this five-apartment, semi-detached at No
28 Mavis Crescent in Kings Park up for sale and within two
weeks it was theirs.

'Apart from some decorating, there isn't a lot that needs doing to it and it will be a great family house for us,' had been Len's verdict after their first viewing.

'Yes,' she'd agreed, as keen as he was that they would be blessed with children, 'and it's good that the houses in the Crescent aren't all identical.' There were semis like theirs, some were terraced properties, with bungalows at the opposite end of the Crescent from No 28.

She took her mug back to the kitchen, a long, galley-shaped room which they'd decorated in pale blue and grey, with blue and white checked curtains on both windows, one on either side of the back door. The next task on her list was to mop the kitchen and bathroom floors. She did the kitchen floor first, leaving the window open wide to allow it to dry. Upstairs, she threw open the window in the large square bathroom and began to mop the linoleum tiles.

Once she'd completed all the chores on her list, Maddie soaked for a long time in the bath and washed her hair before she got out again. It was still a hot day so, when her hair was dry, she slipped into a pair of seersucker trousers and a new white top with a boat-shaped neck, to await Len's arrival home from work.

A couple of hours later, Len walked in the front door to an appetizing smell coming from the kitchen. 'Dinner will be ready soon,' Maddie called to him from the kitchen as he came into the hallway, 'but the oven is switched off so that we'll have time for a pre-dinner drink first.'

She came out of the kitchen and straight into his embrace. She clung to him, feeling as if she hadn't seen him for years instead of only at breakfast time this morning.

'You smell fantastic,' Len whispered, caressing her freshly washed hair. 'I can think of something much more satisfying than a drink,' he said, his voice hoarse with emotion. He smiled down at her and raised his eyebrows.

She smiled back as she took his hands and let him lead the way upstairs.

Chapter Fifty-Seven

July 1969

'Maddie, come and see this Darling,' Len called from the living room as Maddie was mashing the potatoes for their meal. She removed the potato masher and popped her head round the living room door where Len was watching the television news.

'It's amazing,' he said, 'who'd ever have imagined we'd be watching men walking on the moon. You could even hear them chatting and one of them was singing.'

'Fantastic,' she agreed and disappeared back into the kitchen. She smiled at his enthusiasm even though she was unable to share it. Science had been a subject she'd had little interest in at school, doing it only under sufferance, and she still couldn't get excited about the men walking on the moon. What is wrong with the earth we're all currently living on, she asked herself? She smiled again, aware that if science had depended on people such as her, the men would never have got off the ground, never mind reaching the moon.

The news had finished by the time they settled down to their dinner, during which Len told her about his day and of a particularly difficult operation they'd dealt with in the late morning. 'Any ideas for a holiday this year?' Len asked later when they were between the dessert and the coffee stage of their meal.

Maddie shook her head. 'Have you? Don't think they're doing trips to the moon yet.'

'Not yet, but meantime I wondered about us visiting some of the islands during our holidays.'

'Sounds interesting. Had you a particular one in mind?'

'Well, I've only been to two islands so far, Skye and Mull. No, I've actually been to three, I forgot about Iona. I crossed over from Mull to Iona one time. What about you?' He stretched out and caressed her hand as he was speaking.

'Apart from the Clyde islands, like Arran and Bute, none at all.'

'I picked up some leaflets from the Tourist Board yesterday,' he said, getting up from the table to find the brochures in his brief case. He opened them up and placed the page with the map in front of Maddie. Then he moved his chair round to her side of the table so that they could look at it together. 'I wondered about exploring the Outer Hebrides. See here,' he pointed to the islands on the map, 'North Uist, Benbecula, South Uist, Eriskay and Barra.'

'But could we visit all these islands on one holiday?'

'Yep, easily, they aren't so very big and they are linked. There's a short ferry crossing from South Uist to Eriskay and a slightly longer crossing to Barra. I thought if we stayed in a bed and breakfast place in South Uist, then we could travel either north or south to the other islands.'

'Would we take Hilda?'

'We could, although it will probably be expensive to take the car over on the ferry from Oban but we could investigate that. Certainly it would be good with the car to get around, especially as we don't know how good a bus service there will be on the islands. So, what do you think, Darling?'

His enthusiasm was infectious. How could she not want to go? 'Count me in,' she said, the excitement in her eyes mirroring his own.

Chapter Fifty-Eight

August 1969

By the time the holiday came round, Hilda had become Hilda II as Len had finally traded in his beloved Ford Anglia for a spanking new Triumph Herald. The Anglia had been starting to create problems and, more importantly, large bills, so it had seemed wiser to trade it in and put some of their savings towards a new car.

Hilda II was a mustard colour and the upholstery inside was a soft green shade. Best of all, in Len's estimation, it had a sunshine roof. This was just a square that had been cut out of the roof and replaced with a sliding glass panel but Len was like a boy with a new toy. He had plans to drive about in good weather with the roof open but the more pessimistic Maddie wondered if the weather would ever be warm enough to use it. However, she kept her own counsel, not wanting to burst his bubble of happiness.

On a sunny day in Oban they boarded the car ferry 'Spirit of the Hebrides', which steamed its way through the Sound of Mull. From the deck, Len pointed to a castle they were passing. 'That's Duart Castle on Mull. I visited it a few years ago. I'll take you there sometime,' he promised, smiling down at her as they stood at the ship's rail, their anorak hoods up against the strong wind.

They prised themselves away to go down to the restaurant where they ate a hearty meal of haddock, chips and mushy peas, before returning to the deck to view the marvellous scenery.

Len pointed over to their right. 'That's the Cuillin mountains on Skye you can see in the distance,' he shouted above the ferocity of the wind.

'They look ominous, sort of dark and mysterious.' Her voice was swept away on the gale but Len nodded, understanding what she'd said.

'I've done some climbing in the Cuillins,' he yelled back at her, 'but they're not for the faint-hearted.'

'Which islands are they?' Maddie asked, pointing in the direction of two islands that from here looked fairly close to mainland Skye.

Len shook his head, then signalled to her that they should move round to the other side of the ship where it was more sheltered. 'I'm not entirely sure what islands they are,' Len said, once they could hear one another speak. He got out the map and they both held on to it tightly to avoid it blowing away in the strong gusts. 'There's Skye,' he indicated on the map, 'so I'd guess these two are Rum and Canna.'

It was fortunate that the sea remained calm during their Hebridean crossing as they both confessed to being poor sailors in rough waters. They sailed past the island of Barra on their journey to South Uist. 'That's Kisimul Castle we're passing,' Len told Maddie.

'God, it's impressive,' she said, staring at the giant edifice that seemed to dwarf the ferry they were on.

'I've read it's the only surviving medieval castle in the Western Isles. See how it stands on its own little island away from the town of Castlebay. If we visit Castlebay while we're on the islands, we could sail over to the castle. We'd only be on the boat a few minutes.'

They stayed at the rail, arm in arm, as the 'Spirit of the Hebrides' neared Lochboisdale. On this summer's evening, the steamer and its passengers were bathed in a rich golden sunset. They'd removed their anoraks when the wind died down and now wore short sleeved garments only; Len in a t-shirt and Maddie a blouse.

They returned to the car when so directed by an announcement that came over the loudspeaker and once off the ferry they drove the short distance to the guest house they'd booked on South Uist.

*

'Are you sure you don't want a cooked breakfast?' Mrs McNeill, the owner of 'Ferryview', asked the following morning. She stood at the table beside Len's chair. 'A good breakfast keeps you going during the day.'

Len looked up at the middle-aged lady and smiled at her, a smile that Maddie had noticed went down well with older folks. 'It's very kind of you to offer, Mrs McNeill, but we don't eat cooked breakfasts. You don't want one, do you Darling?' he turned to Maddie.

Maddie shook her head and looked over at their landlady. 'I don't eat much in the morning, Mrs McNeill, I'm happy with a bowl of cereal and a slice of toast.'

'Well, if you're sure,' Mrs McNeill said in her beautiful highland accent, almost as though she was singing the words. But she still didn't look convinced about them eating such a meagre breakfast. 'I'll bring you a pot of tea with your toast.'

'That's highland hospitality at its best,' Len whispered after Mrs McNeill had gone off to the kitchen.

When she returned with the tea, Maddie and Len were discussing where they'd spend their first day on the islands.

'We could drive up through Benbecula and North Uist today,' Len was saying. 'Are the islands linked by road?' he asked the landlady.

'Yes, you'll drive over a couple of causeways but they're fine for cars and you won't find a lot of traffic around.'

Maddie lifted her serviette and sat back as Mrs McNeill laid her cereal plate in front of her. 'Are there any places you'd recommend we visit, Mrs McNeill?'

'There are some fine walks in North Uist but not a lot else,' the elderly lady said with a smile, 'and if you watch carefully you might see some otters. Benbecula has a military base and an airport too; a couple of planes a day come in.'

'What are the beaches like?' Maddie wanted to know.

'Alright but there are prettier beaches on Eriskay and Barra and here in South Uist too. We've also got the Flora MacDonald museum at Milton and there's an ancient Broch near here that you might want to see.'

'There's an airport on Barra too, isn't there? Len asked her, as he spread marmalade on to his toast.

'There is indeed and you can watch the plane landing on the beach. Now, if you'll excuse me I'll go and get the bedrooms done. Enjoy your day and I'll leave you to finish your breakfast in peace.'

*

'Let's stop off at the Broch Mrs McNeill was telling us about,' Len suggested, as they were making their way north from South Uist towards Benbecula. 'And we can visit the museum at Milton too.'

'Yep,' Maddie agreed, singing 'Puppet on a String' along with Sandie Shaw on the car radio. It was the song which won the Eurovision Song Contest for Britain a couple of years ago. 'It's such a catchy tune,' she said when the song finished.

Len was concentrating on making a left turn at the sign pointing to the Broch. He parked a short distance down the track and they walked the rest of the way. The Broch dated back centuries and they wandered around the ruins of what had once been home to an Iron Age family. 'You can tell that our ancestors were much smaller when you see the height of the rooms, or what's left of them,' Len remarked.

'Right,' Maddie said, when they'd explored all there was to see in the Broch, 'what about finding the museum now?'

They parked Hilda II outside the museum and went inside to have a look round.

Maddie stood beside Len as they read the history of Milton farm. 'I'm surprised to learn that Flora MacDonald was born on South Uist. I always thought she came from Skye.'

'Same here. There's what the old farm looked like when Flora was living here,' Len drew Maddie's attention to the nearby picture.

They drove north and a short time later Maddie saw a sign saying Benbecula at the side of the road. 'We might see some of the otters Mrs McNeill told us about. Oh look,' she said excitedly, 'this little bridge we are coming to is called

Otter Crossing.'

The sun came out sufficiently to allow them to drive through Benbecula with the roof open and Maddie enjoyed the soft breeze on her face. She looked at the tourist guide. 'It says here that the tune 'The Dark Island' was written by a resident of Benbecula so I guess that's the island's claim to fame.'

'Is that the song the Alexander Brothers sing?'

'Yep. Oh look Len, there's an otter,' she told him, as she saw the top part of its head poke up out of the water at her side of the car. He slowed the car, leaving the engine idling, while his eyes followed where she was pointing. They watched the otter bob up and down a few times before finally disappearing beneath the water.

'Look at that sign,' she said further on and Len again stopped the car. 'Dinna chuck bruck,' it said, the picture of a hand throwing waste into a refuse bin being all the translation that was needed. 'This requires a picture,' Len said, getting out of the car with his camera.

North Uist was almost as flat as Benbecula. It was covered with peat bogs, low hills and lochans. They visited the museum in the main town of Lochmaddy, a fishing port. By the time they came out of the museum, the sky had darkened again and it looked like it was about to rain so they started their journey back to South Uist. They arrived back at 'Ferryview' as the heavens opened and they stayed in their bedroom until the shower passed.

*

'When I'm lonely, dear white heart,
Black the night and wild the sea,
By love's light, my foot finds,
The old pathway to thee.'

Len and Maddie belted out the words of the Eriskay Love Lilt as they drove down a narrow road on the island the following day.

'Bheir me o, horo van o,
Bheir me o, horo van ee,
Bheir me o, o horo ho,
Sad am I, without thee.'

A short time later, Maddie spotted a sign in both English and Gaelic. 'To Bonnie Prince Charlie's Beach', she read out. 'Do you think Prince Charlie landed here in 1745?'

'It's possible, nobody can either prove or disprove it.' Len opened the roof of the car. 'Stand up on the seat and you can take a picture while we're driving.' She did as he suggested, focusing Len's instamatic camera on the view opening up before them. The virgin white sandy beach was surrounded by heather-clad hills.

'Careful,' she yelled, as the wheels of the Triumph bumped over a huge hole in the track and flung her against the roof opening.

'Sorry, Darling,' he took his hand off the steering wheel to steady her. 'Didn't see that big crater coming. There are more holes than road here.' He put his foot on the brake gently and stopped the car to allow Maddie to press the shutter button and capture the scene. 'I think this is as close to the beach as we can drive so let's leave the car here and walk the rest,' Len suggested.

Arm in arm they strolled down the grassy bank and on to the white sand. With Len's arm around her shoulders, Maddie looked across the water to the hills opposite and hummed the Eriskay Love Lilt once more, tears of happiness streaming down her face as she did so.

*

On the last day of their holiday, they took the ferry crossing in brilliant sunshine to Barra, the most southerly of the five islands.

Barra lived up to all their expectations and they were lucky enough to see the midday plane descend on to the beach. About half a dozen people got out of the plane, a couple of them carrying a case. As Len and Maddie hadn't brought the car over to Barra, they got on the same single decker bus as the plane passengers and travelled to the main town on the island, Castlebay.

They enjoyed a light lunch in the Isle of Barra hotel in Castlebay and afterwards took the short sail over to Kisimuil

Castle, the stronghold of the McNeill Clan.

Back at 'Ferryview' they spent their last overnight and in the morning after an early breakfast, they said their farewell to Mrs McNeill before boarding the 'Spirit of the Hebrides' again, bound for Oban.

'I hope we can return again sometime,' Maddie voiced both their thoughts when they were sailing out of Lochboisdale harbour.

'We will.' Len stood behind her on the deck and wound his arms around her waist. 'Let's go to a different island each summer until we've visited them all.'

Chapter Fifty-Nine

December 1969

Maddie's mind was in a fog when she wakened, engulfed in an eerie silence. She hung suspended on her seat belt and her breath came in short, painful gasps. She had a vague memory of a loud bang followed by the crushing sound of metal against metal.

A voice broke the silence. 'Just hold on, I'll get you out.'

She turned her head as far as she could towards the man peering in at her through the space that had once been the car window. He was wearing a tall black hat and with his gloved hand on the handle, he wrenched the door open. The hinges creaked in protest and some of the snow lying on the roof of the car loosened, powdering his black coat.

He stared at her without speaking until she forced herself to turn away from his gaze. Had she died and gone to Hell? Hadn't she always been told as a child in Sunday school that white was for folk who made it to Heaven.

Her focus now fell on to the flap of the glove compartment hanging open. Then her gaze lowered to the glass particles that littered the carpet. They sparkled up at her and lying upside down in their midst was an empty Black Magic box, the contents scattered around her feet. A chocolate sat close to the toe of her boot. It was a long narrow-shaped sweet with an even thinner tail and she recognised it as the orange cream.

'I wasn't ready to die yet,' she wailed through parched lips.

'You aren't dead,' the black-hatted spectre told her, his breath wafting over her as he spoke. It wasn't cold but the warm breath of someone alive. 'You've been thrown against the gear box and injured your leg. I'm going to try and help you out of the car.'

She touched her leg and winced; the wound was open, red and weeping, blood forming a roadway down the outside of her limb. Her skirt was slit open and her tights were hanging in tatters around her bare legs. Slowly, she drew a hand down each of her arms, one at a time. All seemed intact.

'Help me, help me.' The weak murmuring at her side made her turn towards the driver's seat. She tried to move towards the sound but was imprisoned by her seat belt. Her memory pushed through the fog; of course, it was Len, her husband. He was still alive, thank God.

'Len,' she responded to his cry, as she was lifted out of the car seat, screaming from the pain in her leg, and held between two tall men. The man who'd already spoken to her was on her right while, supporting her on the left, was another man, bare-headed, with the collar of his black coat pulled up around his neck. Looking down, she saw that the feet of her knee-length boots were hidden by the snow, with only the upper part of the boots visible above the snowline. When the man on her left shifted his position slightly, the impacted snow crunched loudly under his weight.

She closed her eyes to ease the pounding in her head. The two men carried her over to a nearby car and bundled her into the back seat. 'George here is going to drive you to hospital,' the man in the black hat told her, clicking her seatbelt into place. As she looked up into his face, she noticed for the first time the flakes of snow sticking to his bushy eyebrows.

'Len ... my husband,' she said, her aching ribs causing her to gasp between words.

'Don't worry, your husband's in good hands. The ambulance will be here soon,' the man assured her and closed the door with a bang, once again sending another flurry of snow down off the roof. Then he stood back as the driver started up the engine and the car slid over the icy surface, the wheels juddering on the piles of frozen slush at the side of the road. Once on the road proper, the driver went as quickly as he dared. Coming from the opposite direction, an ambulance passed them, blue light flashing and siren sounding, going towards the crash scene.

'Who are you?' For the first time she noticed the woman in the front passenger seat.

'I'm Ellen, and George here is my husband.' The black feathers on the woman's hat wafted about as she turned round to smile at their passenger in the back. Receiving no response, Ellen fell silent again and peered ahead into the frozen landscape.

They crawled along for a few minutes more, then there was a clanking noise as the tyres came into contact with the hard, impacted surface below them. They came to a grinding halt, the tyres spinning beneath them. 'Damn.' George got out and slithered round to the passenger side.

Ellen wound down her window. 'Are we stuck, George? Do you need a hand?'

'No, stay where you are,' he replied.

Maddie shivered when she felt the icy blast as George opened the boot of the estate car. A couple of minutes later she heard the scraping of a shovel on the hard snow. He was flushed and sweating by the time he got back into the car.

'The man wearing the black hat?' Maddie asked, taking up her previous conversation with Ellen as the car moved forward again.

Ellen turned round again to face her. 'Mr Morgan, the undertaker. He was in the front seat of the hearse.'

There was a silence while Maddie tried to take this in.

'Your car was in front of the hearse,' Ellen explained, 'and all of us mourners were driving in a line behind you when your car was hit. As George and I aren't related to the deceased gentleman we offered to miss the funeral and take you to hospital.'

She turned back to face the front. 'We're nearly there now,' she said, as George indicated right and entered the grounds of Wishaw General Hospital.

The tyres crunched over the piles of snow on the drive. While George and Ellen were helping Maddie into the Accident and Emergency Department, the sound of a siren once again rang in her ears and the vehicle bringing Len to the hospital drove past them into the ambulance entrance.

*

A little over twenty four hours later Maddie lay in Ward 26, the screens drawn around her bed to offer some privacy from the other patients. She was still trying to come to grips with what had happened to them the previous day.

'I'm so sorry, there was nothing we could do,' the Consultant said, shaking his head when he'd broken the news to her the previous evening.

Her injuries weren't serious, apart from her right leg which was painful from its impact with the car's gear box at the time of the collision. She was grateful for the cage over her legs which kept the weight of the blankets off her injured limb.

I've come off so lightly, she thought, bitter tears pricking at her eyelids, if only I could have taken some of Len's injuries. But it was a futile thought as there had been no chance of saving Len's life.

Maddie had only a vague memory of Myra and Norman Singleton visiting her the previous day. 'I'm so sorry, my dear,' Norman said, taking her hand. 'Your loss is as great as ours.' He sniffed in an attempt to hold back the tears.

Myra sat on the edge of the bed, her tears flowing freely. 'We were concerned when you and Len didn't arrive for Boxing Day dinner,' she sobbed, 'and then two policemen came to the house to tell us you'd been involved in an accident. Even as we travelled up from Peebles to the hospital, I was still praying that they'd made a mistake.'

The memory of the happy time she and Len had spent at Fairfields on Christmas Eve and Christmas Day before heading down to Peebles for Boxing Day dinner with Len's family brought a lump to Maddie's throat and a huge wave of pain rose up inside her. She heard Len's happy laughter and his easy banter with the twins and Viv's kids and had to swallow deeply to try and quell the feeling that she was going to be sick.

'Don't worry about Len's funeral,' Norman, ever the practical one, told her, 'we'll make all the necessary arrangements.'

Maddie simply nodded. She didn't have the energy to argue about how her beloved Len's final farewell should be sorted out. She couldn't think of such things right now and was glad that his parents were going to take that task off her shoulders. Now, looking back on that visit from the Singletons, Maddie was sure that she must come across as cold and uncaring but she hoped that they would have realised that shock was rendering her numb.

'We'll come back and see you again soon,' Myra Singleton had told her, as they'd taken their tearful farewell to go to the mortuary to identify Len. Maddie again was grateful that they were dealing with that task too.

Maddie wondered how long she could expect support from Len's parents. She was sure of their support during the days before and after Len's funeral, but whether they'd keep in touch thereafter was anyone's guess. But of one thing she was certain; her beloved adoptive family at Fairfields would be there for her every step of the long road ahead. With that comforting thought in her mind, together with the tranquillising drugs the hospital staff had administered, Maddie drifted off into some much-needed sleep.

*

It was many hours later that it happened.

Maddie had awakened from her deep sleep feeling refreshed, until the memory of the crash and its aftermath assaulted her brain, and the familiar pain started once more.

She sobbed quietly while the other patients snoozed. She could see over the top of the screens to the window on the opposite side of the ward. It was pitch black outside and here in the darkened ward the only light she could make out came from the nurses' station at the bottom of the ward, a few beds down from her own.

How she wished she still had her faith in God. As a

child she'd been brought up to believe in God and Jesus, Heaven and Hell and all the rest that went with church attendance. Over the years her faith had diminished, until it had vanished completely and her heart had hardened. Len's love had melted her bitterness about all the bad things she'd experienced in her life but she was still unsure about the life after death stuff.

How could she ever get over Len's death? 'I'm only 31,' she half said, half thought, 'what if I live for another forty or fifty years. How can I survive without Len?'

She didn't even have a child to comfort her. Their desire to have a family hadn't materialised, although they'd never given up hope that Maddie would in time become pregnant. Now she wept noiselessly, raw with the knowledge that she never would have Len's baby.

Maddie had always envied her mum her deep Christian faith. Even when Mum had known she was dying from tuberculosis, her faith had never wavered. How Maddie yearned to have such a faith to sustain her at this moment. 'Oh Mum,' she whispered into the silent ward, 'if only I could be like you. Please help me, Mum.'

It was as she lay there in the depths of despair and afraid for her sanity that the miracle happened.

Sensing that she alone was aware of it, yet knowing it was real for her, Maddie heard a sound like a pile of dried up autumn leaves being lifted off the ground by a gentle wind. Awestruck, but not afraid, Maddie felt some force enter through the soles of her feet, travel through her body and emerge out of the top of her head. It had taken only a second, if even that, but afterwards she felt the calmest she'd ever been in her life and knew without a doubt that she'd never be alone again.

What had happened wasn't something she could easily describe to anyone else, even Viv, but in that instant she knew she'd get through this dreadful period in her life and come up smiling on the other side of her grief and pain.

Maddie had a happy smile on her lips as she dropped into another, this time untroubled, sleep.

Chapter Sixty

March 1970

Maddie sat cross-legged on the front room floor that Sunday afternoon, hugging her knees, with the sympathy cards scattered on the carpet in front of her. The tears streamed down her face and her shoulders heaved while she listened to the Seekers singing 'I'll Never Find Another You.' The miracle she'd experienced in the hospital ward hadn't left her but there were times like this when she still had to release some of the built up pain and tension following her bereavement.

Maddie was devastated about her darling Len's death. Was his early death a punishment for her past wrongs? But surely God could not be so cruel? Why take revenge for her sins out on Len, who'd had so much to offer the world.

The volume on the record player was so loud that she didn't hear the footsteps coming up the drive. She'd left the front door unlocked and it was only when the music stopped abruptly that she became aware of Viv kneeling down beside her with her arms wound round her tightly.

'Come on, Love,' Viv whispered, stroking Maddie's hair and rocking her gently. 'This isn't helping you, is it?'

'Nothing can. I miss him so much,' she sobbed into the crook of Viv's neck.

'I know, Maddie. At least I don't know, how can I? But I can imagine how I'd be without Dave, so in a way I do understand what it's like for you right now.'

Viv made a pot of tea and they moved into the back room and settled down in front of the gas fire. The warm liquid put a bit of colour back into Maddie's cheeks and her spirits lifted a little with being in the company of her best friend.

'Dad came up with an idea,' Viv told her, 'he thought it might be good for you to have Star here to keep you company. What do you think?'

When Maddie didn't respond straight away, she continued. 'He'd need to be here alone when you are at work, of course, but you could give him a walk before you leave in the morning and another longer walk when you get home.'

Maddie finally stirred enough to answer. 'I'd love to have him here, Viv, but would it work for Star? After all, he's used to roaming around the farm with Zeus.'

'Yes, he'd definitely miss Zeus but you can take him to Fairfields at the weekend so they can have a romp around together. Zeus knows you well too but Dad's had him since he was a few weeks old and I don't think he could bear to part with him, even for you. And although Star's been with us for a while now, he was with a previous owner, so he might not find the move as traumatic as Zeus would. It's worth a try, isn't it?'

'And I could get home some days during my lunch break to let him out into the garden for a wee while,' Maddie said, warming to the idea. 'In fact, old Mrs Edgar next door has my key and I'm sure she'd let him out while I'm at work. Mrs Edgar loves animals, especially dogs.'

'Well think about it and let Dad know.' Viv got up and took the two mugs into the kitchen. After she washed them and put them back into the cupboard, she had a look around. Not too much food in the cupboards and the fridge wasn't overly stocked either. She did hope that Maddie was feeding herself properly.

She had to be careful how she voiced her concerns though as she didn't want to upset her friend so back in the living room, she put her next idea to Maddie. 'Have you prepared anything for your meal yet or do you fancy coming back with me to see the kids and have dinner at ours?'

Maddie's face lit up immediately at the thought of seeing Peter and Sara again. 'Thanks, Viv, I'd really like that but I don't want to be too late home as I have a meeting tomorrow morning and want to get into the office early to prepare for it.'

'That's fine. Dave will run you home whenever you feel ready.'

'I'll just go upstairs and change into another jumper,' Maddie said. 'This one's got a few stains on it.'

While Maddie was doing this, Viv collected all the sympathy cards into a pile. She pushed them into a plastic carrier which she carefully placed behind the settee, out of sight for the moment.

*

On Tuesday evening Charlie arrived with Star plus a supply of dog food to start Maddie off. She was well licked by Star, who seemed excited to see her. He lay on his back so that she could tickle his tummy.

'I've also brought some of his favourite toys.' Charlie dropped a ball, a plastic bone and a piece of well chewed coloured rope on to the carpet. Star nosed the toys for a moment, then moved away into the front room to do some exploring.

'I hope he'll settle here alright without Zeus,' Maddie said.

'I'm sure he'll be fine. It isn't as if he doesn't know you, Maddie, and he'll be great company for you at nights. If you can walk him in the morning and at night and your next door neighbour can let him out for a while in the garden during the day he should be fine. Let's have a look at your side gate to check it is secure.'

'It's fairly strong,' Charlie said when the two of them and Star were round at the side of the house. 'And at least you have the double gates at the front. I'll come over in the next few days and put a new lock on the side gate to strengthen it.'

'That's great,' Maddie said, kneeling down on the gravel path to fondle Star's black head and stroke the thick hair on his back. She received some more licks for her trouble.

'We certainly want to make it as secure as possible,' Maddie continued, getting to her feet again. 'Come indoors,

Charlie, and I'll make some tea before you have to head off again.'

By the time Charlie was ready to go, Star seemed quite at home with Maddie and was sprawled out on his bed in front of the settee. 'Don't think there's any question that you'll be happy here young feller,' Charlie stroked him, 'you've made yourself at home already.'

Chapter Sixty-One

September 1970

Marshall's autumn sale had kept Maddie extremely busy for the past week so she'd been looking forward to her day off. She heard the postman push the mail through the letterbox while she was upstairs doing her hair. Her hair looked dull and lifeless; the natural shine had disappeared following Len's death and had never returned. She decided that next time she was at 'Hair First' in Burnside, she'd ask her hairdresser, Marion, for advice about the problem.

Star sat beside the dressing table stool watching her do her hair. In the months he'd been here, he'd settled well into his new home and loved Maddie, shadowing her around the house when she was in. A few days after his arrival at Mavis Crescent, she'd succumbed to his pleading eyes and allowed him to sleep on his mat at the side of her bed.

Downstairs again, she sifted through the mail and quickly deposited most of it into the dustbin in the kitchen. She carried an official-looking envelope into the dining room and sat down at the table to open it. She gasped when she read its contents and, laying the letter aside, she held the cheque in her shaking hands. She stared for a long time at the figure of £18,000 written on the cheque. Tears slowly squeezed out of the corners of her eyes to land on the paper. '£18,000 for Len's life,' she murmured to herself, 'don't they know nothing can replace my darling Len. He's irreplaceable?'

Star seemed to sense Maddie's state of mind and he rubbed his wet nose against her arm. She buried her face in his soft fur. 'Oh Star,' she wept, 'thank God I've got you, I don't know what I'd do without your company,' she told her pet.

The dog licked the back of her hand and he put his paws on her knee while his earnest brown eyes looked up into hers.

She knew Len had taken out the Life Insurance Policy for this very purpose, to ensure that she would have enough to live on in the event of his early death. But, although grateful for his foresight, all Maddie could think about at this moment was that no amount of money could compensate her for the loss of the only man she'd ever been able to truly love.

She felt no guilt over her involvement in the deaths of Benson and Steve; Benson hadn't deserved to live and Steve was drinking himself to death anyway. Benson had taken more from her than money but his legacy, still sitting in her bank account, would help to cushion her in old age. The irony made her smile. The compensation money after Steve's death was a reward for having put up with his gambling and drinking for so long. She would have been a hypocrite to have mourned their passing. But this time it was different. This was her beloved Len.

The Singletons had kept in touch fairly regularly following Len's funeral but she hadn't heard from them for a few months now and, to be fair, she hadn't contacted them either. Maddie was sure the relationship wouldn't last much longer now that Len was gone and she accepted that. Her relationship with Sheena and Charlie and the family was the opposite; they would be with her through thick and thin.

The thought of Sheena reminded her that she was going to Fairfields for lunch. She pushed the cheque into the sideboard drawer meantime and washed her tear-stained face. She fed Star and let him let him out into the garden to relieve himself.

*

When Maddie opened the back gate of the farmhouse, Star bolted inside, barking loudly. An answering bark came from the front garden and Zeus bounded round the side of the house.

By the time Sheena opened the back door to greet Maddie, the two dogs were running around in circles, chasing one another and rolling in the grass, biting each other in excitement.

'I think they're pleased to see one another, don't you?' Maddie shouted to Sheena over the din the dogs were making.

When Maddie walked into the kitchen, as ever the aroma of home baking came from the oven, filling the place with a welcoming warmth. There were some scrapbooks lying open on the table, with a pile of photographs and a pot of glue sitting near them.

'These look interesting,' she said, picking up the photograph on the top of the pile, one of Viv and her sisters when they were quite young, playing on a beach.

'It's some scrap books I'm making up for Peter and Sara,' Sheena said, as she filled the kettle and switched it on. 'Thought they'd be nice for the kids to have once Charlie and I are gone.'

'Don't talk like that, Sheena. I can't bear to think of life without you and Charlie.'

Sheena laughed. 'I hope it won't be for a very long time but none of us are immortal and I'd like to have our memories live on in our grandchildren.'

'That's all right then, just as long as it's very many years off that we're speaking about.' Maddie smiled at her and sat down at the table as Sheena brought over some sponge cake to accompany their cup of tea.

'I've just put some scones into the oven so once they're cool I'll give you some to take home with you.'

'Thanks, Sheena. The place seems so quiet today.'

'Yes, I always enjoy peace and quiet as it seldom happens. Charlie's away at a cattle sale. He's hoping to get a few more Ayrshires. He'll be home soon.'

Daisy padded over to Maddie's chair and jumped up on her knee, where she purred contentedly while Maddie stroked the fur on her striped head. Sheena got up when she heard the timer ping and took the trays of scones out of the oven. 'That'll be Charlie now,' she said, when they heard the wheels of the cattle truck going past the back door and up towards the fields behind the house. A few moments later there were loud moos from the cows being unloaded to explore their new surroundings.

When Charlie came into the kitchen, he sniffed the air appreciatively, anticipating a freshly baked scone. His face lit up when he saw Maddie. 'I knew you were here lass, when I saw that scallywag Star outside,' he grinned, giving Maddie a welcoming hug. 'Any tea left in the pot?' he asked Sheena as he was washing his hands.

'Sit down, I'm making a fresh pot. I suppose you'll want me to butter a scone for you.'

'But of course,' he laughed and winked at Maddie. 'See how she anticipates my desires before I even express them.'

'Yes, you're one lucky man,' Maddie countered.

'How did the sale go?' Sheena asked as she laid a mug of tea and a scone on the table in front of him.

'Great, I got the ones I hoped for. Good Ayrshire stock. I'll get the vet in over the next few days to check them over but there shouldn't be any problems as they're fine beasts.'

The door, which had been left slightly ajar, was pushed open and Zeus and Star ran in to see what grub was on offer. They went over to Zeus' large food dish in the corner and stood there, one on either side of the dish. Their noses almost rubbed together as they ate.

'I must show you Zeus' new trick,' Charlie boasted to Maddie and disappeared into the living room. He came back with a red balloon which he blew up and tied. He threw the balloon over to Zeus who caught it with his nose and punched it up towards the ceiling. Each time the balloon descended, the dog jumped up on to his hind legs and nosed it upwards again. 'He would do that all day,' Charlie laughed.

'I'm surprised Star isn't getting in on the act,' Maddie nodded towards her pet, who stood eyeing up what Zeus was doing.

'He soon will. Give him time. So how is work going these days?' Charlie asked, turning his attention from the dogs to Maddie.

'Fine,' she said. 'I'm glad to be working as it keeps me occupied and stops me thinking of Len constantly.'

Sheena, standing behind Maddie's chair, threw her arms around her. 'You've done very well, Love, and we all have nothing but admiration for your courage.'

'And you know we're behind you always, lass. And I mean always.' Charlie, his eyes moist, laid his big farmer's hand over her smaller one.

Maddie didn't reply but simply bent over and laid her cheek against his hand.

Chapter Sixty-Two

October 1971

Maddie loved autumn, by far her favourite season. Although it felt more like high summer going by the temperatures. She carried her washing basket into the garden, delighted to get such a good day for drying her sheets and towels.

She wanted to make the most of today as it might be her last day off midweek for a couple of months. With Christmas nearing, staff members were often asked to work on their days off. Still, she consoled herself, she'd have more on her pay slip during that time. Not that she was by any means poor but she enjoyed buying things for Peter and Sara who were constantly growing out of their clothes.

It was only a year and ten months since she'd lost Len and, although she was still trying to get to grips with her return to a solo lifestyle, the miracle she'd experienced in the hospital had never left her and she found herself coping surprisingly well with everyday life. She knew she'd never replace Len, no one could ever take his place in her heart, but she had to admit that her current lifestyle was bearable, thanks mainly to her having so many good friends. Len had been such an unselfish man that she knew this is what he'd want for her.

'Enjoying the sunshine, Star.' The dog lay snoozing on the grass near the back door. From out of the black fur one eye opened but closed again following the effort.

As Maddie pegged out the washing, she planned her day. A scoot round with the hoover, a romp in the park with Star and then she'd settle down on her lounger in her secluded back garden and read her book. She was re-reading her favourite Daphne du Maurier novel, Rebecca, even though she knew the story almost word for word.

She left the washing basket and the peg bag on the grass and started to walk towards the back door. One minute she was back to her childhood pleasures of kicking her way through the crispy, dried up leaves, savouring the crackling sound; the next she was lying flat on her back in a bed of leaves with a pain searing through her left shoulder.

Star yelped and licked her face, his anxious brown eyes looking into hers. From her position on the grass, she could see a magnificent crimson coloured leaf lying beside her outstretched hand. In the filtered sunlight she could trace the veins on the leaf, almost like a road on a map. She knew that she'd tripped on the broken edge of a slab near the drying green, a repair she'd meant to arrange for over a year now and had never got round to.

'If only you could use a telephone, Star,' she whispered to her pet, feeling his wet tongue on her cheek. 'Can you get me help?'

Star gave her face another lick, then raced round to the front of the house. She could hear him barking, no doubt standing on his hind legs at the gate. He barked for some time before returning to comfort Maddie with another lick, then back to his post at the gate.

Her loyal companion repeated this action for a long time without success. Maddie wasn't too surprised as most of her neighbours would be out at work and Mrs Edgar was out shopping with her daughter. She prayed that someone would pass soon and hear Star barking. Then, just as she was drifting away with the pain, she heard a faint sound. A human voice.

'Thank God,' she murmured, before pain made her pass out.

That was the last thing Maddie remembered until she came to in bed. But not in her own bedroom, this was a four-bedded hospital ward.

'Where am I?' she asked a nurse who was passing the bottom of her bed.

'Oh, Mrs Singleton, you're back with us,' the nurse smiled. 'You're in the Victoria Infirmary. You had a nasty fall and broke your collar bone but you didn't need an operation. It should heal by itself.' The nurse straightened up the bedcover as she was speaking. 'We've given you an injection of painkillers and you'll need to wear your sling for a few weeks.'

Maddie looked down at the blue sling supporting her arm. Then she remembered her beloved pet. 'But I need to get home, Star needs me.'

'Star?'

'My German Shepherd. He won't have had his dinner and he'll be starving.'

'Now don't upset yourself, Mrs Singleton,' the nurse soothed. 'I'll try and find out about your dog. Stay where you are till I get back.'

'I can't go anywhere in this state,' Maddie murmured, watching the back of the nurse's uniform disappear through the ward door.

Shortly afterwards the same nurse returned accompanied by a doctor who introduced himself as Dr Nolan.

'Your shoulder will take a couple of months to heal fully,' he said. 'We expect a good outcome but, as you live alone, we'll keep you here for a few more days until we get home care arranged for you. The physiotherapist will start you on some gentle exercises.'

'What about my dog?' Maddie asked, but Dr Nolan had already moved away from the bed, leaving Maddie with the nurse.

'The man who came in with you was a Mr Crane,' the nurse read out the name from Maddie's medical notes hanging at the end of her bed. 'My staff nurse said Mr Crane phoned to say he'd come in to visit you this evening. Excuse me,' she apologised, when another patient called for her assistance.

When visiting time finally came round, Maddie saw a tall man, his dark hair peppered with grey, coming towards her bed. 'Hello again,' he said, his eyes twinkling behind his glasses.

As the man laid a bottle of orange juice down on her bedside locker, Maddie stared at him blankly; she'd never seen him before. He looked about ten years older than her, maybe in his early forties.

'I know,' he said, reading her mind, 'I don't remember ever seeing you before today either. Apart from when I came with you in the ambulance. Your dog did a good job of barking for help.'

'Where is Star? Is he alright?'

'He's fine,' her visitor told her, patting her hand lying on top of the bedcover. 'I've taken him home with me and we're getting on well together. He's a friendly little chap, isn't he?'

'I'd be lost without him,' she said, smiling for the first time since her visitor arrived.

'I'm Rob Crane,' he introduced himself. 'I was nearing your gate when I heard Star barking. I live in one of the bungalows at the other end of Mavis Crescent from you.'

'Strange we've never met before.'

'Maybe not so strange. My wife and I only moved into Mavis Crescent a little over a year ago and at first I was out at work all day. Then we discovered my wife had cancer and I gave up my job to look after her. A few months ago,' he went on, his words becoming quieter and Maddie could see the moisture in his eyes behind his glasses, 'she lost her battle and passed away. I found another job but the firm packed up shortly after I joined their workforce so I'm once again job hunting. I've been feeling a bit lost and depressed so I've really enjoyed Star's company today.'

'Yes, he's great company. I can't thank you enough for all you've done.'

'You've nothing to thank me for. You getting better and back on your feet is all the thanks I need. Now, don't worry about Star, I'll see he's alright until you get home.'

'I've just remembered I left my back door open ....'

'No problem there either.' Rob gave her another reassuring smile. 'Your next door neighbour arrived home as the ambulance was nearly ready to drive us away. She and I went together into your kitchen and collected all the dog food and toys that Star would need at my house. Then we locked the door and Mrs Edgar took the key. She kept Star until I got back from the hospital.

'Thanks.' Maddie lay back on her pillow and yawned.

'Look, I can see you're exhausted with all the excitement. I'll leave you to sleep and I'll pop in again tomorrow. Is there anything you want me to bring you?' he asked but got no reply. Maddie's eyes had closed as he was speaking and she was sound asleep before he left the ward.

*

'Did you have a good walk?' Maddie asked Star a week later, as he bounded into the front room where she was lying on the settee propped up by pillows, her arm protected by the sling. Star remained on the floor with his front paws resting on the edge of the sofa. She laid her book down at her side and patted Star's head. In typical German Shepherd fashion, his ears stood up straight.

Rob came into the room behind Star, the dog's lead dangling in his hand. He smiled at Maddie, totally unconcerned about the muddy paw prints on his trousers. 'Star was well admired by all the other dog walkers we met in the park,' he told her. 'Is it good to be home?'

'Great, peace and quiet after all the noise in the ward. But the hospital did a first class job in getting my care package sorted out so quickly. I've filled the kettle for a cuppa. With only one hand working, I used a measuring jug to fill it.'

'Well done you. I'll go and make a pot of tea,' Rob said, taking off his jacket and hanging it on the door handle. She heard him sorting out the mugs in the kitchen and then he began to hum 'My Way' along with the velvet voice of Frank Sinatra coming over the radio waves.

The song finished and Rob returned to the front room, carrying the tea tray with the two mugs of tea and a plate of assorted biscuits which he'd found in her tins. 'I'm so lucky to have made two new friends in you and Star,' he said, putting Maddie's mug on a coffee table beside her. He held out the plate for her to choose a biscuit.

Maddie picked a bourbon biscuit and then shook her head. 'I'm the lucky one,' she said and smiled up at Rob as she fondled Star's furry head. 'And it's all thanks to my lucky Star,' she praised her pet, receiving another lick for the compliment.

The End

About the author

Irene Lebeter worked as a secretary for forty-five years, in industry, Civil Service and latterly the NHS. Her childhood love of story writing has continued throughout her life and has led to professional creative writing in her retirement. A previous member of Priesthill Writing Forum, she is now a member of two writing groups, Strathkelvin and Kelvingrove, and has completed a two-year creative writing course at Strathclyde University.

Irene has been an award winner in both novel and short story genres at the Annual Conference of the Scottish Association of Writers. She has been featured in the Federation of Writers' anthology 'Making Waves' as well as having multiple stories and non-fiction historical articles published in both UK and USA magazines.

'Maddie' is her second novel and comes following the success of 'Vina's Quest'.

About Author Way Limited

Author Way provides a broad range of good quality, previously unpublished works and makes them available to the public on multiple formats.

We have a fast growing number of authors who have completed or are in the process of completing their books and preparing them for publication and these will shortly be available.

Please keep checking our website to hear about the latest developments.

Author Way Limited

www.authorway.net

Made in the USA
Charleston, SC
20 October 2016